he loves me NOT

BOOK ONE

BOOK ONE

CARMEN ROSALES

Carmen Rosales
Copyright © 2023 by Carmen Rosales
Cover Design © 2023 by Melissa Cunningham
All rights reserved. No part of this book may be reproduced in any form or by any electronic or mechanical means, including information storage and retrieval systems, without written permission from the author, except for the use of brief quotations in a book review.

This book is a work of fiction. All character are fictional. Names, characters, places, and indigents are of the authors imagination. Any resemblance to any of the elements of events, locales, persons, living or dead, is coincidental.

Erotic Quill Publishing, LLC
3020 NE 41st Terrace STE 9 #243
Homestead, Fl. 33033
www.carmenrosales.com

Editing, Proofreading, and Interior Formatting by
Elaine York, Allusion Publishing
www.allusionpublishing.com

ISBN: 978-1-959888-30-7

Manufactured in the United States of America
First Edition April 2023

Also by Carmen Rosales

Hillside Kings Series
Hidden Scars
Hidden Lies
Hidden Secrets
Hidden Truths
Hidden Scion-(Alex & Alina)-June 15, 2023

A Dark Duet
Giselle
Briana

Standalones
Dirty Little Secrets-Coming Soon
Dearly Beloved-Coming Soon
Vows Written in Blood-Coming Soon
Hidden Ties
Like A Moth To A Flame-Coming Soon

The Prey Series
Thirst
Lust
Appetite-May 20, 2023
Forgive Me For I Have Sinned-Coming Soon

Steamy Romance
Changing the Game
Until Her
Until Now

To all the girls and boys who played a game of he loves me, he loves me not.
We all wished for the same thing.

To my husband Junior,

thank you for putting up with me
while writing this book and for not reading it.

Author's Note

He Loves Me Not is book one and is part of a duet which will conclude with *He Loves Me*. It is a dark high school romance. Yes, it ends in a cliffhanger. The list of triggers include depression, death, acts of violence, acts of bullying, mental illness, and suicidal thoughts.

He Loves Me Not book also contains sex scenes that is consensual for the enjoyment of all parties involved. It is intended for mature audiences and is not suitable for all readers. **Reader discretion is advised**. If you are comfortable, please move forward and enjoy.

If you or know anyone you know that is suffering from mental health and needs help. Please call *National Suicide Prevention Lifeline in your local area*.

Forbidden love never felt so right...

Rubi Murray struggles to keep her homelife a secret—even from her best friend and soulmate, Ky Reeves. When the two met as children, social and financial differences couldn't deter their friendship and devotion to one another. But Rubi will not dare admit that her family refuses to accept Ky as her "pretty little rich boy" friend—let alone as her boyfriend. Day in and day out she endures the pain and abuse her stepfather inflicts upon her so she can have just one more moment with Ky.

But all good things must come to an end...

When Ky receives a handwritten letter that Rubi is gone, his anger and abandonment threaten to destroy him. After all of their time together, he deserves more than just a note with a silly dried daisy as a symbol of their friendship. Now, it's up to Ky to pick up the pieces of his shattered heart. Was their relationship a simple game of "He loves me; He loves me not?"

Or was there always more that neither of them could ever confess?

Chapter One

Ky

Dear Ky,

I'm sorry. I have to go away and can't see you anymore. It is not your fault. It is mine. I miss you. I hope you get this. You were the best friend ever. I hope to see you some day.

Oh. I forgot, Superman is better than Batman. Pizza Hut sucks. The big flat pizza is better.

Love,

Rubi

I re-read the letter over and over without tearing it. I've balled it up a couple of times and thrown it across the room, but I always pick it up and flatten the lined school paper. It was the last letter that she wrote me before she disappeared, the last communication I had from her before I never saw her again. Every other day after that letter I went to the treehouse I built with a sheet I took from the hallway linen closet. I was always hoping she would show up, but all she left me was a letter under a rock laid beside a dried-out flower with one last petal on its stem. I kept it in a Ziploc bag hidden in one of my favorite comic books featuring Batman.

I hear a tap on my door as my best friend Chris pushes it, opening it farther. His father dropped him off because he had to be at his office and couldn't take him to school.

"Give me a minute."

"Let's go, dude. My father's going to go ape shit if I'm late to school," he says.

Chris needs me to give him a ride until his car is out of the shop. He got into a fender bender on the way to school recently and he's getting it fixed.

I look up, raising an eyebrow. "I'll be right out."

He knows the look I give all my friends. The *don't fuck with me, drop it* look. I know I have a short temper, and I hate giving him attitude, but I also hate repeating myself. My temper started flaring after that day she left me at eleven years old. The day she left me with a sorry letter and wilted flower like that was enough of a goodbye after everything that we'd shared. A whole year of friendship up in smoke like it meant nothing.

I wait until he leaves before folding the old notebook paper into the Ziploc bag containing the dried flower and placing them inside the comic book and stuffing the entire thing under my mattress. I always take it out when I have the same recurring dream of Rubi. The funny thing is, she is not eleven years old like when I last saw her. Ironically, she is the same age I am each year that I have the same dream. I can't see her face, but I can see her dirty blonde hair and hear her say my name. She calls out to me in the dream, and I answer. But she just keeps calling my name like she can't hear me, and then I'm left hearing her sobbing. That's when I wake up in a cold sweat like I have been looking for her for hours…and I'm exhausted, both mentally and physically.

Swiping my keys and wallet from my nightstand, I stand and grab the strap of my gym bag and head outside, all while remembering the line that has been plaguing me for the last seven years. *It is not your fault. It is mine. I miss you.*

For seven years I have wanted to see her again, to find her. To tell her how I felt as a kid, but I never got the chance. I wanted to tell her how much I loved being with her. I wanted to tell her how much she meant to me. How much our friendship meant to me. How could she quickly just forget about me—only leaving a stupid letter with no real reason?

For the whole year of our friendship, three times a week we would meet in the at the fence line in the backyard of my house where her town ended and mine began. I didn't know her parents and she didn't know mine, but I didn't care. We didn't care. All we cared about were the moments we spent together after school. All I knew about Rubi was what mattered. The things that mattered the most. Not where she lived or what school she went to, but I assumed it was the public school on the other side of town. We talked about everything eleven-year-olds could talk about. The treehouse was right behind my father's estate where the rear of the property line would determine where the rich kids and the poor kids lived. I knew she didn't come from a rich family. Even at eleven years old when I saw her climbing the fence, I could tell that the type of clothing she wore and the shoes that were on her feet were secondhand. The threads of her shirt were thin and frayed, and her shoes were dirty and not name brand like the ones I wore every day.

But money doesn't always buy happiness. Living with my father after my mother left was a testament to that.

My mother left me and my dad—abandoning us for another life after my tenth birthday. So the only other person I could call a friend at the time was Rubi. She was the only one I could tell my secrets to. As a young kid, when things got rough or people in your family disappointed you, friendship like the one I had with Rubi was the only thing that mattered. My best friend mattered, and she was it.

I never forgot the disappointment I felt with my mother that day. It had been raining for a while, and the sky was dark and overcast. I could still recall the distinct odor of fertilizer mingling with the damp grass. My father standing in the entryway of the mahogany-colored front door, wiping away the tears that were streaming down my face, and I knew in that moment...she was never coming back. I would never see her again. I would never smell her lovely perfume, or taste her home-cooked meals that would not be made again under this roof. I would never feel her touch me with affection again.

She stooped until our eye levels were aligned. I would never forget what she said that day. With lips painted like a pink rose, she said, *"It is not your fault, sweetheart. It's mine. You're better off with your dad, and try not to give him a hard time."*

I hiccupped, wiping my face and not understanding the reason why she was leaving. "Are you coming back. I promise to be good, Mommy. I promise," I pleaded.

She gave me the impression that I was bothering her as she shook her head and didn't answer my question. Straightening while exhaling a breath, she looked up at my father standing behind me with a glare. *"Get him inside, Richard. You're making me look bad."*

I turned my body to look at my father, hoping he would tell her not to leave. Not to leave me. I watched him, but all he did was nudge his head for me to get inside.

When I turned back to see my mother one last time, she was already in the car that was idling in the driveway. She was leaving me. She left us both. She was gone.

I followed my father inside the massive house, devastated. He gave me a stern, emotionless stare before pushing the door shut behind me, the knocker's distinctive thud the only sound that either of us could hear.

He reached out and put his hand on my shoulder, gazing into my eyes as he said, *"Don't ever trust a woman with your heart. They will take advantage and then they will abandon you like you mean nothing. Always remember that."*

After Rubi left that letter, I knew what my father told me that day was true. I would never forget the way she left me. The way Rubi abandoned me...just like my mother.

How quickly they left by choice because you didn't matter enough. Their promises broken––only to be rewarded with my blinding hate. It is just a reminder of how much you meant to them. A reminder of what happens when you become complacent.

"Are you going to put the top down?" Chris asks, as he slides into the passenger seat of my matte black BMW M8 convertible.

I place my gym bag in the back leather seat and slip inside the driver's side at the same time. Looking at him, I shut the door and press the ignition button as the engine of the powerful car revs to life.

"Didn't you say you couldn't be late, and your father was going to go ape shit? Putting the top down takes a couple of minutes, dude," I mock.

"Just drive, asshole," he belts out as we both laugh.

Chapter Two

Rubi

I'M SITTING IN the office with my social worker, a high school official, a court liaison, and a man whom I didn't know still existed. My sperm donor...also known as my father.

The smell of old wood and carpet makes the room feel even stuffier than it already is. I look out of the dirty, peach-colored blinds and take note of the sun streaming in through the window, the rays shining a spotlight on the white cup of tap water they offered me when they brought me here after my court hearing. It's so bright I can see the dust particles floating in the air. You can tell no one cleans this place. It's like every place I have been to since they took me away from my mother and stepfather when I was eleven years old. I thought what my parents did to me was bad, but being forced to leave my best friend was the worst thing ever. The rest I could live with...but that, that was the hardest thing I've ever endured.

The female court liaison shuffles papers in a manila file with my name in big black letters scrawled across it. Rubiana Murray. Most of my close friends call me Rubi, but there are only a handful of people I could call my friends nowadays, and they are all from juvenile detention, or floating around somewhere lost in the foster system. Some of the social workers, well, the nicer ones, call me Rubi Ray. When I was younger I wanted to be called something different, maybe a way to forget about my past. So, I shortened my name to Rubi Murray.

"Mr. Murray, are you aware of Rubiana's history?" the court liaison asks.

No, of course not. He wouldn't know shit about me or my history because this is the first time he's seen me in I don't even remember how long. Looking over at him now, I realize that he has the same dirty blonde hair that I have, but where his complexion is fair, mine is tan like my Colombian, meth-addicted mother.

"No." His coffee-colored eyes glance in my direction, but I look straight ahead, ignoring him but still listening. I have learned how not to be seen but to always listen.

He looks down at the stack of papers that contain numerous incidences of my abuse, pictures that show how much my mother and stepfather neglected me, my arrests, the foster homes I have been in and out of, and most importantly, my psych evaluation. It even includes my stellar grades in high school, although they won't focus on that. I'm not a genius, but I can manage good grades if I stay in one school long enough.

"Well, besides the fact that Rubiana has a juvenile record and will be turning eighteen in eight weeks, she has to stay under your supervision until she graduates high school as part of her sentencing from her last hearing. The judge ordered that if she didn't abide by the terms of her sentencing, she would be tried as an adult and need to serve her time in a female correctional facility at the county level."

"Do you understand what is at stake here, Rubiana?" The social worker from the Georgia department of child services addresses me in a stern tone.

I can see the court liaison shaking her head at the social worker to let it go with the questioning; The social worker's brown suit jacket creased, and the spot of coffee that she spilled on her cream-colored blouse screaming at me. But still, I stay silent like I usually do.

They know that I'm not going to speak. I don't break. Not anymore. The liaison was there the whole time I had therapy, and also at the hearing. I was curt and only spoke when I had no choice.

Everyone in this room—obviously not including my father—who has dealt with me and my case knows I will just sit here and let them make decisions for me because I'm technically still a minor and am a ward of the state. That is, unless the sperm donor seated to my right has decided to take me in and finally take responsibility because they found him and forced him to.

The last time I was abused, the pictures they took hit a soft spot with the judge. So they searched for my father, and the only relative they could find besides my mother and uncle was him. I was told he received a letter from officials with the State of Georgia, and I guess he finally grew a conscience. Why? I have no idea. So, the plot continually thickens.

What a fucking hero?

I could not care less at this point. One house is as good as a foster home, or even juvie. It's a place where I can eat, sleep, finish school, and bide my time until I can legally be on my own and not have to serve time for the crimes I committed. Stealing mostly. It was easy, and no one ever got hurt.

So I sit there and I keep quiet, wear my black hoodie over my Dutch braids, and ignore everything that they are saying. It is all white noise to me. I'm just a charity case, and now they have found a way to dump it on someone else. One less expense for the State of Georgia. One less problem on their desk of files with pictures from my childhood that would make a grown man throw up.

"So…" The high school official from an elite academy whose name I recognize from across town, where I used to live with my piece of shit mother and stepfather, turns to me, giving me a fake smile, and addresses me. I know it's the same school I heard about as a kid because of the royal blue uniform jacket with the gold Westlake Preparatory Academy logo stitched on the right breast pocket. My eyes focusing on her perfectly tailored dress shirt with blue stripes and her necklace of pearls hanging from a neck that has seen better days.

"Rubiana, I see that your grades when you actually attended school are good and that you have passed the state standardized test which will allow you to finish your senior year at Westlake Preparatory Academy." I roll my eyes and look away. "I'm Mrs. Lane," she places a hand over her chest to introduce herself. "And I am in charge of getting you enrolled. Your father–"

My head snaps up, and my jaw hardens as I point to the man I refuse to ever acknowledge as my father. Interrupting her, I say, "That man is not my father." I look at his hard face knowing he is pissed off because I'm embarrassing him. Well, guess what? Too fucking bad. Where were you all my life? He has no right."

"It's okay, Rubi," the social worker from children's services says. "I understand you are angry." She glances at Stephen Murray and continues. "Under the circumstances, we all understand that you have been dealt the short end of the stick, and many people have disappointed you and let you down, but Stephen Murray is your father. Genetic testing from each of you confirmed he is your biological father and is here to take custody of you and will remain as your guardian until all requirements from the court are met."

I snort. More like they wished I never existed, like the asshole to my right obviously does, and his act of kindness is an act he's putting on for who, I can't imagine. Hell, maybe he is twisted like all the others, and he wants to stick his hands in the cookie jar. A small ounce of fear rises in my belly.

"Have you checked to see if he is a good fit to raise me? Ran a background check?"

"Are you serious?" Stephen, the sperm donor, growls.

I pull myself up from slouching in the uncomfortable chair as I turn to my right to face him. "Does it look like I'm not serious? How do I know you're not perverted just like all the others?"

An audible gasp is heard around the room as I call out the very crimes that were committed against me for them all to hear.

"I know you have been through a lot, young lady, but I will not have you disrespect me in front of anyone. Are. We. Clear?" he says through clenched teeth.

I have never before hated someone I just met. It usually takes a bit of time, or when they show their true colors and use me in some sickening and abhorrent way.

"Mr. Murray!" the social worker scolds. His head whips in her direction. "This is not what we discussed. This is new for her, and I'm not going to condone her attitude, but under the circumstances, she has a right to question. She has a right to ask."

He places his hands up in mock surrender. His gray suit jacket tightens around his arms from the movement. Stephen obviously works out and doesn't have a pot belly. I can see what my mother saw in him other than the U.S. citizenship she was after when she became pregnant with me. It doesn't take a rocket scientist to figure out my mother, Mariana Hernandez, was in the states illegally when she was involved with him. She found a replacement when Stephen left, though, my piece-of-shit stepfather.

"I know––I'm sorry." He faces me with his coffee-colored eyes and straight dirty blonde hair. "I apologize for my outburst.

This is not how I wanted this to go. I–" He closes his eyes, and I tilt my head and give him an I-don't-give-a-fuck expression. I truly don't care. He had seventeen years to be involved in my life, and now he suddenly shows up like my fucking savior.

This attitude is all you know when you have been in the system long enough. Changing environments disrupts the way you know how to process things. Things you have had to do to survive. I never thought I had a living relative to come here and take me in. I never once thought my deadbeat of a father would show up after all this time, or attend a school I thought I would never set foot in. I was wrong. Now I have to survive in a new environment with new people in a place where I know no one. Again. Every kid in foster care or juvenile detention wants to go to a stable home to live a better life. In my experience, being placed somewhere else is not always paradise. You think you are escaping one hell only to be sent to a lower level that breaks you all over again.

Like when I was eleven years old and first learned what heartbreak and loss felt like. My thoughts return to my best friend I had to leave behind because social services found out about my living conditions and how I was abused for so long. I left Ky a note hoping he would understand. Telling him how he was the only true friend I had at the time. He was everything to me.

Every year I wondered what he was doing. If he lived in the same house where the estate homes began. His backyard was so big it reminded me of a forest. It was easy to climb their fence and meet him three times a week when my stepfather left for work.

I would climb the fence after crossing the street near the bus stop on the outskirts of West Park, where I lived. West Park was the poor town on the left side of West Lake. West Lake was the rich part. Like everywhere, there is always the rich part of a county and the poor side of a county.

Our friendship started one day when I was running away from home and jumped the fence. I didn't know it was someone's backyard. I was eleven years old with a very worn backpack that was duct-taped on the bottom. I landed hard on the ground in my worn, dirty shoes I'd found in a dumpster. I looked up, dusting myself off, and that is when I saw him for the first time playing in the yard with a stick, trying to catch bugs.

"I can assure you that Mr. Murray is an exceptional member of the West Lake community and donates to multiple charities, including Westlake Preparatory Academy. He has an impeccable background and is a very successful businessman." I hear a man's voice.

I look up, snapping myself out of my thoughts. I see a man in a black suit handing each person in the room a folder while Stephen signs papers. I didn't even see him come in, and now they are finalizing all the legal paperwork and handing me over to Stephen. I must have been thinking about Ky. Thinking about our time as friends is what has kept me going. It is how I survived. How I have been coping mentally with everything I have gone through since I left almost seven years ago. The thought that someone out there cared was everything to me as a kid.

Maybe Ky goes to WestLake Prep. I wonder if he still the same boy with the same heart I have cared about since I was eleven? The best year of my life was spent with Ky, even if I was a snot-nosed kid with stringy hair, a dirty face, and dirty, worn clothes. I wonder what he looks like now. Does he have the same dark hair and expressive eyes that promised to keep all my secrets? As a kid the things I liked and didn't like were my secrets, and Ky was the only one I told them to. He would listen and then he would share his. These were things we told each other. Things that only we knew and no one else and it brought us so close together.

One thing he promised me was that he wouldn't turn out to be a bully like the kids in my school did who made fun of me in West Park. I know Ky, and deep down, I know he wouldn't be like that, but time has a way of changing people. If I run into him at Westlake Prep, I hope I don't hate what I find if I see him. My heart flutters at the thought and I try to hold back the grin despite myself, eager to know if he attends the same school and what a shock it will be for him when he sees me.

Chapter Three

Ky

I KICK THE bag in the boxing gym over and over, ending the combination with a kick to the bag that has it swinging with the distinct sound of the chain holding its weight. I train in the boxing gym every day after school with a couple of my closest friends, Tyler and Chris.

My father took me to Thailand on a business trip over my summer break when I was twelve, and I fell in love with Muay Tai, or what is known as *Thai boxing*. We traveled to *Soi*, in the Chalong Phuket area in Thailand and I learned so much while there. Some people in the States refer to what I'm doing as kickboxing, but I have learned they are quite different. Kickboxing is a four-point striking technique, while Tai boxing is an eight-point striking technique. My dad saw that I stuck to it because it was a way to channel my anger without getting into meaningless fights. It is also a bonus that I can defend myself if needed.

When I met Tyler and Chris in sixth grade, I told them to hang out with me at the boxing gym my father opened, and the rest was history.

I glance to my right where I see Tyler assaulting the bag with a combination of fist blows. Sweat runs down my neck and

I rub my forearm over my sweaty brow to keep the sting from my eyes as I saunter over.

I give him a nod with a chin raise when he spots me a few feet away. He gives me an expression that tells me he is battling some internal issues, so I walk over to check up on him. "Yo, you good?"

He turns to the bag and continues his assault as if he didn't hear me or see me standing right near the bag. His breaths are coming fast from the effort, and I can tell whatever is bothering him, it's some deep shit.

I have no idea what the fuck has him in this mood. We usually tell each other almost everything. What girls we fuck so we don't hit on the same one, or which ones we don't care about if we wanted to make a move. Either way, we always tell each other when something has us down. Well, almost everything. No one knows about Rubi. No one. She's mine, even if I hate her to this day.

I turn my head and spot Chris on the mat teaching moves to another fighter.

When he gets up, he notices me looking over. I point my thumb toward Tyler as the sound of taped knuckles hitting the bag over and over echo behind me. "What's with him?" I ask Chris.

He shakes his head. "Some shit about his dad. Family problems. It's all I know. I don't know the details." He shrugs as if it's not his problem.

The sounds come in rapid succession mixed with grunting and deep breaths. I turn around, and Tyler's arms drop like dead weight as a look of exhaustion crosses his face as he holds the bag like it's a lifeline as he tries to catch his breath.

He screams, and it's then that I walk up to him and growl, "Locker room. Now!"

He can't be bringing that shit into the gym like that. It raises questions he won't want to answer.

I walk toward the locker room located in the back of the gym and he follows behind with Chris in tow.

I slam the door shut with my foot. "Alright, what has you all fucked up like you're trying to exorcise a fucking demon out there?" I ask him with my hands crossed over my chest.

"Yeah, dude. You're hitting the bag all sloppy and shit," Chris teases.

"Fuck you, Chris," Tyler grumbles.

Chris sits down on the metal bench with his legs on either side, grabbing a towel to dry off the sweat from his back and chest. "I'm messing with you, brother. What's up?"

I walk around to make sure no one is inside who can overhear our conversation. Once the coast is clear, I walk back and lean against the pillar. "Alright, spill."

Chris slides his fingers through his hair that's full of sweat from his sloppy training sesh, and lets out a puff of air. "Man, all I know is I want to kill my father right now. I can't stand to look at him."

I quirk a brow. What the fuck is he talking about? Stephen Murray is a stand-up guy. Everyone likes him, including my father, and that is saying something. My father is a pain in the ass and doesn't have many friends outside of business. Chris and Tyler's father are basically the only ones he would trust. There is nothing that man could do that could have Tyler feeling this way.

"Fuck, man, I have a sister and we are like three months apart, " Chris blurts, raising his head to the ceiling in frustration.

Okay. I take that back. Stephen Murray has some explaining to do.

"What the epic fuck?" Chris bellows. "Are you serious?"

Tyler nods, confirming what we are hearing. What we are all assuming, that he cheated on his mother Caroline.

I pinch the bridge of my nose with my taped fingers, not believing this shit. "Okay. Now what?" I ask with my eyes closed, picturing Tyler with a sister.

He faces the wall and places his forehead against it. "I have to meet her at the house tonight. You guys cannot show up under any circumstances. Apparently, my father had a thing with her mother before he met my mother. Her mother was supposed to move back to Colombia or some shit, but never did, obviously."

"Why?" Chris asks.

I was about to ask the same thing. Why did he let her move back if she fell pregnant? Why didn't he say anything to his mother or to Tyler until now?

"According to my father, the lady wanted U.S. citizenship and was trying to get my father to marry her for papers when he just got out of college. She saw my father as a meal ticket, and when he found out what her motive was, he told her to fuck off and go back to Colombia. She was supposed to terminate the pregnancy and go back before my father threatened her with Immigration. In my father's mind, he thought she had the abortion. She even assured him that it was terminated."

"Damn, what a bitch. She actually got knocked up on purpose to stay in the U.S.?"

Tyler pushes away from the wall and turns to face us. "Yeah, man. That's the story. If it's entirely true or not..." He shrugs his shoulders and grabs a clean towel from the shelf and throws me one, "I wouldn't know for sure. All I know is the chick has been through some serious shit."

"What kind of shit?"

Not that I give a rat's ass, but I'm curious.

"Foster care, juvenile detention is what my father said, and that is just skimming the surface. She's a handful and not easy to deal with according to him. He wants to do the right thing by taking her in until she figures shit out. She was dealt a rough hand. She got into some trouble, so she has to stay with us until she graduates high school as part of a sentence the court gave her."

"Damn, dude. She sounds like she's pretty hardcore," Chris says. "I can't wait to meet her," he adds sarcastically.

"Whatever you need, brother. You know we got you," I chime in. "It sounds like her crimes weren't all that bad if she went to baby jail."

Tyler sighs. "I don't care about her. I care about how my mom is taking it. In my eyes, I'm an only child. I don't have siblings. The people I call my brothers are you two assholes."

I smile. "Damn, right. Fuck her. She's probably just like her mother and sees a meal ticket and is hoping to cash in on it."

"I agree," Chris says.

"I think so, too. She's obviously going to our school for our senior year. Let's make sure she gets the Westlake Prep welcome."

But wait...if they're three months apart, it means she starts her senior year at West Lake Prep, and we have to deal with her until the end of the year. In other words, let's make sure she knows her place. Chris, Tyler, and I rule West Lake Prep. Not even the football players fuck with us because they know we will kick their ass. Wrestlers, either. They know better. We might be considered bullies, but we are much more than that. We don't let anyone fuck with us. Whatever we say goes, everyone else falls in line. We aren't some preppy rich kids who get good grades and only go to second base with girls. We are the guys their fathers warn them about who fuck them when no one is watching. The most important part is that they like it.

The girls call us the Gods of WestLake Prep. We are more like the sinners with a fat bank account and too much power passed down from our families. We aren't the goods kids. I know I'm not. Right now, we have an intruder. Someone trying to fuck up our dynamic. Our boys' dynamic.

Good thing for Tyler, I don't have a soft spot for females. I fuck 'em and leave 'em, and if they try to fuck me back, I destroy them. One time is all you get unless I say so—and the second time is just on their knees. Chris sees things the same way I do. Tyler is the lesser evil because he still has his mother around. Chris only has his sister, Abby, who is the only exception. The only reason none of us has touched her is because of the bro code and all that.

I could only imagine what Tyler is going through right now with his father. A long-lost sister suddenly showing up and not knowing he knocked up a chick right when he met his mom. And then didn't say anything about the woman, or that it was remotely possible that he had a bastard kid in the world. I would be pissed at my father, and let's not talk about the trust issues that stem from finding out a dirty little secret like that this late in the game. She's practically an adult. A complete stranger.

"How's your mom taking it?" I ask.

He shakes his head. "She feels like all women would feel if they found out their husband had a kid around the same time that she had a child with him, devastated. Betrayed. Confused. Ashamed. Guilty." He wipes his hand over his face. "I can't believe her. She actually feels bad for the chick."

I shake my head in disbelief. If I had a choice to choose a mother, it would be Tyler's mother Caroline. She's an excellent mother any kid would die to have. I hope she can survive this. I hope Tyler can survive this. His father had a secret child who popped up out of nowhere—well, we know where, obviously. He doesn't deserve this right now. I mean, we are about to graduate and go off to college.

"It's supposed to be our year," Chris says, standing up and placing the white towel around his neck. He looks between us, his brown eyes trying to understand. "Don't let some female wannabe thug who is trying to get one over on your Pops mess up your life. Fuck her. Don't let this shit get to you. It's not your mom's or your problem. Besides, it happened before he got together with your mom. If what he says is true, he didn't cheat on your mom."

Tyler nods. "You're right. Fuck her. If she wants a free ride, we'll make sure she pays for it."

It's then that I realize he's right...fucking shit up is what I do best.

Chapter Four

Rubi

I WATCH AS the trees pass by through a neighborhood I had no idea I would ever visit. Every kid on the other side of town knows where the rich neighborhood is now that I'm back in my old stomping ground. They can see the tops of the nice roofs and trees that surround lush landscapes, and what every poor kid can't imagine is how much nicer it would look once inside one of those massive homes. Who would have thought my biological father lived in that same neighborhood with his posh family. The closest I got was to walk through a yard that belonged inside a magazine spread showcasing the rich and famous.

I never went inside his house for fear that I would be kicked out. We kept to the edge of the property where there were many trees that blocked the view from the back of his house. I always wondered what the inside of Ky's house looked like. Now apparently, I would get the chance to live in my own dream home... but I have a feeling it'll be more like a nightmare.

Judging by the car my sperm donor drives, it is the nicest vehicle I have ever been in, so the interior of his home must be equally as luxurious, I'm sure. The leather inside the car is the color of vanilla, and the smell is nothing I have ever experienced. It can only be described as rich and sophisticated.

My mother didn't even own a car. The only vehicle I have ever been in was my stepfather's beat-up old Ford that smelled of death and cigarettes. The smell of death is best described as the smell of methamphetamine and heroine when smoked from a pipe. It smells awful. There were times I couldn't get it out of my nose. I'm almost positive it clung to my clothes. I was so embarrassed I would visit the store and spray whatever tester they had over my clothes every chance I could. Especially before I would visit Ky. He always smelled good. Not that I would put my nose to his skin or shirt—even though the thought crossed my mind from time to time. I never attempted to do it out of fear he would think I was being weird and would stop being my friend.

"I'm sorry we had to meet under these circumstances, Rubi," my father, speaking to me awkwardly, pulls me from my own thoughts. I'm still pretty angry. I get that he didn't' know where I was or how I was raised, but he also knew a child he helped create possibly existed. A child he never cared enough to look for or find out for sure that I was aborted. He took my mother Mariana's word for it after she lied to him. If he only knew I was closer than he thought.

I roll my eyes and cup my hands together, pressing my short nails into my hand making little half-moons in the skin of my palm. "It's Rubiana," I respond dryly.

"What was that?"

I know he heard me. Only people who know me call me Rubi, and those few are the friends I have made along the way who have helped me survive in juvenile detention and foster care. Kids like me who have shit parents and no opportunity. Kids like me who have mothers and fathers who know they exist and don't give a shit about them. The fathers who don't care to look for them and prefer for them to be terminated. A man like the one next to me who was content to erase me like a mistake written in pencil.

"I said my name is Rubiana."

"The social worker said that you like when people call you Rubi."

"That's reserved for people who care about me. To you, I'm Rubiana."

I hear him expel an audible breath. I never asked him to acknowledge my existence. I didn't ask him to respond to the court summons, although legally he probably had to, so he did that on his own. I was accepting of the idea that I didn't have a father, and now I have to accept the fact that he exists and is right next to me.

"My wife Caroline is excited to meet you. I understand you're angry with me, but all I ask is that you do not take it out on my wife or my son," he says, almost as a warning. At least that's how I take it, but I'm a little bitter and everything he's saying makes me see red.

I smirk sarcastically. There it is. I was wondering when he would break down the rules and regulations of living under his roof. What an asshole. I thought my mother was a piece of work, but my father, he is in a category all on his own.

I turn my head to look at his side profile while he steers the car down the street. "Why don't you do all of us a favor and take me back."

He glances at me briefly. "What?"

"I said, take me back to social services and leave me there, or you could just let me out right here. You can tell them I ran away. And you won't have to deal with me another minute."

My eyes sting with tears of anger. I wonder why he even bothered to take me in. I'm almost eighteen, anyway, and I would prefer to serve my sentence literally in any other capacity. Why does he even care what happens to me when he never cared for the last seventeen years?

"I'm sorry, Rubiana. I can't do that."

"Why not? You don't have to take me in, you know. The government has taken great care of me for years."

He snorts. "I doubt that since we were just dealing with judges and court sentences." He looks at me, scrutinizing my baggy pants and black faded hoodie that I found in a box of clothes left for the homeless.

Clothes that no one would wear because they have outlived their usefulness and are riddled with wear and tear. But they are good enough for the rejects in the system. I stopped caring about the colors or the holes in the clothes I would get. But I draw the line if it doesn't fit. And if I'm going to steal––borrow—it might as well be something nice enough to not look like I'm a complete charity case.

"It would be for the best. You don't have to show up to your house with your perfect wife and son with a daughter you clearly never wanted. I could be like one of those dogs you leave at the shelter when the owners no longer have a use for them. I mean, I wouldn't think any less of you than I already do."

I touched a nerve because he glares at me, gripping the leather steering wheel and watching it turn while his expensive gold watch gleams. I turn my head and see him pull into the driveway of an impressive home. White exterior walls, black trim around the windows, green lush lawns, and beautiful square carriage lights that must sparkle when the lights turn on. The driveway is white concrete with green artificial grass dividing the squares evenly. There is a Mercedes SUV parked to the left, and a late-model lifted Dodge Ram truck to the right with a black paint job and big tires.

He then presses a button on his Mercedes sedan and places the car in park. He bends his head and looks at the dark wood double doors of the impressive two-story home. He wipes his hand over his face and turns his head to find me looking straight ahead. I don't owe this man or his family shit, to be honest and don't want them to give me anything either. I get that it's not his precious wife or son's fault, but it's not mine either and I didn't ask for any of this.

"Rubiana, I'm sorry for what you have been through. I don't know what to say or what I could say to make anything right. All I know is that I have made a decision and I'm going to stick to it. I don't expect you to like me or forgive me in anyway. You have every right to feel disappointed and angry with me, but please direct it at me and not at Caroline or Tyler. They have accepted my decision and they both feel that I have made the right choice to take you in...and each of them acknowledge that you are my daughter. I talked to the judge at the hearing, and she agreed that this would be good for you. I know you have had a hard life, and had I known..." he trails off, taking a deep breath, and continues. "I'm just sorry. I don't know what I'm doing or how to even talk to you. Just, please try. It is all I'm asking. When you graduate, you can do whatever you want. Go wherever you want. I won't hold you hostage any longer than what the court requires."

I cross my arms over my chest listening to him. All I hear, though, is his guilt. This isn't about me, but himself. I get it. It's all good. It's pity. So I do what I've done for a long time...I look at the house in front of me like it's my next prison. At least it's better than foster care, I guess. I have a few boxes to check off: complete my senior year, graduate, and then I'm outta here. I can start my life on my own terms then, and answer to no one but myself.

"Fine, I'll play house. Don't expect me to be all grateful and giddy that you swooped in to save me because I'm not."

He lets out another breath he must have been holding. "Fair enough. I do want to tell you that we have a few more rules." I quirk a brow. "No boys in your room. I need to know where you are at all times. Curfew is at eleven p.m. on school nights, and midnight on weekends, unless you are out with Tyler. He knows to keep you out of trouble. No fighting at school. Show us respect, and everything else will fall in line. It's not too much to ask. There is a cellphone in your room, uniforms for school, and I will take you tomorrow after school to get anything else you need."

I rest my head against the headrest and look out at the dark wooden front doors like they are a portal to my impending doom. "Anything else?"

"Yeah, remember not to give Caroline a hard time."

There he goes again about Caroline. He must really love her. It's a shame I don't know what that emotion is like.

"I have one rule," I say, closing the door with a small thud and meeting his gaze across the roof of his black car.

"Okay, what is it?"

I pull the hood of my sweater off my braided hair and look him in the eyes. "You read my file?"

He averts his eyes and clears his throat. "I did."

He must have seen the pictures that tell half the truths of my past. What could be seen from the things I went through. Physical things that appear on your skin that are hints of the suffering you endured, like notes left on your flesh that tell a story that no one should have to read. How can he possibly understand or know. Only a person who has gone through something similar could recognize the signs of evil. Everything that he must have seen in my file is proof of the physical part. The mental part is the greatest pain of my story...and that can't be read in a file or put into words.

It's a pain no one would ever know.

The secrets you keep.

The secrets that define the memories you play in your head.

The ones that have you not giving a fuck anymore.

"All I ask is that you make sure you keep my past to yourself. I already have your pity. The last thing I need is theirs."

Chapter Five

Ky

"SO HOW WAS the meet and greet?" I ask Tyler in a sarcastic voice.

"Nothing like I expected," he says, gripping his Algebra 2 textbook in his right hand and watching me grab mine from my locker before slamming it closed.

"What do you mean?"

He runs his hand through his dirty blond hair in obvious frustration. "She doesn't talk much. Clipped answers. Yes, no, thank you, hello. That's it."

Chris walks up to us, obviously only hearing the last part. "Is she hot?"

Tyler snaps his eyes at Chris. "Dude, what the fuck? The last thing I was doing was checking out a girl who shows up in my house as my half-sister. You don't see me asking you the same about your sister Abby. It's weird as fuck."

Chris tenses at the mention of his sister, who is the only chick we protect on the cheerleading team. She's pretty but not my type, and too nice for her own good. I've caught Tyler checking her out a bunch of times but keep that to myself. I don't think Chris has noticed, but I'm not going to put Tyler out there like that. We all have eyes, and they are meant to look, to watch. If a fine ass chick walks by or shows you something, it's your God-given right to admire. I don't give a fuck who you are. It works both ways. Girls check out guys all the time too.

Chris places his hand in a friendly way on Tyler's shoulder. "My bad, brother. I was trying to make light out of a messed-up situation. I appreciate you respecting Abby." His gaze finds mine. "Thanks for helping me out with her and keeping these assholes away from her since eighth grade."

Abby is short for Abigail. She is only one year and a few months younger than Chris. We call him Chris for short, but she prefers to call him by his full name Christian. I can tell it annoys him sometimes, but he loves his sister and protects her as he should. Up until now, Chris was the only one with a sibling, but now Tyler has a sister. So that leaves me being the only one who is an only child.

"So when do we get to meet your sister?" I ask Tyler.

His face turns into a scowl. "She is not my sister. She's my father's mistake, not mine. I don't know her, and I'm not interested in getting to know her. So you guys getting to meet her has nothing to do with me."

Chris raises his brows at Tyler's hostile tone. "Damn. That bad, huh?"

The bell rings, signaling the five minutes students have to get to class. I'm surprised she isn't hanging around him. I'm sure Tyler's mother, being as caring as she is, would have asked him to show her around, or at least walk her to class.

"She is his problem. I refuse to play the doting brother. I don't care. The faster this year is over, the faster I can leave and go to college. And I don't have to see her face again or deal with my father feeling guilty."

"How did your mom take it when she actually met her?"

He shakes his head. "She feels bad and is acting like my father didn't keep the fact that he fathered a child with an illegal immigrant from her when they met. Or that he failed to mention it at all since she got pregnant with me, and then they got married. Knowing my mother, she will treat her like the daughter she never had, though."

Tyler's mom couldn't have any more kids after she had him. She wanted more children. I think she wanted a daughter after Tyler was born, but apparently suffered from multiple miscarriages based on what Tyler has mentioned in the past. It sucks how some women who don't deserve kids have them, and the ones who are excellent mothers have trouble conceiving. It's like God's cruel joke or something. Drug-addicted mothers who sell their kids for the next hit can conceive, but poor souls like Caroline can't have more kids.

"So where is the evil spawn?" I ask sarcastically.

"I don't know. Probably getting oriented in the office."

A group of girls on the cheer squad pass us, checking us out. Tina, Jen, and Nicole are among the cheerleaders. Jen thinks she is my favorite because I fuck her whenever I feel like it, and she thinks she is the only one I have dipped my dick in. But she is just the more willing of the bunch. If she only knew last night that it was Nicole I was fucking at her house when she texted me goodnight, she'd flip out.

Nicole gives me a little smirk like she is special or some shit. I don't think Jen got the memo that I have fucked every girl on the cheer squad and dance team, except for Abby, of course. Thing is, though, they all have one complaint: I don't do serious boyfriend shit, whatever that means.

But it's true...there isn't a girl in this school who will tie me down, so it's best that they all realize it and let me have my way with them.

Chapter Six

Ky

I WALK INTO Algebra 2 with Chris, Tyler, Jen, and Nicole trailing behind me. We take a seat just in time as our teacher, Mrs. Keller, walks in. Mrs. Keller is one of the few who teaches the same subject for more than one grade. Most of us have attended Westlake Prep and know her from previous years. She's wearing the staff version of the West Lake uniform. Pencil skirt and blouse for the female staff, and polo shirts in a deep blue with slacks for the male staff. The male students wear white polos and dark blue slacks. The female students wear my favorite, red and blue plaid skirts with white shirts. The skirts are mid-thigh, and what I like to refer to as convenient for a quick fuck. The white shirts allow the male or female students, depending on what you're into, to take note of whether a girl has a decent rack. Most of them don't mind wearing different-colored bras under the white shirts to show off their assets when they take off blazers. It's a win-win for the guys.

"Welcome to Algebra 2. Most of you already have had algebra with me." I take a seat in the back with Chris and Tyler to my right, and Jen and Nicole trying to see who gets to sit on my left directly next to me. Apparently, Jen won the coveted spot today. "For those who don't know me..." She stops as the door opens and a girl enters the class with a dark blue hooded sweatshirt with the hood over her head, hiding her face. I can tell it is a girl because of the uniform skirt she is wearing. I take note of the way her tan legs move as she walks inside the classroom, which causes me to lick my lower lip. She's obviously new because I would have noticed those sexy tan legs.

Her head is bowed. Mrs. Keller watches along with everyone in the classroom as she makes her way inside and finds an empty seat in the back toward the far-right corner of the class. Tyler tenses and his hands grip the edge of the desk. It's obvious from his reaction that it's his half-sister. The one he wished never existed.

Mrs. Keller clears her throat and continues. "For those who don't know me, I'm Mrs. Keller and I will be teaching Algebra 2 this year." Her eyes dart to the back as she takes notice of the girl who walked in who has kept her hood over her head, obscuring her face from everyone. The new student doesn't move, and just stares straight ahead. She also didn't come in with a bag or a notebook, which is odd because I know Tyler's mom and dad would have made sure she had the necessary supplies. "I would like for each of you to take out a sheet of paper and write a paragraph that tells me what you did this past summer." Mrs. Keller walks toward her desk and leans against the edge, placing her hands in front. "It can be a trip or experience with your friends or family. What you liked about it. What you didn't like. The story is yours to tell. This is I can get to know you before diving in."

Everyone opens their backpacks, and the sound of paper being flipped in notebooks and others tearing out sheets of paper becomes the sounds that surrounds us. I reach in my pocket to grab my favorite pen and open my notebook to a clean sheet of paper to write down what I did all summer. Basically, train, hang out with my friends (*fuck girls*), go to parties, sleep, and repeat.

I hear Mrs. Keller begin to call out names as I'm writing, and I tune her out until she says Tyler's name. Knowing my last name is not far behind, I pause. But the name I hear next makes me stop. My pen begins bleeding into the sheet of paper when she repeats the name.

"Mur...Rubiana Murray."

My heart drops and my stomach clenches when I turn my head to my right in disbelief. No. Fucking. Way.

"Rubiana Murray. Could you please let me know you are here?"

The girl raises her hand, and I see the blue hoodie is old and faded with marks on the sleeves. My eyes look down to a pair of old Converse sneakers that have seen better days. My eyes trail to the dirty laces and socks that have been washed so many times, it's a wonder they are still able to stay on her feet.

"Eww. Gross," Jen says from my left. "Who the hell is that?"

She says it loud enough that Tyler shrinks in his seat.

"I'm here," Rubiana says in a soft voice that goes straight to my dick.

Fuck. It can't be. This must be a sick joke.

"Are you two related?" Mrs. Keller asks her after Rubi places her hand down. "Could you please take that off your head in my class? I would like to see who I'm talking to."

Her fingers slide the hood of her sweater off, revealing the same dirty blond hair I remember as a kid, except she is wearing braids , the ends tucked into the back of the sweater so you can't tell how long her hair is.

Her face is tan with the same small nose, and lips the shade of red. Her bottom lip is slightly bigger than her top, making a little pout that brings back memories of her. I could never forget those lips that are the perfect shade of red. Not too deep or bright, just right. The shade any girl wants when applying the color red but has to blot their lips with a napkin a few times to get it the right color but not Rubi. On her, it's all natural.

"That's better. Thank you, Rubiana. I asked are you and Tyler related?"

She keeps looking straight ahead, but everyone is looking in her direction. Wondering. Waiting for the answer. The gossips are waiting to eat up the knowledge that one of the popular guys in school has a sister no one knows about.

"No."

Everyone's attention is now on Tyler.

"No," he repeats. "We are not related. We just have the same last name."

"Oh, okay. I'm sorry." Her eyes flick to Rubi. "Rubi, could you please begin writing. I notice you don't have a piece of paper or pen out on your desk."

Some people snicker, including Chris, Jen, and Nicole.

Tyler opens his book bag with more force than necessary and grabs a sheet of paper and a pen with a scowl on his face. He gets up and walks over and places the paper and pen on Rubi's desk. "Don't embarrass me. Come prepared next time," he whispers to her.

Her eyes flash in his direction, and I swear I can see the corner of her pouty lip lift in a snarl.

Jen laughs. "Please, Tyler. Her shoes are enough to embarrass anyone. What are those?"

Everyone laughs at her joke. "She has a lot to be embarrassed about, and it has nothing to do with you," Jen says.

"Come on, guys, give her a break," Mrs. Keller scolds. I don't feel bad. She deserves it. "Ky Reeves."

When she hears my name, she turns her head, eyes opened wide, and that's all the attention that I needed. Recognition. Checkmate. She remembers. Her eyes find my dark ones and

I glare at her. My reaction must surprise her because her lips part. Her brows slightly pinch together.

"Here," I call out, never breaking eye contact. The look I'm giving her is not forgiving. It's full of anger. I'm not happy that she is here, though, and soon enough she will learn to keep it a secret from the others that we know each other. I'll make sure it stays that way. She is not going to have it easy. I'm not going to make it easy for her. Here she will realize she is on her own. I'm the bully I told her I would never be. The good friend was flushed out the window when she left me her stupid little letter after I told her things about me no one else knows. My secrets. My goals. I was stupid and fell for her friendship, when at the time she was everything to me. I'm glad I never told her the truth of how I felt about her when we were kids. I admit I told her I liked her, and that I thought she was pretty and special. She probably thinks I'm the same stupid eleven-year-old she left with a broken heart. I'm going to make sure she knows I'm not that kid anymore. I'm the exact opposite. The sooner she realizes it, the better.

After ten minutes, the teacher clears her throat. "Alright, the next twenty minutes of class I will call on some of you so you can read what you wrote. This will be part of your participation grade. I have written your weekly assignment on the board. It is due by Friday, no exceptions."

She begins to call out names randomly around the room, and I know she will call on Rubi since she is new. I can't wait to hear what she says she did during the summer. I mean, I shouldn't care, but I'm interested in seeing what she has been up to these days.

"Probably went dumpster diving," Nicole says under her breath to Jen. I know they are talking about Rubi and how her dirty-looking hoodie and sneakers stick out from the brand-new school uniform she is wearing. Looking at her from the corner of my eye, not to make it obvious I'm staring at her, I notice her sexy thighs and wonder how soft her skin is. I also notice the way she slides her tongue over her bottom lip every so often.

One thing I have to hand to Rubi, they can make fun of her shoes or hoodie because they are dingy looking, but she is still hot as fuck. She looks like a schoolgirl fantasy in a porn video, where the lady dresses up in a naughty schoolgirl outfit before she spreads her legs, waiting for you to take her on the desk. That vision makes me wonder if her breasts are full and perky. I can't tell a thing with that hoodie she's wearing.

"Rubiana, please share with the class what you did over the summer."

I raise a brow when I see Tyler shift in his seat uncomfortably. He pinches his nose with his fingers, and I wonder what has him all flustered.

Who gives a fuck what she did? It has nothing do to with him. Why should anyone care. He of all people can't stand her existence. I'm just a nosey prick who wants to know what she did. I also want to break her like she broke me. Make her hurt the way I did.

She stays quiet, and the initial shock must have worn off by now. The shock of us crossing paths again. We're in the same room. After all these years of wondering where she went.

The what if.

What not.

The stupid little flowers I gave her the second time she came to meet me by the edge of the fence in my backyard, like a lovesick idiot begging for her attention. Trusting her. Promises we made to each other. They were all lies that spilled from her tongue. And I hate her for it. I hate her for using me and then throwing me away without a reason.

Some might think I'm stupid for hating her the way I do right now. It was just a stupid letter, but to me it was more.

She was all I had left at a time when I was a different person, a better person.

The class waits for her to speak. She raises her eyes and looks straight ahead, but stays silent as everyone waits. And waits.

"You heard her," I say in a harsh tone that has her turning to look directly at me. I wave my hand in Mrs. Keller's direction, indicating that the teacher asked her to do something. "You're not special here. If everyone has to do the assignment, so do you."

Her bottom teeth snag the skin of her bottom lip. Her leg twitches underneath the wooden desk with the attached blue plastic chair. She's pissed that I called her out, but I don't care. I raise my brow in challenge.

She rolls her eyes as she stands and walks up to the teacher, handing her the piece of paper. Mrs. Keller scans the paper while Rubi walks back to her desk, catching the eyes of Jimmy, the asshole up front. I didn't miss the way he looks her up and down.

Rubi sits back in her seat, and when Mrs. Keller looks up from reading whatever Rubi wrote, I notice her eyes are glassy. My interest is piqued. I want to know what she wrote. To see if her writing is any different from the note she left me all those years ago. I feel like a fucking psycho, but maybe I am a fucking psycho. I'm crazy, cold-hearted, and unemotional, but I still want to know what she wrote about her summer. But just like everything in my life. The timing is just off.

Because just then the bell rings.

Fuck.

Chapter Seven

Rubi

I'M WALKING INTO the lunchroom, which is way nicer than the public schools I have attended. The smell is even different. It smells like real food in here, and not frozen meat that looks like it was created in a lab somewhere. Although, it was still edible, it was better than what I had wherever I was staying. Growing up I became a creative culinary artist with the scraps I could find just to keep the hunger pangs away.

I take a seat at the long bench tables that are set up in rows of five. I notice the jocks with their letterman jackets sitting at one table. The cheerleaders are there and I know they are cheerleaders because one of them has a pin that says cheer captain on her school jacket, and at another are the emo kids to my right. Then I notice a guy sitting alone with no one around. His head is lowered as he eats in silence.

I take a seat after getting a tray of food and placing it in front of me, even though I'm not hungry. I don't think I'll be able to eat as I replay what happened in English class. I can't believe I ran into him. Ky. I knew it was a possibility, but I wasn't prepared for the sight of him. His dark eyes bore into my skin like the sun heating me up from the inside. I was nervous. My leg wouldn't stop twitching at the sight of his muscled arms with random tattoos peeking out, or the fact that he practically didn't fit in the chair with the wooden desk. I wonder how he talked his parents into allowing him to get the ink. Kids from where I'm from get them because they know a tattoo artist that could care less about how old you were as long as you had money. He has changed. He has changed a lot. All grown up into this dark, sexy badboy, but what had me holding my breath in class was the way he looked at me with pure hatred in that moment. I mean, it looked like hatred.

I knew he recognized me, and he noticed that I did too. I remember the letter I left him with the flower that had one last petal hanging on it that was dried up from keeping it flat in a book. It was the only way I could say goodbye. It was the only way I knew how to communicate with him so he wouldn't forget me. I was hurt and scared. I didn't want to lose him, but I knew I had to give him up. It never crossed my mind that he would get mad at me. Upset. Maybe. He was the only person in my life who knew me. He was the reason I kept going, never giving up, but how he treated me and looked at me back there in the classroom, I know his feelings toward me have changed.

People change for different reasons. Obviously, I've changed too. I just hope he has changed for the better. I hope he is happy. I saw the way the girl sitting next to him just stared at him. I felt a pang of jealousy, but I pushed it down. I have no right to be jealous. I haven't seen or talked to him for so long, but in my mind, I guess Ky was always mine. When I had no choice but to leave, I kept the memories we shared inside of me like a silent whisper, constantly telling me to fight and hold on. To fight for another day. Because when you fight for another day, you hope there is something or someone waiting for you once you come out on the other side. Telling you they care. Telling you that everything will be alright. I kept fighting, but now I think I will never have anyone there waiting for me. Especially not Ky.

I scroll through the cellphone that was left on the nightstand in my room. I've never had a phone of my own before, so I distract myself by trying to get familiar with it. I'll learn, though. I just know the basics of texting and calling.

Silence falls in the cafeteria as Ky enters with my half-brother, and another guy I noticed in algebra class who walked in with the stuck-up girls who were laughing at me. I see Ky, with his dark hair and tight polo shirt fitting his frame perfectly, greet the jocks, and notice Tyler has a letterman jacket on his arm. They must be on the football team, but I notice Ky doesn't have one. Interesting. Maybe he doesn't play football. He never told me he was interested in any sports, but that was a long time ago and interests change.

Me. I like dancing. Hip-hop, mostly. I found out I like it when I was sent to a family that fostered eight kids. They were of different ages—three boys and five girls, making me the eighth one of the group. They taught me dance moves for a year until the couple turned out to be shit. That was when I started stealing—I mean, borrowing. I had to. I couldn't let the other kids go hungry.

My eyes look at my food and I start to eat like it's my last meal. Some habits are hard to break. After I take my last bite, I glance around the cafeteria and see a paper ball with something on it fly across the room toward the guy who is sitting quietly to my left. It hits him in the forehead and falls on the plate and landing in his ketchup, causing it to splatter down the bridge of his nose. The cafeteria erupts into laughter. My head snaps around, and I see the jocks at the football table laugh. My eyes find Ky, and he is laughing along with them.

Asshole.

The poor kid doesn't have a napkin, and he is stiff like a statue. His brown hair is covering his eyes, and I can't see him properly because he refuses to look up. I can't blame him. As a foster kid, I understand getting bullied all the time. We are used to it, but we also make alliances with the misfits. The ones who don't give a fuck anymore. The ones who end up in gangs. They aren't bad. They just don't have a choice. The system fails kids like us all the time. You can't even blame the system because where would that leave the parents. The ones who brought you into the world.

"I hate them. Every year is the same," the kid mumbles to himself, loud enough that I can hear him.

I feel bad and know what it's like. I hand him the clean napkin from my tray across from me. He looks up and takes it.

"T-thank you, "he says, wiping the ketchup off the best he can.

"Hey, Patty! I told you to stop leaving your tampons in the bathroom, you dirty fuck."

My head turns, and I see a blonde prick seated at the jocks' table, laughing and smirking. I roll my eyes at his crude remarks. Prick. My eyes dart over to see Tyler watching me from where he is sitting, doing nothing to stop the idiot. What a bunch of immature, rich assholes.

"What are you looking at, Street Rat? I heard all about you showing up for a free meal ticket. I'm not surprised you sat over there with P-p-patty," the blonde prick mocks.

Motherfucker. I turn my head around and glare at Tyler. If I had any doubt of how he felt about me, this is all the proof I need. I'm not stupid enough not to believe he is one of the popular ones, he obviously is with where he is seated. The girls hang around him and Ky like they are waiting for scraps. I'm already public enemy number one on my first day. But I won't let it get to me. If there is one thing I have experienced plenty of, it is to be the unwanted and the outcast. A bunch of rich pricks won't ever get to me. Especially a stuck-up half-brother who is quick to talk shit about a situation I have no control over. He doesn't know me, and I don't want to know him. He can kiss my ass. They can all kiss my ass.

He thinks I want to be here. If he only knew I preferred to stay where I was. At least in the foster system I knew to never expect much. I wasn't required to act a certain way for the benefit of others either. I was real. I was me. Rubiana. The difficult teenager with a juvenile record who has been through enough shit in her short life to make any psychotherapist wealthy from the weekly visits alone. Who are they to think allowing my sperm donor the right to bring me here would fix my inner turmoil from the abuse I have suffered? They have zero idea of what I've endured.

"D-d-don't let them get to you."

My head spins back around to the poor kid they called Patty. He is looking at me, and I can see that his eyes are actually a soft brown. Almost a honey color. He has attractive features, and could easily pass as a good-looking guy if he had a dose of confidence. I wonder what his story is, being at this school among these elitists.

"Let who get to me?" I ask, playing it off.

I know he means the assholes sitting at the table, including Ky. I want to glance over in his direction but don't want to make it obvious, so I stay with my back turned, facing Pat.

"What's your name? And why do you let them get to you?" I volley back the last part, even though I obviously know his name.

He slides his long hair that's covering his eyes to the side as he studies me for a second before he answers. "My n-n-name is Patrick." He takes a deep breath before he continues. I feel something hit me on my back but I remain still, not giving anyone the satisfaction, facing Patrick and waiting for him to continue. I have no choice but to Ignore the fact that they are throwing things, trying to intimidate and make fun of me. It's a test. When bullies push, it's to see how far you let them go, and they gauge it based on how you react. Sometimes ignoring it works, but other times it just gives them the right to keep doing it.

Confronting them and standing up for yourself is necessary, but right now I want to hear what poor Patrick has to say. I get why he doesn't have confidence and allows these assholes to make fun of him and put him down is because he stutters. People who are trying to hide their own insecurities sometimes prey on others to make themselves feel better, and in this case, it's Patrick who is the victim because of his speech impediment. It's not like he wants to stutter. He just does. As a decent human being, you can choose to ignore it and not make it obvious that he has the disability, but people are not nice. They love to focus on the negative.

In my case, it's because I'm not from here and come from the other side of the tracks. The poor side, and let's not forget that I also trespassed into Tyler's idyllic life and caused ripples in the water for his family.

Patrick takes a deep breath, I guess it helps him stutter less with the way he tries to calm himself down. "They are all bullies and love to pick on others who a-a-are not in their ci-circle."

"Who's they?"

I already know the asshole who threw the ball of paper at him, and it's probably the same one throwing things at my back.

"C-conner plays football and is the quarterback. Tyler, Chris, and Ky. The p-popular girls in the cheer squad. It's a tight group."

I turn my head to my right and close my eyes briefly, remembering the promises we made.

"*Will you promise not to be a bully when you go to school?*" I ask.

I had jumped the fence again for the fifth week in a row with the understanding that Ky and I would hang out three times a week. The sting of my back reminds me not to make sudden movements as I sit cross-legged on the old blanket on the grass. Lying down, I break the stick in my fingers into tiny brown pieces taking in the smell of grass, flowers, and trees. Ky placed two flowers with the little white petals I love so I can make my wishes near me on the blanket. I never even knew those flowers existed.

My mother's house on the other side of town doesn't have grass that smells like fresh earth, or have any types of flowers in the yards. It's just the scant remnants of brown, dried-out grass that looks like flames have torched the ground, and all that is left is dirt that makes you sneeze and dirties your shoes.

"I promise," he says when he looks up at me with his dark eyes. His eyes are so dark they are almost black. Just like his hair.

He reminded me of my all-time favorite movie Cry Baby starring Johnny Depp that we had on VHS tape. Maybe because it was the only thing I could watch at home because the TV screen was all white and fuzzy every time you tried to change the channels. But still, it was a great movie.

Ky looked like he was growing into a young Johnny Depp. Every time I would watch it on the old VHS my mother had in my room, the tape got stuck and it was the only movie it would play. The first time I saw the movie, it reminded me of a boy I met wandering on the edge of town, hoping I could get a glimpse of how the more fortunate people lived when I jumped the fence and came face to face with a boy. A boy who listened to everything I had to say. There were times when he was lost in thought, the expression on his face would go blank and then he would look like he was worried. I always wondered what worried him. He would never tell me, and I would never ask.

He didn't ask where I came from, or where I lived exactly. I think it was obvious I didn't live down the beautiful tree-lined street filled with expensive homes that he lived on.

"*I promise. Especially you. I could never bully you, Rubi. If anyone tries to bully or hurt you, I'll beat them up.*"

I smiled at that admission, looking down at my dirty fingernails from breaking the twigs into tiny pieces. My real-life protector. I know he was just a boy my age. But it was nice that there was someone who was willing to take on that role. I looked up and his dark eyes would follow the movement of my fingers as he watched me make a mess on the blanket.

"*Promise?*"

"*I promise. Always.*"

"Hey, are you okay?" Patrick whisper-yells.

My eyes quickly opened, and I realized I was trapped in one of my memories, one of the good ones, at least. "Yeah."

I see him stiffen, and his head lowers like he wasn't just talking to me. It's then I realize what caused that reaction when I feel the bench vibrate as someone sits to my right.

My head angles and my heart begins to beat like a drum in my ears. My stomach clenches in knots, and the scent of his cologne makes me aware that he is real. That he is next to me.

Ky.

His lip curls into a sneer. "I want to make it clear that just because I'm friends with Tyler, doesn't mean it applies to you."

"It's nice to see you, too, Ky."

Even though he is being a total dick to me right now, it doesn't change the fact that he is even more gorgeous now than when we were younger. I knew even as a young girl that he was going to be drop-dead gorgeous when he got older. He's dark and intimidating, and for the first time being around him, I'm nervous. I'm nervous because this is not the same Ky I knew. The Ky I knew would never make me feel inferior. He would never make me feel the way he is right now. Alone.

Funny how the people you want to change don't, and the ones you least expect to change, change for the worst. In the end, they leave you disappointed. It is like a personal betrayal hoping their heart was in the same place as yours.

"Wish I could say the same." He gets close and my muscles tense waiting for the blow I know he is going to give me. "I didn't come over here to say hi or reconnect. I came to make sure you get the message from me and not from anyone else. Stay the fuck away from me and my crew, that includes Tyler. You have done enough simply by showing up out of the scum you came from to fuck with his life. No one wants—or needs—you here."

My eyes dart in his direction. Anger simmering in my veins from his words. Words that pierce me inside replaying in my head. The change in him. I knew just by looking at him today that he had something dark lurking inside of him. My ideal guy would never be a person I couldn't stand the sight of, but like everything in my life, everyone I've ever known has left me with hurt and disappointment. I can't change people, and I won't be able to change what he has become. Someone who doesn't want me around.

"You know you can't hurt me any more than other people have. I can see that you have changed...and not for the better."

He chuckles and lowers his voice so no can hear his next words. "You don't have to play pretend, Rubi. I know you're just a pathetic loser who was probably only trying to get something out of me back when we were eleven, but realized the only thing I had to offer was a conversation by a tree in my backyard. You don't know me, and I don't know you. You're like an unwanted rat looking for the next home to rob. Am I right? Isn't that what you are into? Stealing." I suck in a breath trying to contain the anger I want to unleash. He doesn't know anything. He doesn't know me or know what I have been through. If he only knew I had to steal just to survive, but he doesn't care. Nothing about this Ky is the Ky I knew all those years ago.

I didn't mean to steal... I have a list of all the things I stole so when I get a job I can pay it back.

It was for things like food and for clothes that I didn't have. It was pure survival. I got caught, but so what. I knew it would only be a matter of time before I would get caught again. It's getting harder to steal with cameras and technology. I didn't look like I belonged in the store to begin with. My threadbare shorts and t-shirt I was wearing looked like I stole clothes from a five-year-old. When I changed into the new clothes in the fitting room and walked out, the stupid lady in the changing room alerted security, and they called the police.

I had snuck out of my latest foster family's house that day because they loved to collect the checks, but didn't pass the fruits on to the foster kids. Typical drunk assholes milking the system for money. It is always the same. They put on a front to be able to foster kids who have been abused or abandoned somewhere, but it's all a lie.

I'm realizing Tyler is just like him, a heartless asshole. Ky looks down with a look of disgust at my shoes and my baggy blue sweater that has seen better days, all the while making a gesture like he smells something rotten. "You stink, but then again, you always did. You always smelled like the piece of shit you are. I should have known better. I've been waiting for the day our paths would cross so I could tell you what I truly think of you. If you think you had it bad in whatever sewer you crawled out from, it will be nothing compared to what I have in store for you."

"Fuck you," I snarl. "Stay away from me."

His eyes travel over my face, and then down to my legs, angling his head like he is checking me out, but I know he is doing it to intimidate me. "Nah, I wouldn't think about fucking you...I have standards. The girls I fuck around with are more my style. Clean, pretty, and the type who have something going for them.

Everything you are not. Maybe you could play with Patty over here if he tucks his nut sack back since he's a little bitch and wished to have a pussy."

"L-leave her alone."

Ky quirks a brow and raises his eyes to Patrick. "What was that, asshole?"

"Leave him alone," I blurt, but Ky ignores me.

I'm surprised Patrick is sticking up for me against Ky, but the stricken look in Patrick's eyes tells me he isn't so sure of himself. I can tell that Ky could hurt Patrick with his height and muscular build as he leans over the table.

"This is not middle school, bitch. I will kick your ass all over this cafeteria so everyone can watch how I use you to wipe the floor."

I realize I have to stop this, and without thinking, I place my hand on Ky's forearm, hoping he doesn't really mean it. The expression Ky has aimed at Patrick says he isn't fucking around. The heat from his skin can be felt through my fingers and crawls up my arm like heat from a torch.

He suddenly jerks his arm from my touch like I burned him. "Don't fucking touch me."

I pull my hand back, taking a deep swallow. His jaw tics and his hard gaze is directed at me, and all I see is anger, hate, and disgust. All in that order. He no longer sees me as a friend, and that's fine. I don't know what I did wrong except leave him a letter. It was the only way I could tell him goodbye. It was the only way I could keep my secret.

"I'm sorry. I won't touch you ever again."

He smirks at my response. A condescending smile that tells me he wants me to feel inferior. For me to bow down to him like he is some deity.

"I think that's for the best. I wouldn't want to catch anything that meds won't cure."

I look around and notice all the attention in the cafeteria is on our exchange. He must feed off of it and wants to make it known that I'm in the same league as Patrick. That's fine. I couldn't care less. It hurts me that he, of all the people I cared about, turned out this way. That he thinks so low of me when he doesn't know a thing about my life. The promise he made about not being a bully went unfulfilled, and it makes me wonder what other promises he broke besides this.

"So that's what you do now." I lift my chin and shake my head. "Bully people to feel better about yourself. Threaten people. Beat them up for sport when they don't do what you tell them."

He smirks. "Nah, just you and that prick in front of you. And anyone else I find the need to set straight. But for you, I'm going to make your stay here extra welcome."

His eyes flick behind me, and then I feel something wet and cold spill over my head and down the back my hoodie.

I stiffen and watch as Patrick tries to stop them, but he fails. Ky grips his wrist so tight that Patrick yelps. "Ahh. L-let go."

"This doesn't concern you, Patty. Fuck off. Don't let me catch you interfering in what doesn't concern you. You got that," Ky snarls, shoving him back.

Patrick grips the edge of the table to keep from falling while I whip around to see who poured the milk over my head. I notice the blonde girl with green eyes from algebra class laugh along with the rest of the students seated in the cafeteria. I think her name is Nicole. The same one who was looking at Ky with longing when her other friend sat next to him, beating her to the seat first. Bitch.

"Go sit," he demands, nudging his chin toward the table where Tyler and their group is seated.

"Yes, baby," she says with a hint of saccharine to her voice.

She must be his girlfriend...or maybe one of them. I wouldn't be surprised. He must have them eating from the palm of his hand.

I try to get up, but the liquid seeping down my back has me wincing. Damn it.

I want to kick Nicole's ass, but all that would do is get me in trouble, and it's the last thing I need, another stint in juvenile detention.

If I want to taste freedom once I graduate, I have to lay low and stay out of trouble. It's like a bright light leading me out of the dark prison I was sent to after experiencing hell. The year I spent sneaking off to meet Ky was a reprieve from the mess that was my childhood. A childhood I knew was full of pain.

Now I wished I never met Ky so I wouldn't be so disappointed. I'm so angry with myself for thinking he was the only person in my life who was real. The one person who understood me. This is just another blow in my life. I guess some people are just born unlucky, and I'm one of them.

I stand in the aisle and give him a look of hatred and disgust for who and what he has become. My eyes sting with hurt and disappointment for the boy who is now a man whom I find gorgeous still, but his attitude toward me diminishes his appeal. How could someone who looks so beautiful and have everything be such an entitled prick?

I lean in close, bending slightly at the waist while hating the mid-thigh skirt I have to wear. Not my style, but what choice do I really have? My eyes are at the same level with his, not caring if I smell like milk. "Thank you for making my stay here extra welcome. My name is Rubiana. Get it right. Only my close friends call me, Rubi. Asshole."

He gives me a grin and shrugs his shoulders. "Good. I'm glad we established that we aren't friends. We aren't anything. I'm just making sure you know your place while you're here."

He turns his head, but then whips it right back. "And one more thing. I hate repeating myself, but I'm going to say it for the last time. Fuck with Tyler, and I'll end you."

I blink at him like his threat doesn't faze me in the slightest. I don't care anymore. The only person I can count on is myself now.

Chapter Eight

Ky

THE REST OF the day goes smoothly until I'm heading out to my car parked in the senior row at the front of the student parking lot. I see Tyler's worried expression as he's looking at the students coming out of the school who are walking out in groups and going to their cars, getting ready for whatever afterschool activity they are running off to.

I haven't seen Rubi since lunch, and I'm relieved that I don't have her in any other class except Algebra 2. I didn't think seeing her again would bring out these savage feelings of anger toward her. I've been in a funk ever since finding out that she is here, and I know I'm handling it pretty bad.

I face Nicole before Tyler walks over. I had to wait until school was over so I could call out Nicole for the little stunt she pulled spilling milk all over Rubi's head. I didn't want it to get that far in confronting her.

"I didn't ask you to do that," I snap.

She shrugs her shoulders and smirks. "I was just helping out. Since you don't like the fact that she is here, I did it for you," she purrs.

"Well, don't do things for me I didn't ask for."

She rolls her eyes dramatically and my left eye twitches in annoyance. I'll deal with her later.

My intention of confronting Rubi was to feel her out to find out what her real purpose is, not make things worse for Tyler. I can tell Tyler is stressed about his father showing up at the school after Rubi's little milk accident. He is worried about how his mom will take it when she finds out her son was being a dick when he probably lied and said he was cool with Rubi living with them. Tyler's a good guy and he doesn't need this right now.

I never told them about Rubi and I don't intend to tell them about how I know her. I hate keeping secrets from them, but I don't want to let anyone know that we have a complicated history. I don't want them to know that she is the catalyst for my anger and the reason why I don't have girlfriends or want to get married. Ever.

I walk up to Tyler, leaving Nicole standing there as he watches the front doors of the school. Waiting.

"What's up?" I ask.

He shakes his head. "I'm pissed at you for what you did at lunch today. I have to wait for her to come out so I can give her a ride home. Father's orders. I know I will have to explain what happened to her." He turns his head to look at me. "Why did you do that?" Tyler asks.

I raise my hands in mock surrender. "I didn't tell Nicole to do that. That was all her. I told her to lay off and not to get involved."

"Yeah, man, but your little side chick, or whatever you want to call her, just fucked me at home. My father is going to give me shit about messing with her. It's like I have to babysit her and make sure she stays out of trouble. Court order."

"First... Nicole is not my side chick, because that would mean I have a main chick, which I don't have. I'll take care of

Nicole's little infatuation with me. She just needs to know she isn't special because I fucked her at Conner's party over the summer. It was supposed to be on the down low like most of my hook-ups, but I guess she can't accept it. Not my fault." I'm not the type of guy to let it be known who I sleep with. I guess some of them want to brag that I slept with them. "I wasn't trying to make it hard on you at home. I was making sure she knew how her year here will go...and what do you mean by a court order?"

Tyler told us a little about Rubi being his half-sister and how his father found out about it, but he's kept pretty silent on the details.

"I overheard my father talking to the principal. She has a record, like I mentioned before...all underage misdemeanors. Stealing, I think he said."

I play it off like I don't know anything about the situation. I knew it was for stealing. I sent a text to my father's lawyer when I found out that she was here in algebra class. He said that she had a record for stealing. That is all he could tell me since she is a minor. "What the fuck for?"

It doesn't matter. It's not like I care that Rubi turned out to be a criminal. *Liar*. It's not my problem, but apparently this is something that affects Tyler. That's what I keep telling myself.

He unlocks his truck and opens the driver's side door, and I walk around to my car and do the same. I'm able to see him over the roof of my car with my height advantage and the fact that his truck is lifted. "My dad doesn't say much about her past. It's like some big fucking secret he doesn't want known. Not even my mom knows. Like I said before, all we know is that she is biologically his and technically my half-sister, she's been in and out of foster care for whatever reason, and has gotten into trouble a couple of times for stealing. She has three stints in juvenile detention. I overheard them say when I was in the principal's office.

"He let allowed her in your house when she's a thief?" I blurt. What the fuck? How could his father trust her, but then again, maybe he doesn't trust her, so he has Tyler babysitting her before and after school like a child.

"My father was defending her to the school. He said she had it tough and that she only did those things for food and clothes. The last time it was for the other kids who didn't have anything. I guess not all foster families are good. She was in for two months this past summer and just got out. Hence, the court hearing my father showed up to. If she gets caught doing anything illegal, she will be tried as an adult. My father is on his guilt trip and assured the judge that he would make sure she graduates high school and stay out of trouble as part of her sentence. That's all I know. The last thing I need is my father getting on my shit about her."

So, she does have a heart. Just not for me. She never bothered reaching out to me. Ever. I can't lie and say I didn't wonder what happened and why I wasn't good enough for her. We live in a modern world. Facebook or IG. She could've searched for me online. It's not like she didn't know where I lived. I guess I have to face the truth…she thinks I'm not good enough for her.

Now she expects me to be civil or friendly. Fuck that. Fuck her. Thinking those two words has the thought of Rubi's tan thighs wrapped around my hips as I punish her for not wanting me. I told her she smelled and was not pretty like the other girls I hook up with, and it's all bullshit. Rubiana Murray is hot as fuck.

The front doors of the school suddenly open, and she appears wearing a boy's polo uniform shirt I'm sure they gave her from the lost and found. My brows pinch together as she has a plastic grocery bag hooked on her finger that must contain her wet school shirt and hoodie. To my surprise, she turns to the left and throws it in the trash. It must smell like vomit by now. It's not going to go well when Tyler has to explain to his father that it was my fault Nicole stuck her nose in where it didn't belong.

She makes her way toward us with a blank expression and walks up to the door on the driver's side of his truck. She is facing me with the door open as I watch her cross her arms, and that's when I notice them. The tattoos of the flowers. The same flowers I gave her the second day she showed up in my backyard. The flowers she once told me were her favorite. I always placed them on the blanket near the tree that held our treehouse. We built that treehouse together. It was our spot. At least it was until the third summer I got tired of waiting for her to come back and burned it. My father almost lost it when he saw the smoke and flames. I burned the tree practically to the ground. Ashes was all that was left. Just like my feelings for her.

I wonder how she was able to get the sleeve tattoos of all the daisies. It was obviously done by a professional, but where she comes from and the fact that she's not eighteen, I'm sure she hustled it out of someone. Maybe fucked the tattoo artist. The thought of her spreading her thighs for someone has me clenching my hands into fists. I also notice that she has a Band-Aid covering a spot on her forearm. I wonder how she hurt her arm. Nothing about her should bother me, but it does.

I guess all the thoughts about her I had pushed down are resurfacing again. Let's face it, I need to fuck someone. It's been a while.

"I'll walk. Don't bother waiting for me after school anymore to go to your house."

I notice she doesn't say home. I guess she doesn't consider Tyler's house her home.

"It's a three-mile walk to the house, Rubiana. I don't have time for this shit. Get in the truck," Tyler demands.

Looking at both of them, they have the same hair color. Dirty blonde like their father. The only difference is that Rubi has tan skin where Tyler's is more fare.

"No te preocoupes, caminare," she mumbles underneath her breath.

Woah, she just spoke Spanish.

I watch Chris and his sister Abby walk up by the front of my BMW after they leave the main building.

"Oh my God, is that her?" I hear Abby ask Chris.

"Yep," Chris responds behind Abby, causing Rubi to turn around. Her eyes find mine and then dart over to my car, recognition hitting her. I wanted a car that looked like the Batmobile. The BMW M8 convertible is close, and even has the windows blacked out. She obviously hasn't seen the Lamborghini my father gifted me for my eighteenth birthday. Yeah, Rubi. Superman sucks dick. He doesn't have swag like Batman. Doesn't get pussy like him either.

"Tyler, she's gorgeous." She looks over at Rubi and walks up to her. "Hi, I'm Abby. I'm Christian's sister," she says with a big smile on her face.

I roll my eyes because Abby can be clueless sometimes, or maybe she plays it off for Tyler's benefit. One thing about Abby is that she is a good girl. She's a junior, so she doesn't know what is going on, or what transpired at lunch today. She even looks at Rubi's shirt but doesn't ask why Rubi is wearing a boy's uniform shirt.

Rubi looks over at her and then at Christian. Her head turns in my direction, and I absently rub my tongue over the front of my teeth. She realizes that Abby isn't a threat and turns toward Abby with a smile. A smile that I could have sworn made my heart skip a beat. Fuck. She is gorgeous. Her straight white teeth peek out between her reddish lips, causing my dick to swell inside my pants.

Chris glances at Rubi with an expression that tells me that she is having the same effect on him. *Over my dead body.*

"Rubiana was just leaving. She has to get home," I say, making a note to call her by her full name since we aren't friends. "She——"

Rubi ignores me and cuts me off, directing her comment to Abby, "My name is Rubiana, but you can call me Rubi."

"Rubi," Abby repeats. "I like it. It's pretty."

"Thank you. I obviously didn't pick my name, but thanks," she responds, teasing her.

Abby smiles like she just made a best friend. If she only knew we are trying to avoid anything that has to do with her.

"I was just about to head home. I'll see you around. It was nice meeting you, Abby. I guess not everyone here at Westlake is a stuck-up snob."

Abby looks at her brother and then back at Rubi. "If they bother you, let me know." She looks at Tyler. "I can't believe you would allow anyone to pick on your sister. What is wrong with you? You know how Ky and his flock of admirers get."

"She's not my sister, Abby. I hardly know her," Tyler argues.

"Whatever." She looks at Rubi. "We need to hang out some time. Forget about the guys. They can be temperamental. It's a hormone thing."

Rubi glances at me and responds, "Yeah, I can tell. I guess that their nuts are finally dropping."

Chris chuckles.

He knows she meant that last jab at me. I have to fix what I did at lunch for Tyler's benefit. It is my fault about the milk incident, even if I wasn't the one who poured it per se.

"Get in the car," I demand, sliding inside my driver's seat and starting the car. I see her standing there and begin to get annoyed.

I lower the window and look out at Tyler's confused face. "I'll handle it. I'll take her."

He shakes his head. "I need her to get back home, or my father will have my ass, Ky."

"I'll deal with it. It's my fault anyway," I tell Tyler as I lean closer over the console to look out at Rubi with a raised brow. "Get in, Rubiana."

She reluctantly stomps over and opens the passenger door and slides in, causing my hands to grip the steering wheel as her skirt slides higher up her thighs, teasing me. Her hand grips the seatbelt as she buckles herself in.

She wastes no time after sitting in the seat as she says, "Alright, say what you have to say quickly and take me to their house."

I place the car in reverse, not caring that people are staring at us as I drive out of the parking lot and onto the street. A spur of the moment decision I made was that I decided to get her a new hoodie to replace the one that was ruined. She can send me the bill from the school store for a new school shirt. Either way, it's a win-win. She gets a new hoodie and school shirt on me, and Tyler is off the hook with his dad, and I'll feel better for not fucking my friend over because of what happened at lunch.

"Where are you going? Tyler's house is that way." She points her thumb with the arm full of tattoos in the opposite direction that we're heading. Tattoos with history. Our history. Her favorite flower. The one I gave her first.

I glance at her briefly. "I'll make you a deal. You keep your mouth shut about the hoodie and school shirt getting ruined, and I'll buy you a new hoodie, and you can have the school send me the bill for the uniform shirt."

She laughs.

It's a beautiful laugh, but I keep a straight face, not giving away the fact that I find it sexy. Everything about her is sexy.

Yeah, I definitely have to get laid. I usually don't go this long without having sex, but I haven't hooked up with anyone recently because I have been busy with my father helping him with his business.

"What's so funny?"

"I guess your boy doesn't want to tell his daddy what an asshole he really is by spreading rumors about me and getting his friends to bully me on my first day. He can't fight his own battles." She scoffs. "I can't believe you rich kids. You think blackmailing people because you have money is the answer for everything when you fuck up."

My nostrils flare in annoyance as I pull in the parking lot of the upscale mall in West Lake and find a spot. I turn and face her, my eyes sliding over the polo shirt she's wearing. I notice that her breasts are small but not too large. My eyes slide back up and I'm met with a knowing expression. *Busted.*

"Are you done ogling me?"

I snort. "Please, I have already established what I think of you...and attractive isn't one of them."

"Then you're just a creep. Not only do you like to intimidate people, but you also like to bully, blackmail, and probably spread lies about them."

"Don't flatter yourself, and the last thing I am is a creep. I don't need to blackmail you for shit. I think my offer is in your benefit. You get a free hoodie that was better than the homeless-looking one you were wearing earlier."

She shakes her head and averts her eyes. "You are such an asshole. I'm trying to figure out how anyone puts up with you."

"That's because I'm not a liar, and I don't need to pretend to be anything I'm not."

She pulls her head back like I slapped her. I know I'm being a dick, but I can't be nice to her. I hate her for what she did to me. People like her are the way they are because they refuse to be better. She thinks people should feel sorry for her. It doesn't give her a free pass to show up and fuck someone else's life up because her life was so shitty. She should be grateful her biological father took her in and that she will at least graduate from an elite high school.

I hear her hand fumbling with the door, and she manages to open it and slide out. Fuck. This is not how I planned for this to go. I lower the passenger-side window. "Get back in the car, Rubiana."

She stomps off with her back turned as I watch her school skirt sway with each step, making me want to grab her and throw her over my shoulder like a caveman.

"No, I'd rather walk. I don't want you to buy me anything. Like you said, I'll just continue to be a piece of shit and steal one, right? Go fuck yourself, Ky. I hate you! Do yourself a favor and leave me the fuck alone."

Chapter Nine

Rubi

I FINALLY MAKE it to the house and am hot and sweaty. I am also in need of a shower, and have to thank whoever created locks for the front doors that require punching in the code. It is the first time I have used one, and I have to say, my sperm donor must make good money to afford a nice home like this.

When I shut the front door, I'm greeted with a Hawaiian-scented candle that is burning somewhere in the house. It beats the meth and cigarette smell I'm used to from when I was younger, or the old mildewy smell from the houses I was placed in foster care.

The gray wood floors are a big contrast to my dirty, worn-out Converse sneakers. The white walls complementing the gray and white carpet and nude-colored furnishings. I make my way past the foyer and up the stairs to a room, the likes of which I have only seen in a magazine, but not before I'm interrupted.

"Hi, Rubiana. I thought Tyler was bringing you home?" Caroline says in a soft voice.

I turn, facing her with my hand on the white wood railing of the staircase. She furrows her brows when she notices the polo shirt that is similar to her sons. If my day couldn't get any worse, Stephen Murray steps up behind her, looking at me over her head with a hard expression in his eyes.

"Where were you? And why do you have a boy's school shirt on? I was clear about the rules."

I shake my head at him and turn away—he thinks I was with a boy—and begin to climb the stairs. I don't need this shit. "Why don't you ask your son? And hello to you, too, Mrs. Murray."

I make it to the landing and turn the silver knob to the room I'm told is mine and I hear Mrs. Murray's voice before I close the door with a thud. "It's Caroline."

I call them Mr. and Mrs. Murray out of respect, but mostly because it's formal, and I don't consider them my parents or guardians, to be honest. I don't have parents. I never did. I gave up on that notion when I was eleven.

Sixteen was the age I realized I was truly alone and had no family. My mother was still in jail for drug use, possession, child neglect, and child abuse from when social services took me away at eleven. My stepfather was tried for the same, but his sentence was a lot worse.

I look at the soft white comforter I had used as a makeshift bed the night before that still remains in the closet. I look at the mattress like it is the first time I laid eyes on it. The mattress looks soft, and it's a full size, not like the hard twin mattresses I was used to, but when you are accustomed to hiding while you sleep, it's a hard habit to break.

I open the two wooden doors the rest of the way to the wall-to-wall closet. It only has my school uniforms hanging inside, and the black trash bag I keep my other clothes in, and push it to the side to make some more space. I adjust the comforter on the floor to prepare to go to bed after I take a hot shower.

I started sleeping in the closet when I was nine. It was so my stepfather wouldn't easily find me when he was high on whatever the drug of choice was at the time. When he was in that condition and couldn't see me in the bed, he usually left me alone. The closet was my haven. Hiding would also give me time to get away if someone was looking for me, or give me time to sneak out the window. Sneaking out of the window was relatively easy. I would always make sure to leave the latch unlocked just in case. Being abused practically all your life leaves lasting effects. It makes you realize how alone and helpless you are in a room full of people. You never know which monster around you is more evil than the other.

In this house, I'm not so sure about the monsters, but I'm not taking any chances. I've learned not to trust anyone, even If they say you are their daughter. I have had plenty of wannabe fathers in my life so far. Tyler is also two doors down from my room, and I don't trust him either. He didn't waste any time letting everyone know how unwanted I am in his life at school.

Stephen Murray doesn't know me, and he doesn't care. If he did, I wouldn't be so fucked up. I wouldn't have people look at me like I'm a disease that is invading their perfect little lives. I wouldn't have been left with a mother who only cared about her next hit of meth with anything she could sell or find.

After a hot shower, I hear a knock on my door. "Yeah." I call out.

"My mother says dinner is ready." I hear Tyler's muffled voice through the door.

I sigh and turn the knob as I open the door with more force than necessary. He stands at the threshold and lowers his chin to his chest.

"Are you going to tell them what happened?"

"Why? So you can add that I'm a snitch to the list of crap you have already told everyone about me?"

I cried in the shower. I couldn't help it. It's been an emotionally exhausting day. My eyes must be red and puffy, but I don't care. I just want to leave. Not be stuck in a never-ending system. A cycle of lies and neglect.

I want to have friends, get a job, maybe a boyfriend. Someone who likes the real me and can see past my history. I didn't ask for a meth-addicted mother who hated the fact that I was born, or a father who could not have cared less about me. Or even a half-brother who sees me like a threat to his existence.

I didn't cry and pity myself because of what Tyler said about me, though. I cried because I held on to an image of a boy who turned out to be someone I don't recognize. The love I had for him is what kept me going. I never reached out or looked for him because what would be the use? I was stuck in a government system and too young to do anything about it. We had a pact. A bond. At least that was what I thought we had. I guess I was lying to myself. Maybe it was best that I had to leave so I didn't see how he became the person he is now, a person I don't recognize. A guy who hates me. He could never love a girl like me. My beautiful boy has turned into a monster. One thing about being around monsters is, you don't run from them, you face them when the time is right. At eleven years old, it wasn't the time.

"Look, what happened today was not me. It was Ky and Nicole. She has this thing with him since they——" He trails off when he looks up.

Shit. He probably sees my eyes and could tell I was crying. What he almost said was since they fucked. I'm sure Ky has hooked up with most of the girls at school. I wouldn't be surprised with how good-looking he is. I get it. I've seen it from where I'm from. Except where I'm from, guys don't come from money and have nothing to lose except their freedom. They end up in gangs and sell drugs to make up for the lack of direction they never had. The gangs become their family...selling drugs their career. When you have a record, there aren't many options when you become an adult.

"Fucked," I finish for him, and he blinks. "You mean to say since they fucked. Good to know I have to watch some chick with a hard-on for Ky trying to go after me when he's around. She's lucky I didn't break her face."

He raises his brows. I must sound like I'm jealous, but I'm not. I can't be jealous of someone who thinks a girl like that is even attractive. A girl who is attractive and has a great personality would be a girl like Chris' sister, Abby. The one who secretly glanced at Tyler with longing. The one Tyler obviously fails to notice, but that is not my problem. I don't know them, and maybe I'm reading it all wrong.

"You didn't hear me say that. I really meant what I said. I didn't send Ky over to you or Nicole. That was all him, and I told him to leave you alone."

I believe him because Ky has kept a secret of his own. A secret I'm sure he doesn't want out. The one that says we met as kids. That we spent every week together for a year when we were eleven years old. That we were best friends and shared things. Things like my first kiss. It was a peck on the lips, but still a kiss. A kiss I remember. The one kiss that was better than any of the forced ones I received in a group home when I was a teenager from boys who don't know how to take no for an answer.

"Can we go downstairs and act like nothing happened. Please." He raises his eyes, pleading for me to go along with it. "For my mother." He swallows. "She's fragile, and I'm not sure how she is taking all of this. I'll tell my father you had an accident in the cafeteria, and after school you got a ride from a friend after they loaned you a shirt from lost and found. It's not a total lie."

If he means his mother is fragile, that can only mean one thing, she suffers from depression. That is what rich snobs call being fragile. I know that much watching TV. Caroline Murray most likely suffers from depression. I'm curious.

"Why is your mother fragile?"

He averts his eyes and slides his hands inside the pockets of his gray sweats. "She couldn't have children after having me," he says in a low tone.

Damn. That means she must not want me here, or the fact that I exist must bother her. She plays it off well though. Caroline has been very nice and has only shown kindness since I showed up. He is probably telling me so that I can be on my best behavior.

"Alright, I'll go along with it. I'm not here to disrupt your perfect little life or your mother's, and my plan is to leave after I graduate. I don't want a brother, and I'm not here to take your daddy away from you."

"Then why are you here? The truth."

I give him a side grin. "I don't know. I told your father to leave me with social services, but he refused. I never wanted to come." I lower my voice and he watches me as I speak slowly. "I... don't... want... to... be... here. Totally out of my control."

He steps aside while I close the door to the bedroom. I walk toward the stairs and I turn my head to look back as he stands there in his white t-shirt and gray sweats with a confused look on his face. "Let's go, *brother*," I say sarcastically, nudging my head in the direction of the stairs.

I can play fake with the best of them. If it gets me my freedom, and Tyler and his crew off my back, so be it.

Chapter Ten

Rubi

I WALK TOWARD the dining table that can easily seat ten. The largest table I have ever sat at was at a table for four, and we had to take turns. I take a seat on the cream cushion of the wooden chair in front of Caroline. Mr. Murray is seated to her left, and Tyler is seated to my right like we are an actual family and have been doing this for years.

Mr. Murray eyes me curiously as I look at the perfectly dressed table with matching plates and serving dishes filled with fluffy, buttered mashed potatoes and meatloaf. There is even warm dinner rolls and whipped butter on the side, and an array of different options to drink: soda, lemonade, and ice water. After scanning the perfectly placed food, I look up at Caroline and notice she is nursing a glass of wine.

"After dinner, I'll take you to get some things you need like I promised," Stephen says as I push my chair forward.

"Okay," I reply.

Tyler begins serving himself a hefty amount like he is eating for three instead of one. Mr. Murray goes next, and then Caroline. I stay frozen like a statue, unsure of what to do. I've never tasted meatloaf. The closest I have ever had was a Banquet frozen meal from the freezer, and it was the ninety-nine-cent kind you find at the Dollar Tree. The mashed potatoes I have eaten came from a box mixed with water and salt like the kind you get from a fast-food place. I never had the luxury of soda as I watch Mr. Murray pour a generous amount. This is all foreign to me, sitting here watching them eat and not worrying about if tomorrow they will have enough food.

I sit at the table and think about Emily, the six-year-old who is currently in a smelly house with barely enough food to eat, much less the luxury of different kinds of drinks.

"Rubiana, sweetheart. Is everything alright? I hope you like meatloaf and mashed potatoes?" Caroline asks in a soft, caring voice.

I blink back the sting of tears for the other kids who were left behind. I nod. "Yeah. I'm fine." I give her a wry smile.

How could I sit here and eat this glorious food when others little kids are going hungry? Kids I tried to protect but couldn't.

"Do you not like meatloaf?"

I swallow and look at the swirls of steam coming out of meat that looks so tender and delicious you can cut it with a fork. The scent of the flavors hitting me all at once causes my stomach to protest.

"I-I have never had meatloaf before."

"Oh. I should have asked if you liked meatloaf before I made it," she says, giving Mr. Ray a worried look.

I'm thankful she cooked a nice meal. It's more than anyone has ever done for me, and I do not want to seem like I'm ungrateful for her hospitality. So with my plate in hand, I serve myself a slice of meatloaf I know will taste amazing. I do the same with the mashed potatoes and grab a dinner roll. My mouth watering before I've even had a bite.

I give her a smile when I cut a piece and briefly close my eyes to savor the taste of a delicious, home-cooked meal. "It's very good. Thank you, Caroline."

Her lips lift in a warm smile as she takes a sip out of the glass of red wine. Mr. Murray gives me an appreciative nod. I didn't say that to be fake. It really is good.

"So what happened to your shirt today?" Mr. Murray says.

Tyler stiffens at his question, but I remain quiet. I plan on keeping my word as long as Tyler keeps his.

Tyler clears his throat. "She had an accident and ruined her hoodie and school shirt. The office was nice enough to give her a shirt from the lost and found."

Stephen looks taken aback, and maybe a little guilty for the way he treated me when he walked in. He automatically assumed I was already causing him trouble and hanging out with random boys. If he only knew his friends' kids are the trouble. Tyler gives his parents the impression he is an All-American kid by playing football. Bright future.

"Oh, that makes sense, but how did you get home?"

Before I can answer, Tyler speaks up. "Abby."

"That's great. See, Stephen. I knew she would get along with Tyler's friends. Abby is a great girl. I wonder why she didn't come inside to say hi. She always does, but anyway, she must have been busy with practice. Her brother Chris is a big softy when it comes to Abby. Oh, did you meet Ky?"

I stiffen when she mentions Ky's name. Tyler senses me tense and looks at me from the corner of his eye, and then at his mom.

"Yeah, they met," Tyler says quietly.

I'm sure they are wondering why Tyler is answering every question for me.

"He can be a little rough around the edges, but once you get to know him, he really is a nice guy underneath. Loyal to a fault."

I almost choke on the piece of meat in my mouth. Loyal, my ass. A traitor is more like it. An asshole is the best word to describe him. I take a sip of water and swallow, remembering the ride to the upscale mall he pulled into. And how he tried to blackmail me to make himself feel better.

The way his arms flexed. The random tattoos inked on his arms that I know have a meaning. I remember he told me when we were kids that everything meant something special. That everything you do should mean something. I didn't understand what he meant at the time.

"Be careful with Ky," Mr. Murray warns. "He has a temper, and as much as he is a good-looking young man, he is more of a heartbreaker. Sometimes, a troublemaker."

I snort. "Don't worry, Mr. Murray. I have no intention in getting involved with anyone while I'm here. I'm just passing through."

He stiffens, and I notice Tyler places his fork down and raises an eyebrow. I guess he thought I would call him Dad or some shit. There is nothing he has done for me to earn the title. He is Tyler's father...not mine.

Caroline looks nervously between us and clears her throat. "Well, I know it's a little early, but your eighteenth birthday is coming up and I wanted to know what flavor cake you would like. I know this great place, but you have to place your cake order months in advance."

I bite the corner of my lip trying to figure out how best to answer. How do you tell someone that not only have you never had meatloaf before, but you also never had cake before—much less your own birthday cake? The closest I had was a cupcake I stole from the package to give to Billy and Gene before they were legally adopted. They were six and seven years old with birthdays in the same month. The foster couple we were with at the time didn't give a shit about our birthdays or Christmas. Those were the worst days for kids like us. It was a reminder that no one cared or was coming to help us.

I look around the table, Mr. Murray seems pissed that I won't acknowledge him, and I could not care less. I glance at Tyler, and he slouches in his chair, probably waiting for me to say what my favorite flavor of cake is. My eyes land on Caroline as she smiles at me, waiting patiently.

"Um. I wouldn't know." I pour water in the glass cup in front of me and raise it, taking a sip and liking the way it cools my throat. I place the glass back on the table. "I've never had an actual cake before. I've also never had a birthday cake. The closest I ever had was a cupcake, and it was vanilla, I think. So I guess vanilla would be okay." I shrug my shoulders. "You really don't have to go to so much trouble. It's really no big deal. It's just another day."

Her smile falls and she looks at Mr. Murray, and then at Tyler. Silence. No one says anything. I've made them feel bad, that much is obvious.

Caroline blinks rapidly and places her napkin on the table and gets up. I guess I fucked up and said something to upset her, which wasn't my intent.

I get up from the table and begin to clear my dishes and head to the kitchen to wash my plate, my appetite all but gone. It's the least I could for the nice meal and offer of a birthday cake from Caroline. I'm not used to eating so much at dinner anyway.

"That's okay, Rubi. I'll help clean up," Tyler says.

I pause and look up to see Mr. Murray and notice he is also upset. I look over at Tyler, and he is just staring at his plate like it holds the answers to all the world's questions.

I place my plate and glass back down on the table and decide to be nice and address her by her first name like she asked. It is my way to smooth things over. "Please tell Caroline I'm sorry."

"Get some rest. I know I said that I would take you to get some things you needed at the store, but I promise to take you tomorrow."

"Don't trouble yourself, Mr. Murray. I have everything that I need."

Much like the meatloaf and cake, you can't miss all the things that you never had.

Chapter Eleven

Ky

IT'S FRIDAY AND I'm hitting the bag, getting my work out in at the boxing gym with the guys. After Rubi walked off in the parking lot and made the three-mile hike to Tyler's house, I followed her to make sure she made it home safely. My pride wouldn't allow me to make it known I was following her. I don't follow girls. Ever. Until her.

I followed from a safe distance making sure she couldn't tell I was following her. I know the Murray's family routine, and the usual time Caroline makes dinner. So I waited until I knew she would be asleep, but the funny thing is, when I climbed the tree on the side of the house up to her room, I didn't see her sleeping in the bed. I'm not sure if she snuck out, or if she slept somewhere else. I knew it was the room she was staying in because Tyler mentioned she was sleeping two doors down and was complaining he couldn't have girls over because her room was too close.

Tyler comes up behind me and I lower my arms from hitting the bag. I wipe the sweat from my forehead, shaking my tense muscles. Rubi coming back into my life has stirred up so much shit. I had nightmare with her in it. It was someone trying to force themselves on her, and all I can remember was wailing on the fucker. Blow after blow felt like lifting heavy weights, but I could see the man's face, I can hear her calling out for me, but I couldn't see her.

I woke up in a cold sweat reaching out for her, but she wasn't there. So I re-read the old letter wanting to rip it to shreds, but like always I couldn't do it. Because I can't let go as much as I want to but there is something about her that doesn't let me.

"I need to talk to you."

"What's up?"

"It's about, Rubi."

At the mention of her name, my head snaps up. Did something happen? Did she do anything?

I play it cool like I could not care less about Rubi. "What about her?"

He looks down like he feels guilty about something. "I know I told you about her showing up and it messing things up, but I need you to leave her alone."

"Wait. Is this about the other day? Did she say something?"

He shakes his head. "No. We talked, and she agreed not to say anything. She doesn't plan on staying with us past graduation anyway. It was all my dad's idea for her to come stay with us."

Why would she leave? Where would she go? I shouldn't care, but I can't let her go again. Not yet. Not until I break her like she broke me. I want her to feel like I felt. Hurt.

"What happened? Did she do something? Is Caroline alright."

"My mom is fine, Ky. Trust me. Just leave Rubiana alone."

Wait. Hold up. Is he defending her?

"Why the change of heart? Did she threaten you?"

"Nah, stay out of it, Ky. I know how you get, you think you know best, but this is family shit and I'll deal with it. I know you're lookin' out, but I can handle this."

I shrug my shoulders in agreement. Like it doesn't bother me he is warning me off of Rubiana. No one warns me off of Rubi. No one. Not even my best friend who is also her half-brother.

The following week is Conner's first party of the year. He's the popular quarterback of the school who loves to throw parties. He loves to host them since his parents are away a lot. I walk in with Jen. Her arms are wrapped around my waist and she's already feeling the effects of the coke she snorted and five shots she took out in the driveway. She loves to pre-game in case there isn't any alcohol or coke available at the parties she attends. She gets it from Travis, Westlake's wide receiver and resident drug dealer. He gets shit from West Park through our connection. Well, my connections at West Park.

Jen sees Nicole and saunters off, giggling in her direction. Nicole's eyes travel over my black Armani T-shirt and black jeans. Not happening, sweetheart. I need to nip this shit in the ass fast. I look over and see a chick walk in whom I recognize from the dance team. I think her name is Roxanne, but she goes by Roxy. Roxy has a nice rack in a tank top paired with a very short jean skirt.

I turn my head in her direction and bingo, eye contact. I give her my signature grin, and she looks around to make sure it is aimed right at her. When she is sure that I'm checking her out, she walks over and places her hands on my chest.

"Want to hang out?" she asks in a sexy voice.

I give her my panty-melting smile. "Sure. What do you have in mind?"

She slides her fingers in my hand and pulls me toward the bathroom in the hallway. Her wedge heels make her ass sway as she walks toward the door. From the corner of my eye, I see Nicole glare at Roxy as I follow her to the bathroom and close the door.

She leans on the black marble vanity, and I can tell she is a little tipsy. I have a light buzz going from the shots of whisky I took with Jen before walking inside. The music begins to blare outside the door, making it vibrate from the bass of the speakers. Even though it's loud, you can still hear laughter and people screaming over the music.

"Are you good?" I ask. I don't want a girl to do anything if they aren't game, or if they're too drunk.

"Yeah. I'm good. It's about time."

I tilt my head. "Time for what?"

"For you and me to hook up."

"Oh, yeah?"

She nods and licks her lips, attempting to look sexy. She isn't what I usually go for, but I'm not the type to turn down easy pussy.

She turns around and moves her long brown hair over one shoulder and bends at the waist. Fuck yeah. Her hands lift her jean skirt to reveal a black lace thong.

I pull a condom out of my wallet and tear it open with my teeth. "Are you sure?"

"Yeah, I've been wanting this for a while now."

Greenlight. She's down to fuck. She rubs her perky little ass over my hard cock feeling the length over the fabric of my jeans and she moans. I unbutton my jeans and pull it from my boxers and slip the condom on to rub the tip over her slit and Jesus, she is dripping wet.

"You want me, don't you?" I say to her.

"Since tenth grade."

I chuckle and slide the tip in gently so she can adjust to my size. Some girls can't take it and I don't want to hurt her.

"Shit, Ky. The rumors are true, you are big."

I slide in deeper and begin to pump inside her while she holds on to the edge of the vanity.

"Fuck, yes."

I pump into her some more and she stiffens. "Too much, Ky. Back up."

I ease up and drive into her without going all the way in. I tilt my head back and control my pace as she moans. I slide my hands up and play with her tits, wanting to bust my nut and get it over with. She will have to do. She moans and I can feel her pussy as she comes.

"Hmm, it feels so good. Damn, Ky."

For you, maybe, sweetheart. After she comes, I thrust a couple of times and spill into the condom without a sound.

When I'm done, I pull out and she cleans herself after I dispose of the condom. Mission accomplished. She will now go around and tell everyone she fucked Ky Reeves tonight. Nicole will then realize she is just like the rest of the girls I hook-up with. Random. She was probably thinking I was into her because she thought I hadn't hooked up with anyone since the summer.

"That was amazing. We need to do that again," she says, kissing me on the lips. I give her a smile and move to the sink to wash my hands. I look at her through the mirror and say, "I'll call you."

There is a knock on the bathroom door. I dry my hands and she adjusts her skirt. When I open the door, my chest tightens. Pretty brown eyes meet my dark ones, and then drift to the girl I just fucked, realization dawning on her face about what we just did.

"My bad. I didn't know the bathroom was taken."

Roxy walks up on her tippy toes and gives me a kiss while my gaze never leaves Rubi. What is she doing here, and who did she come here with?

"The bathroom is all yours. We are done. Call me?" Roxy says, leaving pink lip gloss on my lips.

Fuck.

Rubi averts her eyes and turns around, but I grab her hand, keeping her from walking away.

She snatches her hand back, her jaw is set. "Don't touch me. Who knows what you were touching in there."

I give her a satisfied smirk. "What's wrong, Rubiana. Jealous?"

She laughs through her nose and says, "Let me guess, you're going to do bad things to me and fuck me to death because you think that's what I want. But here's the thing." She moves closer and says loud enough over the music. "I don't fuck preppy rich boys who are on a power trip because of daddy's bank account."

I grin. "Oh, let me guess. You fuck broke bad boys with a record."

She scoffs. "Who said I fuck anyone. Those are your thoughts. I'm not one of your groupie airhead types you can impress with a bad haircut and shitty attitude," she says, sucking her teeth on the last part, her eyes looking me up and down like I don't measure up to her standards.

I pull her inside the bathroom, and she yelps when I close the door and push her up against it.

She glares at me. "What the fuck are you doing? Step off."

I push my knee between her thighs, and I look down and notice her really short shorts, and the same dirty Converse she wears. I see she has another one of those dingy hoodies. This one is red, though. I tower over her. Her hair is in those tight braids I want to unravel so I can run my fingers through the strands.

I lean into her, and she tries to wiggle her way out, but I'm bigger and stronger. There is no way she can get out of my grip. My nose involuntarily travels along her skin so I can memorize her scent. Her skin feels so soft, I want to lick and suck on it until I make sure I leave my mark, so everyone knows who did it. Who marked her?

"Do you know what I'm doing, Rubi? I'm breaking you. I will destroy you in the most beautiful way. And then you will understand exactly what you mean to me."

"Fuck you."

"Is that want you want? For me to fuck you?"

I slide my hands down her throat, feeling her pulse throbbing erratically under my fingers. She's nervous. She wants me. She wants me the same way I want her, but we are too stubborn to admit it, and refuse to give in.

"I want you to leave me alone. Remember, I hate you."

"You don't hate me. You hate that you don't have power over me. I'm a preppy rich boy, huh." I lick her neck with the tip of my tongue, and she stiffens, but the rise and fall of her chest is telling me a different story with every breath she takes. Every inhale and exhale makes my cock throb. It's like it knows this is where it should have been, and not trying to bury it to the hilt in that poor excuse of a quickie I just had with Roxy. I push into Rubi so she can feel my hard-on, but the look in her eyes is full of something else. Something I can't put my finger on. Her eyes begin to water, and I frown.

I look down at the position I'm in, and I tilt my head, and a feeling comes over me that crashes into me like a wave. Someone has done this to her before. They tried to hurt her. And my nostrils flare. What the fuck am I doing?

I know what she is doing. Self-preservation. I hurt her with what I said, but there is something different here. I can't listen to the little voice in my head telling me to stop right now. I want to push. I want to hurt her. Not physically because I would never hurt a woman, just emotionally.

"You're right. You are definitely not my type but I'm not yours either. Your type is a dirty thug, or maybe it's one of your foster daddies."

I see her hand raise to smack me across the face. Pain explodes down my jaw. I look at her with rage and I catch her hand just in time as she goes for round two.

She pushes against me, and I release her. "You're right. I had plenty of those. They loved me so much." Her eyes so lost and broken find mine. "In all the wrong ways," she says, her voice cracking on the last part as she storms out of the bathroom.

I pinch my nose with my fingers and place the palm of my hand to my cheek to keep the burn from stinging from the slap. What the fuck just happened? Why did I say that to her? My anger got the best of me like it always does.

Instead of getting what I wanted, all I got was words from her lips I didn't expect to hear, and a look on her face I never thought I'd see. So much pain there. I wonder how she is still holding on.

I make my way out of the bathroom and look around the area of Conner's house that is full of people grinding and dancing to the music. The party is in full swing as my eyes scan around looking for her. Her words replay in my head. *"They loved me so much. In all the wrong ways."*

Fuck my life.

It's then I see Chris.

"Hey, man. Have you seen Tyler?"

He takes a pull of the beer he must have grabbed from somewhere. "Yeah, I think he was taking Rubiana back home. She looked like she wanted to leave."

I play it off and respond with a shrug. "Damn, that sucks."

He nods, looking around at all the girls who wave at him as they pass by. Some of them giving me knowing looks. Roxy moves fast.

"Heard you hooked up with Roxy."

Yep. There it is.

"Yeah, there wasn't too much I had to do on my part. Just another hook-up."

"That bad, huh."

He knows it was too easy. Some girls don't realize that a guy needs a challenge.

"Yeah, it was."

He takes another pull of his beer and leans in. "At least now Nicole will be off your back, or at least finally get the idea that you're not hung up on her."

"Whatever, man, she did serve her purpose. I served hers, obviously. No hard feelings."

Except for the girl I had pinned up against the door after I fucked some other chick five minutes before. A girl whom I made believe is too dirty for me to fuck. To want. One who realized what I just did before she knocked on the door.

The only thing I can think about from my encounter was the softness of her skin. The way she tasted. The way she felt in my arms, but then the thought infiltrates my mind like a hammer.

Some asshole touched her.

Without her permission.

They hurt her.

My hands ball into fists just thinking about it. I shouldn't care. Rubi is not my problem. She never was. But then I think about my nightmares that involve a girl. A girl I thought was real, but all you see when you look into her eyes are shadows of something you don't recognize. Something is missing. A big chunk of the puzzle.

And Rubi, somehow, is the missing piece.

Chapter Twelve

Rubi

TYLER DIDN'T ASK me questions about why I wanted to leave. I guess he figured I felt uncomfortable, not that he probably minded since me leaving came with the added bonus of not having to babysit me. He could drop me off and be free to go do whatever it is he does. Smoke or drink with his friends, or even fuck in a bathroom. I noticed some of the kids who attend Westlake Prep are not the stars their parents must think they are. I saw drugs being snorted, smoked, and even pills popped. They are just as bad, or even worse, than the kids at West Park. At least the kids there know what drug use can lead to, and either choose to sell it for profit (to the kids on this side of town) or use it to forget the shitty life they were handed. It's pretty ironic that these snobs think they have it so bad with their fancy houses, cars, and lavish lifestyles.

The thought of Ky cornering me in the bathroom flits through my mind. The way he felt against me. The way his mouth felt along my neck. He didn't hide the fact that he was turned on. His hard length pressed against my thigh was evidence that he doesn't find me as dirty and ugly as he claims.

What got me was what he said about foster daddies. His accusation of what I must like them to do to me. He has no idea what I have been through. Someone like him would never understand. All I could do was learn from the experiences I have had. At one point, I wanted to go back to help the others as much as I could when I turned eighteen. I didn't know how exactly, but I figured out that would be impossible.

As much as I find Ky attractive now that we are older, he obviously doesn't see me the same way as when we were kids. He sees me as a threat for whatever reason. Maybe he likes to toy with people he finds beneath him. The way he dismissed that girl named Roxy was proof enough what he thinks of girls. He's a player

As much as I like or feel attracted to Ky, I need to make sure I don't fall for him. I'm not the type to lie to myself and say that I didn't want him to kiss me, because I did. I wanted it more than I thought possible. I was jealous he was screwing someone else. He saw it in my eyes, and that is dangerous for a guy like Ky to know you want them. It is how you lose yourself and become vulnerable. And I don't have that luxury of showing vulnerability.

After I make it home, I look at the gray walls of my bedroom. I'm sitting in the closet after my shower and staring at the empty bed. The moon casting its light across the room. The shadows from the trees on the side of the house make it seem like the walls are moving closer.

I'm supposed to feel safe here, but this room is foreign. I could scream, yell, cry, and no one would understand or really care. They would send me to the nearest psychotherapist like they have before; when they realized the home they sent me to was unfit because of the people in it. One home and then the next, like a never-ending cycle. They sent me to the clinic that offers free mental health for kids who have gone through trauma. None of it helped.

So, I hide. I hide the memories as best I can. I hide the pain, the tears, and the screams, locking them inside my head. They are like a living, breathing disease left by the people who created them.

Like every night, I wait. I wait to drift off to sleep thinking of a better life. A life where there wasn't a little girl or boy going to sleep hungry or cold. In pain or scared to go to sleep, afraid of the monsters they are sure will come for them as they drift off. That is what I always dreamed about when I closed my eyes every night since I was a kid. The past hoping for a better life where I could create beautiful memories.

A life where Ky would hold me and never let me go. Where he would smile and be the friend I dreamed of for so long. Maybe end up being the boyfriend a girl wishes for. I always thought of Ky as the only person who never judged me from where I came from.

But man, was I wrong.

The light streams through as my eyes flutter open. At one point, I felt like I was floating up until I landed on the bed, but that's impossible because I slept inside the closet. It wouldn't make sense because it's the dark that greets me every time I wake up.

I sit up and my heart pounds inside of my chest. I look around and notice I'm not inside the closet. I'm on the bed. I raise the comforter and look down at my leggings and extra-large shirt that has seen better days. I look at the door and notice the lock is still secure and the door is closed.

A knock on the door has me clutching the sheet with my hand. I must be sleepwalking because there was no explanation for what happened. That must be it. It must have been my subconscious wanting me to sleep on the fluffy mattress.

"Rubi," Mr. Murray calls through the door. "Are you awake? I wanted to know if you still wanted to go to the store? I'll be waiting downstairs if you still want to go."

"I'll be right out," I answer.

I wait to see if he tries to open the door. One. Two. Three. I hear his footsteps retreating and sigh in relief. *Okay, he isn't a creep.* I tell myself. He doesn't seem like one, but I can't trust anyone. It's Saturday and I have avoided Stephen as much as possible, but I do need to get a couple of personal things that I'd rather pick up myself.

My phone vibrates from an incoming text on the nightstand. I reach out and grab it. Hoping it's Cesar responding to me from the text I sent giving him my new number and letting him know where I was and what school I was attending.

Cesar: Good morning, beautiful. It's been a while. Are you ok?

Rubi: Yeah, this is a new number for however long I can keep it.

Cesar: I heard about your reunion. Is everything ok?

Rubi: For now.

Cesar: You know what to do if you're in trouble.

Rubi: Call you.

Cesar: Anytime. Anywhere. I'll come get you.

I smile. I met Cesar when I was fifteen. He was seventeen and already part of a gang. He would protect me when I went to juvie. No one picked on me or said anything because of Cesar. He is now the leader of the gang that runs the West Park area. He isn't a saint, but when I didn't have anyone, he was there to fend off the sickos. Not all foster kids my age were nice. They saw young girls like me as an opportunity.

When Cesar turned eighteen and was legally an adult, he couldn't help me out anymore like he promised.

Rubi: I know.

Cesar: Anyone I have to go fuck up in that preppy school you go to now?

I think of Ky and the other kids who talk shit as I pass them in the halls. It's nothing I can't handle. The only downside is that I can't say anything back that will get me in trouble. The Ky situation has gotten worse, but I don't think he would physically hurt me. I mean, I slapped him, and he didn't retaliate.

Rubi: Nothing I can't handle.

Cesar: We need to meet up.

Rubi: Why, miss me?

Cesar: I'll always miss you, Rubi.

Rubi: Soon. I miss dancing with you and hanging out.

We used to dance together. Hip-hop, mostly. Cesar came from Puerto Rico. His mother ditched him when he was fourteen and went back to Puerto Rico supposedly. That was the story they told him, at least. His father was running with gangs over there and was shot and killed, leaving his mother to take care of him. I guess she couldn't handle Cesar. He is intense. But he was always sweet toward me and told me never to give up. That I was better than those people. Better than my mother and the father who didn't bother looking for me.

I freshen up and make my way downstairs, tucking my phone inside the front pockets of my hoodie. I'm glad I memorized Cesar's number when he left. He said he would never change it. That I could call him if I was ever in trouble. It's too bad he hangs around drug dealers and other kids who have no way out. I worry about Cesar sometimes. I know it is only a matter of time before he ends up in jail...or worse, dead.

"Ready?" Mr. Murray says, seated at the dining table and nursing his cup of morning joe.

"Yeah."

He gets up and makes his way around the dining table, picking up his keys in the side table by the front door.

He gives me a small smile. "Let's go."

After shopping at the local drugstore, I notice a pet store advertising free pet adoptions for cats. There's a black and white cat pawing at the glass next to the sign. I bend slightly and place my hand on the glass like I am giving him a high five. *I know, little dude. I understand your pain.* Unwanted. I would love to have a pet. I never had one of my own. I did have an alley cat I nicknamed Mo because I liked it even though he was orange and reminded me of the cat in *Puss in Boots*. He would wait until I came home from school to see if I could find him something to eat, or give him a rub on his dirty fur. It was better to be greeted by the dirty cat that most likely had fleas than the putrid smell of burning meth, cigarettes, and the dirty home that greeted me every day I would go inside.

My stepfather saw me pet it one day and I never saw it again.

I knew the real reason. It was my fault for petting it. I cried all week over Mo, wondering where he went. I hated my stepfather even more after that. I knew that day moving forward to never show him I liked something, or he would make me pay by taking it away.

"Do you like him?"

I look up at Stephen, afraid to answer. I want to say yes, but I know what happens when I like something. It always gets taken away, or I have to give it up. I stay silent, straightening my hoodie. Looking between him and the window at the young cat meowing and rubbing itself against the glass. Hoping.

I rub my lips together and look at my dirty sneakers, and then tilting my head to glance up at Stephen, he knows. Yeah, I like him. It's obvious, but he wants me to say it. He wants me to admit I like the cat. But what will he do if I say yes? I guess there is only one way to find out. The cat is safe inside the store. What would my biological father do if I liked or showed interest in something? He looks at the window, and then at the front door of the pet store, and back to me.

I guess I'm about to find out.

Chapter Thirteen

Rubi

I WATCH AS the black and white cat purrs as I pet it while it's laying on the bed. I sit and he nudges his head and flips over on his back so I can rub his belly. I named him Hope.

Stephen was excited I wanted him to adopt the cat for me. If he only knew it was the first time someone got me something that I actually wanted, he'd be even more excited. I didn't know how I would be able to buy food or pay for his annual check-up in the future, but I was about to turn eighteen and would figure it out. The actual cat didn't cost Stephen anything to adopt except for the litterbox, food, water bowl, and kitty litter. The store gave away a free bag of food when you adopted a cat.

I couldn't hide the smile on my face when they handed me the cardboard box carrier that had I'M GOING HOME WITH MY NEW FAMILY written all over it. It felt good, and it made me look at Stephen in a new light. I know he was trying to have a relationship with me by being nice, taking me shopping and spending time with me, but how could you erase all the time he was absent. How do I forget the part that he moved on and didn't look for me when he knew there was a child he created somewhere. If the court hadn't sent him a letter because my mother listed him on the birth certificate, would I be here? Would I have met him? Deep down I know the answer. But is there room for forgiveness for past mistakes?

After playing with the cat and setting up his food bowl in the en-suite bathroom where I also placed his litter box, my stomach was protesting in hunger, and I realized I haven't had anything to eat except for a bag of potato chips and a bottle of water from the drug store. I put away the items Stephen purchased, as well as the new Converse sneakers he insisted I let him buy for me. He said it was for school, and the pair I was wearing was in violation of the school uniform, so I gave in. It's funny to think the first clothes I have ever worn that weren't second-hand or worn by someone else would be a private school uniform. Now I have new Converse sneakers to add to the list. I didn't care that that uppity bitch Nicole and her friend Jen made fun of me. I'm used to it. It's part of the charm of being in the social services club and they can both fuck right off.

I can hear male voices coming from downstairs but I can't take the hunger pangs in my stomach anymore. When you don't have food on a regular basis, your body acclimates and stores what it has to, and you get used to eating when you can, but when you eat food three times a day, after a few days, your body screams for food. Like right now, I'm starving.

I place a kiss on Hope's furry head and make sure I put away anything he can't get into. I close the door behind me to keep Hope from sneaking out and getting lost in a new environment, especially a house of this size. I make sure the door is closed by double-checking the handle and smile to myself as I make my way down the staircase. I have a pet and it sort of makes everything a little better. I won't feel alone in my room.

My smile falters when I see into the family room through the arch that divides the massive open concept of the house. Ky is leaning back, stretching his arms and smiling at something Tyler said. He is so tall, and his arms are wide and muscular. He overpowers the off-white-colored sofa. Actually, he overpowers everything.

What is he doing here?

Since I have been here, I haven't seen him hang out here with Tyler and the other guys the house. My eyes dart over to the other sofas and see that Chris is seated with two other guys I have seen at school who are players on the football team. I have also seen them sitting at their lunch table, and I know one then is named Conner. The starting quarterback on the football team and the one who threw the party last weekend.

My foot meets the floor with a thud after taking the last step, and Ky turns his head toward me, his smile fading, his midnight eyes watching my every move as my feet shuffle in my new sneakers toward them. I don't notice if the others see me approaching because our eyes are locked on each other. It's like I'm transported back to the time when we would meet on the edge of his backyard, reminding me telling him Pizza Hut. My stomach recoils at the thought of eating it. It is the only pizza that I have tried that I don't like.

I would eat it if I didn't have anything else to eat, of course, but the memory of our heated debate about the best-tasting pizza when we were kids play in my mind like a movie.

"Pizza Hut sucks," I say, making a face and sticking out my tongue. "I heard it's not really pizza, but just some baked bread with cheese."

"Oh yeah, how would you know."

"Because," I say, thinking about the offending pizza. "This girl in my class named Cindy, her parents are divorced, and her mother brought New York-style pizza and her father

brought Pizza Hut for her birthday party last Friday. We got two slices, one of each, and I was able to tell the difference. New York-style pizza is thinner, tastes better, and the slices are bigger. Pizza Hut pizza taste like cheesy soap, and is thick with more bread than cheese. One kid named Lance said that it sucked, and I agree."

"Well, Lance is an idiot and doesn't know what he is talking about. If I see him, I'll tell him that to his face."

"Why are you getting so mad?"

"I'm not. Lance is stupid and doesn't know what he is talking about, and you don't either. Pizza Hut is the best because it tastes the same wherever you go," he says, making his point. "New York-style pizza is a style of pizza and doesn't mean everywhere you go it tastes the same."

I stayed quiet not knowing that. How would I know? He doesn't know it was my first time trying any type of pizza from anywhere. So, I let it go and notice by the way the sun was setting that it was time to get going before my stepfather showed up at the house. If he found out that I wasn't home, there would be hell to pay, and I was just recovering from the last time.

"I gotta go."

"Why?"

"My dad is about to get home and I have to make sure I get my chores done."

He makes a face like he smelled something bad. "Chores?"

I nod. "Yeah, chores."

He shrugs his shoulders and dusts his khaki pants as he stands from the wooden crates he placed between two trees to begin making a treehouse. "Will you come back tomorrow?"

I pick up the bag with the empty plastic water bottle I use to get water from the water fountain by the public park on the way home, and place one foot on the wooden fence before hoisting myself over the panel and look across. "I'll try, but I will come back."

He looks at his feet and then looks up at me with his straight black hair and pitch-black eyes. "Promise? It's okay if you don't like Pizza Hut, but I still think that kid Lance is a dick."

I grin. "I promise."

"What is she doing here?" a girl says to my left. I think her name is Trish. Part of the cheerleading team. Total bitch and part of Jen and Nicole's little squad. Dumb as a rock. She got a C on the last quiz in class, and that is because she has some other kid giving her the answers to the test questions. They were on the board.

"She lives here, genius." Abby's voice floats over from my right. I didn't see her sitting on the chair because of the column.

Abby turns to look at me and gives me a soft smile. "Hey, are you hungry? Ky ordered pizza. I thought maybe Tyler knew what you liked, but he didn't, so Ky just ordered."

I look at the Pizza Hut boxes spread out on the massive coffee table, and then Tyler speaks up. "Sorry, Rubiana. I wasn't sure." He swallows, and I think he feels embarrassed for some reason, but I could have it all wrong.

He points to the boxes, and I can tell that there isn't much left. It's also obvious that no one had any intention of offering me anything, including Tyler, but that's okay, I'll find something else in the kitchen. I'm not used to being around this much food, much less having anything delivered. "Go ahead. You can have some."

I back up a couple of steps and Ky's eyes meet mine. "It's Pizza Hut. Everyone likes Pizza Hut."

My eyes narrow at him because he remembered. Out of all the things he could have ordered, he made sure he ordered something he knows I don't like. My stomach decides to betray me and growls.

Ky raises a brow. "Hungry?"

His tone has a hint of sarcasm, and I know it's his way of making fun of me without making it obvious that we have history. He wants to force me to take a cold slice of pizza that he knows I don't like and eat it. But I won't give in.

I have been forced to do things I wasn't comfortable with all my life, and I'm tired of people using me, hurting me. There is a reason I hate that type of pizza, and it wasn't just because of Cindy's parents. It was something more disturbing than that, and my mind drifts back to that place.

"Come sit on your daddy's lap. I'll buy you Pizza Hut if you do. I'll even get you your own pie." He smiles and his eyes are like two saucers staring off into space. "Come here, Rubiana. Sit here. Your mommy and daddy are passed out." I look at the dirty brown couch, and they are both on their sides. I found out why they always end up on their sides when they smoke the glass pipe. It's so they don't choke if they throw up. It must be heroine this time. My eyes find my stepfather's friend from work named Mike. "They won't know. You can call me Daddy Mike."

"Rubiana?"

"Rubiana!"

I look up and my eyes are blurry. I blink and place a trembling hand over my face, feeling the wet tears I hadn't realized were sliding down my cheeks. "I-I'm sorry," I whisper. I slide my hand across to wipe the moisture from my face and look up and see Stephen.

His concerned expression turns angry when he looks over at Tyler. "What did you do?"

Tyler raises his hands up. "I didn't do anything. We asked her if she wanted some pizza. That's it. She just backed up and spaced out. Then she started crying." Tyler shakes his head. "No one has done anything to her. I swear."

Ky has his brows pinched in confusion, and he just stares at me. I grip the sleeves of my faded red hoodie and glance at Stephen. "He's right. They didn't do anything. I'm just––"

Stephen's expression softens. "It's okay, Rubiana. You don't have to explain anything. How's Hope? Is he doing okay?"

"Who's Hope?" Tyler asks.

I glance at Stephen, and then at Tyler and everyone else seated in the family room who are waiting for his answer.

Stephen smiles. "Rubiana adopted a cat."

"Oh my God. How cute," Abby squeals before standing up. "Can I see him, Rubiana? My mother would never let me have a cat inside the house. You are so lucky. What color is he?"

I glance at Tyler, who looks shocked and confused. "You let her adopt a cat and keep it in her room?"

Stephen flicks his gaze at his son. "Yeah, I did. You have a truck that cost over a hundred-thousand dollars. You have a bunch of friends who hang out with you. You get to go out whenever you want and have a hefty allowance. You have had everything you have ever wanted. So, yeah. I let her adopt a cat. Is there a problem?"

"No, what does Mom say?"

Mr. Murray chuckles sarcastically. "She said I should get Rubiana whatever she wants," he replies. My cheeks heat in embarrassment.

I never thought of Stephen and Caroline wanting to be nice to me since they decided to take me in. I guess they aren't so bad after all. At least, so far.

Abby walks over. "Could we see him?"

I bite my lip. "I-I'm not sure if it's a good idea to bring him down since it's his first night here."

"We could all go up to your room quietly, then. Just to take a peek at him," Abby offers.

"Well, you know the rules, Rubiana." Stephen looks at Tyler. "No boys in her room. I'm firm on that," he says, looking at the other guys. "No boys are allowed in my daughter's room. Got it?"

"Yes, sir," they all say in unison.

"It's not like any boys actually want to go up to her room," Trisha adds.

The other guys snort, and their attention is aimed at me. Conner winks at me, but I avert my eyes.

"Tyler, come to my office, please. I need to talk to you about something," Stephen demands.

Tyler gets up and nods. "I'll be right back, guys." And then he says quietly, "My father is going to chew my ass about the pizza."

When Tyler and Stephen leave the room, I see the TV remote fly across to where Ky is seated, hitting Conner in the chest. He winces from the contact.

"Fuck around and found out, asshole," Ky growls.

"What the hell, Ky?"

Ky turns to him. "You know exactly what I'm talking about, Conner."

Conner is the type who loves to throw parties where students from Westlake Prep can drink, get high, and fuck around. Typical rich boy jock who feels entitled, and these are their friends. I thought the handful of friends I have were shitty. My thoughts fly to Cesar because he must be selling the drugs to these rich assholes. That is how Cesar makes money and what he does running the gang. I haven't seen Tyler, Ky, or Chris do any of that stuff I saw at the party, but it doesn't mean they don't though.

I'm not dumb to think that they don't smoke weed, but I'm talking about the hard stuff. The stuff that makes people crazy and not act like they normally would, or draw out how they really feel deep down inside. Meth, coke, or heroin.

"Are you okay?" Abby asks with concern in her voice.

I give her a wry smile. "Yeah, I just thought of something sad."

She is asking because she saw me crying. Not a total lie. I couldn't tell her the whole truth. Not about how I know Ky, or the truth about the stupid pizza. I take a deep breath because what could have happened with Mike didn't. He just used the fact that I was hungry to get me to do the unthinkable...he molested me.

My stomach protests in hunger but one thing about hunger is that you can get used to it and fight it. The body finds a way to preserve itself. Like right now, the feeling of hunger has my stomach screaming but I can fight it off. I have done so many times since I was a kid. I can do it again. And like always, no one will notice. No one will care.

"I would love to see your new cat. Is he nice? How old is he?" Abby asks, reminding me about seeing Hope.

I smile at the change of subject. "I'll bring him out, but if he gets anxious, I'll take him back up."

"I can't wait."

Five minutes later, Abby is on the wood floor sitting cross-legged in front of me and petting Hope as he lays between my legs for a stomach rub. He begins to purr from all the attention.

Conner gets up, and so does the other friends of Tyler's. Ky stands behind me, and I can't think. The hairs on the back of my neck stand up under my hoodie.

"I have never been so jealous of a cat before," Conner teases. I guess Ky gives him a look because his eyes widen, and he glances at me. "I'm playing around. The little guy is lucky, is all."

I can feel Ky leaning close behind me, and Abby looks up with a smirk. I don't know why she is smirking at Ky behind me. It's then that I see his strong hand reaching around me, his face inches from the side of my neck, scratching the cat on his stomach. I'm tense. My heart is pounding and I'm aware of the heat of his body behind me. I'm even more aware of his strong forearm by my thigh. The cat peeks at him next to me and nudges his head for him to rub his neck.

"He likes you," Abby says, looking at Ky with a smile. "He is purring so loud."

Conner reaches out and tries to pet him, but Hope swipes his paw and scratches for him to stop.

"Ow! Stupid cat. He scratched me," Conner barks, snatching his hand back.

I pick up the cat and clutch him to my chest in case Conner tries to retaliate. "I'm sorry. I guess it was too much for him, and he's just not used to all the attention."

Conner gives me a hard stare, but I glare at him. Cats have to defend themselves when they feel threatened. It's not like he stabbed him and drew blood. It's the only way they know how to communicate. He was in a shelter and was found hungry and covered with fleas. I read the adoption papers that had his medical report attached to it, and I feel this connection to him even more because of the life he's endured.

"It's a stupid cat and he should know better."

"Stop being a pussy, Conner. He probably doesn't like you for whatever reason," Ky says.

"I should scratch his punk ass and see how he likes it."

I clench my jaw and realize I should have never brought him down. It was a mistake. Petting and rubbing my nose against his fur to soothe him, I want to make sure he feels safe.

"Touch her cat and I'll break your face. It's your only warning," Ky warns in a hard tone.

Woah, where did that come from?

Conner's expression turns to pure fear, and I wonder why. Conner is not a small guy. He is a douche, and I would never give him the time of day, but he also seems a bit immature. Ky towers over him by about two inches. Trish raises her brow and stands, jutting her hip out and shaking her head as she gives me a knowing look. She looks behind me and I want to turn my head to see Ky's expression, but doing so would make it obvious that I care about what he thinks. I'm also relieved he stood up for the innocent little fur baby in my arms. He is only eight months old and loves to cuddle, and I'm positive he will keep me warm at night. He is a sweetheart and doesn't deserve Conner's wrath.

"He's a cool cat. I like him," Ky says, surprising me at how soft his tone is when talking about Hope.

"Thank you." I look up at Conner. "I'm sorry Hope scratched you. I don't think he was ready for all of the attention, but touch my cat and I'll make sure it's more than a scratch you get."

Abby raises her brow and looks between me and Conner. I'm sure she is surprised by my threat. I'm not eleven years old anymore. I will protect Hope. I have to make sure Conner and his friends don't think I can't protect myself—or protect what is mine.

"What are you gonna do?"

I spit the same words Ky did earlier. "Fuck around and find out, Conner."

Ky chuckles behind me. Connor looks up, and I'm not sure what look Ky is giving him, but he quickly looks away.

Chapter Fourteen

Rubi

THE FOLLOWING MONDAY at school, I close the locker and spin the lock with a frustrated sigh. It's the second time in a row that I've found a block of cheese that smells like someone threw up inside my locker. It makes all my school supplies smell, and whoever did it attached a picture of a street rat onto it. They also decided to decorate my locker with the word FREAK. Dickfaces. I hate these people.

The slams of lockers can be heard all around me as the bell signals a warning that students need to park their asses inside class. I make my way to algebra class, dreading seeing Ky and his group of skanks, and the way they give him knowing glances.

I make my way down the aisle and stiffen when a girl from the dance team snickers at the girl seated in front of her. "Did you hear last weekend at Conner's party that Ky fucked Roxy, and she complained his dick was so big he could hardly fit. It's not the first time I have heard that."

"I know. I keep hearing that his fine ass has this huge cock. I wonder how big it really is?"

I roll my eyes because of course that is all they care about. That and how popular they are and how much money they come from.

"There is a party this weekend at Zain's. Everyone will be there, including Ky," the girl to her right says.

I haven't heard about it, but then again, I'm no one to these people. Just an unwanted pest they want to get rid of. My locker smell can attest to what they all think of me.

I pass by them, and then the other girl to their right adds, "I just saw him go into the empty lab classroom with Jen. I think he likes her since they are always somewhere getting each other off. I heard he might make them official."

The other girl snorts. "I doubt that. Everyone knows Ky doesn't believe in having a girlfriend. He just likes to hook up."

So, they have been friends for a long time. Probably not long after I was taken away by social services. It's crazy to know that he is now best friends with my half-brother, even if I don't consider him my family. I wouldn't know since Tyler doesn't say much on the rides to school, except this morning he asked if I wanted breakfast. Of course, I declined.

I take a seat in the corner like the first day, and the classroom door opens. Ky walks in with Jen in tow, and it's obvious they were screwing in the lab. My stomach sinks because she is the meanest out of all the girls who go here, and I still can't believe he would want a girl like that. Nicole looks up and her mouth turns into a frown.

"Sorry I was almost late. You know how Ky gets," Jen says breathlessly, adjusting her skirt and making it blatantly obvious what they were up to. Nicole gives her a smile that doesn't reach her eyes, and it's apparent Jen doesn't know about Ky screwing Nicole. Interesting.

Ky takes his usual seat and raises his brow when he sees Jen and Nicole talking. Probably laughing about it to himself. Typical player. Jen looks over at him and licks her lips, and I swear I'm about to throw up. It shouldn't bother me. I shouldn't care, but Ky was everything to me for so long, and it hurts.

I take my book that smells like puke and open it. If I spray something on the textbook to lessen the smell, I'll ruin it, so I have to be creative to get the smell out.

"Oh my God, what is that smell?" Jen says, making a face and scrunching her nose as she looks at me while covering her face with her hand.

I guess I know who was behind the cheese and the rat pics. Bitch.

"It's that street rat." She looks over at Tyler. "Do you at least give her some advice about hygiene?" Her eyes find mine and Ky is grinning.

He thinks this is funny. What happened to the sensitive Ky who was defending my cat? Judging by the look on his face, that Ky doesn't exist. This is the real Ky.

"Leave her alone, Jen," Tyler tells her.

"I'm just pointing it out. You should explain this to her. I mean, her snatch stinks."

"I think you should be worried about where the dick you just rode has been before you talk about anyone else's snatch. Stop being an insecure, snobbish skank. It only leads to desperation, but skanks like you can't handle things you can't control. That is why you let guys treat you like shit," I snap.

"What did you say to me?" she snarls.

I get up from my chair and in her face with the book that she ruined. "You heard what I said," I say through clenched teeth, holding the book up to her face, her eyes widening. She never thought I had a backbone. I've been watching myself, but there is only so much I can take. "Keep putting cheese and shit in my locker and see what I'll do next, you dirty cunt. I'm sick of your childish games."

"Sit down, Rubiana."

My head whips around to look at Ky sitting behind her, defending her. Rage runs through my veins like poison. His face is hard, and his ebony eyes are and unreadable.

I lean in closer to him, the hood of my hoodie sliding off. "Or what?" I threaten in a low tone. "What are you going to do, huh? Kick my ass? Tell me not to fuck with your little piece of ass?"

"Don't threaten me. It will not go in your favor."

Oh, this motherfucker. I laugh through my nose sarcastically. "Bring it. I'm not scared of you." I turn my head toward Jen. "None of you."

"You touch me, and I'll have you arrested like the little thug you are," Jen warns.

I tilt my head. "Bitch, you wouldn't be able to dial 911 when I'm done with you. But let's not get ahead of ourselves." I lower my voice to a whisper. "People are watching us now. But it's when they are not that the real fun will begin."

"Fuck you. That is why no one wants you here. You're nothing, it is why your parents don't even want you. You're just a waste of space."

"At least I'm not an easy lay who spreads her legs for anyone."

She laughs. "You're just jealous. One of the hottest guys at this school wants me all the time."

The class is silent, and my eyes find Ky as he slouches in his chair with a smug smile on his face. "Interestingly enough, I'm not interested in a cheating, backstabbing liar."

He stiffens and his nostrils flair. "Sit down before I have you thrown out of the class."

"Don't bother. I was on my way out."

I walk over to my desk and Tyler gets up. "Rubiana, stay in class. Don't listen to them," he pleads.

I grab my stuff. "I'm good."

"Why are you leaving? You can't skip class...you know that."

"Don't worry. You can tell your father I fucked up as usual." I turn and make my way down the aisle.

"Let her leave, Tyler. She is good at that. Like Jen said, no one wants her here. She stinks anyway, dude," Ky says sarcastically.

Everyone laughs and my chest goes tight. My eyes find Ky's, my nostrils flaring.

He makes a motion with his fingers, shooing me away. "Run along, freak."

The word *freak* tells me he was also behind the word written on my locker. He knew about the cheese and Jen's little pranks. That's fine and I'm game...

He wants a battle; I'll bring him a war.

...

I'm sitting in the cafeteria alone. I'm sure word is going to get around about my threat to Jen and Ky, but I don't care. It was weird how Tyler was trying to defend me and not laughing along with his friends, though. He was probably just worried about getting into an argument with his father about how he is allowing his friends to treat me. So he can go to hell too.

I left the classroom because I didn't trust myself around Jen and the others. I would have punched her square in the face. I can't wrap my head around why Ky has to treat me like dog shit. I left him a letter. I told him goodbye. Big deal.

I don't have another class with him, but the next time I see him, I'm going to confront Ky because I want to know why.

"H-hey," Patrick greets me before taking a seat in front me like he does every day at lunch.

"Hey," I say, taking a bite of the hard chocolate chip cookie they had in the lunch line. It tastes like cardboard, but I've had worse.

He looks at the cookie I'm holding and swallows after taking a sip out of his Thermos. "That tastes n-nasty. How can you eat that?"

I look at the cookie before turning it in my hand and then looking back at him. "It's better than nothing...and I've had loads of that in my life."

He points. "Anything would be better than that cookie."

I rub my lips together after taking another bite. "Where I come from, you're lucky you get a taste of anything. Trust me, it's not that bad."

His eyes soften. "I-I'm sorry."

I angle my head. "What are you sorry for? You didn't do anything."

Why would he be sorry? I wonder why an attractive guy like Patrick doesn't have a steady girlfriend, or why he isn't seated at one of the popular tables. Maybe even have a table of his own with friends he has things in common with.

"I criticized your choice of food. I don't know the s-specifics of where you lived before or your situation."

I point my spork at him before digging into the tasteless cafeteria mashed potatoes. I'm actually really hungry, but I keep that to myself. "How could you not. There are plenty of rumors about me floating around the halls and in the classrooms."

He shakes his head. "I prefer to hear it from your lips."

I quirk a brow. "My lips?"

His face flushes beet red. "I-I didn't mean…"

"Why do you stutter when you get nervous?" I interrupt him.

It's none of my business, but I had to ask. It only happens when he is nervous, and not all the time. He looks embarrassed, and I want to kick myself for being nosey. He stares down at the plastic table, and then his eyes find mine.

"I-It——" He takes a deep breath and continues. "It started when I turned fifteen. It just happened."

"Oh." I swallow the mashed potatoes, not really tasting them. "Why do you sit alone and not with anyone?"

"I sit with you."

Is he flirting with me? I grin, and for the first time he smiles. It's nice. He has straight teeth, and his hair falls over his left brow. It doesn't give me flutters in my stomach like it would from a guy you find hot and want to get his attention and you are finally getting it. It's more friendly than anything.

"Why don't you play sports? Have a girlfriend? You must get bored."

"I draw."

"Oh. Maybe you can show me sometime."

He smiles. "Sure. D-Do you want to go out sometime?" he asks. "I-I know I'm not your type, but as f-friends."

Is he flirting with me? I wear a hoodie every day to school. I don't wear makeup and I'm made fun of regularly. He couldn't possibly find me attractive.

"How do you know my type? What is my type?"

He looks up nervously and then his eyes move past me. I have no idea what or who he is looking at, but I don't want to turn around.

Patrick's eyes land back on mine. "I-I thought maybe someone like Ky is more your type, or maybe one of the football players."

I snort, shaking my head. "Absolutely not. They think I'm a freak and they make fun of me."

"But you never said they were ugly or found them unattractive," he volleys back.

"I don't need to compliment them. I still haven't been able to get past their winning personalities to even get a good look."

Patrick starts laughing, like a full-on belly laugh.

I would never admit I found Ky remotely attractive. The memory of him and how close he was to my skin that night at the party is imprinted in my memory, but then his words to me earlier in class tells me that he isn't who I thought he was.

The fact that he slept with Roxy—and then Jen—tarnished my feelings for him.

"Would you look at that? Patty has a grin on his face." Ky's voice has me looking up to my right.

"Fuck off, Ky."

He chuckles. "Not until he tells me why he is grinning like an idiot. He stares over at me from across the cafeteria, and then is laughing while lost in conversation with the likes of you. So I'm curious as to what this little bitch is saying about me."

"I said, fuck off, Ky. Leave him alone." He leans close to my ear, and I watch as Patrick gives him a glare but doesn't move. "Or what?"

Turning my head, Ky's lips are close to my cheek. If I move one centimeter, I would be able to feel if his lips are firm or soft. If they are warm or cold. The tension between us builds like an invisible band, stretching and stretching until it's about to snap. His dark eyes trace my lips, and my heart is pounding in my ears. I can hear ringing as all the voices fade, and it's just us. Why? Why is he such an ass?

"Why don't you tell him the truth?"

My eyes widen. He can't mean about our past. "What truth?"

"The truth that you want me. Since the first time you laid eyes on me, you have wanted me." He nudges his head slightly. "Go on. Tell him the truth."

He is so full of it. Full of himself. Before I would admit to anyone that I find him attractive, or that he makes me go crazy, I'd rather eat the block of cheese they left in my locker.

Having made my decision, I look over at Patrick and I answer his earlier question before we were so rudely interrupted. "Yes, Patrick, I'll go out with you."

Patrick's eyes widen and he looks at Ky. I feel Ky tense, but I don't care. Patrick has been the only person who has been nice to me besides Abby. I'm done with Ky and his shit.

My eyes meet Ky's pitch black eyes and I notice his jaw is hard. He takes a deep swallow, and I could tell me accepting to go out with Patrick bothers him more than he'll admit. "I think it is best you head back to your table, your girlfriend is waiting. Maybe go for round two in the lab. That's all she seems to remember when it comes to you, am I right?"

"For the record, she isn't my girlfriend, and who I fuck in the lab or anywhere else is none of your business. Be careful, Rubiana. It looks like you spend too much time keeping tabs on where I stick my dick."

"It's pretty easy when every available female in the school advertises it for you. So fuck you if you think I'm keeping tabs on anything at all about you."

He stands up and looks down at me like I'm nothing and scratches his dark brow. "Pass. I might catch something, or worse, smell like you."

I bite the inside of my cheek, tasting blood to keep my bottom lip from trembling. His words slice through me like a knife. But his words have their desired effect. They break me apart inside, and my next words are solely based on self-preservation.

"Gee, Ky. It looks like you're too strung up on how I smell. What would your girls think?"

He chuckles. "They would know I would never give you the time of day."

I know, Ky. You have made it clear I mean nothing to you.
I only wish I knew why.
I wish it didn't hurt so much.
But it does. For the first time, I wish I never jumped that fence. Then maybe, I would never have to walk around with a hoodie hiding the scars from my past.

Chapter Fifteen

Rubi

AFTER SCHOOL, I wait until Tyler takes off for football practice and make my way down the block toward Ky's house. His backyard ends on the edge of the upscale neighborhood. What separates the back of his house and the street is a space that has grass and is lined with trees like an access route. I didn't know what it was when I was kid, but my curiosity was piqued when I saw the roof of his house between the trees.

The roof of his house looked like a massive building. It was huge, but I never saw inside his house. I guess he wanted to keep my visits a secret. I didn't know why, but at the time, I was afraid his parents would call the police on me or something.

I finally reach the back fence of his house and place my foot over the fence and swing my leg up and jump down, hitting the leaves on the edge of his yard and making a crunch. I walk around the massive tree and make my way to the other corner where the two trees would meet, making it easy for my ten-year-old skinny self to climb over. It seemed so tall back then, but now that I'm older it's only a six-foot climb.

I jump down and turn around and my eyes water. Where the pallets of the treehouse were that we built when we were kids is now burned. The trees are charred and black, ruined. Dried leaves are falling, and I'm surprised the trees didn't fall over in the fire. Wood pieces are in a pile on the ground, some still the color of wood, others rotted by years of rain, snow, and the sun making it look like a pile of rubble. Instead of cleaning it up, it's still there like a memory.

I hear the crunch of grass and leaves behind me and I turn around. Ky is standing there with black sweatpants on and a black hoodie that is unzipped, showing his hard chest and ab muscles. It looks like he was working out.

"What the fuck are you doing here?" he asks in a hard tone. "Get the fuck off my property?"

"Why?" I blurt, my voice breaking. "Did you burn it?"

He stands there watching me, crossing his hands over his chest. His gaze unflinching. "Leave."

"No. Not until you tell me why? Why do you hate me so much? I never did anything to you."

"You're right, you haven't. I just don't like you, and I burned it when I knew you weren't going to come back. I got your letter, and it made me realize I was a stupid kid who made friends with a girl who was a liar. A girl I didn't really know, and have no interest in ever getting to know again."

"I couldn't. They––"

He walks forward and I look up as he towers over me. "I want you to leave me alone. I want you to get off my property. I don't want to be your friend, and I have no interest in you whatsoever. Not even for a pity fuck. Stop being pathetic and let it go. We are nothing. We never were."

I nod as hot tears slide down my cheeks, blinding my vision. I don't want to cry, but hearing him say these things is breaking me.

I take a deep breath and move to the side to walk past him, but he blocks me. I thought I could get out down the side of the house to walk back to Tyler's house.

"Nope. You go back the same way you came. The next time you jump over the fence, I'll call the cops, and I don't give a fuck if you spend the rest of your sentence in jail as an adult. You are not my problem."

He walks closer and I take a step back, but he backs me up against tree. "Don't do this to us," I plead.

He smiles, but it's not warm. "There is no us, Rubiana. There never was an us. I was just a stupid kid who didn't know any better who allowed a dumb girl to hang out with me to pass the time. You are nothing. You mean nothing. I don't know how clear I have to make this for you."

I sniff and I try to swallow a sob that is trying to escape. I close my eyes, hoping this is a nightmare. But when I open them, he is in my face. His beautiful face rigid, angry, and dark.

"Why do you hate me?"

No answer. He remains silent, his eyes close in a slow blink. He steps back and I slip past him to make my way over the fence. But his words stop me from jumping down. "Oh, and Rubiana. Behave or I'll retaliate."

My temper rises and I look at his handsome face, wondering where things went wrong with him. "Don't threaten me, Ky. I have dealt with worse assholes than you. You wouldn't even scratch the surface."

It just hurts that he just became one of those assholes on a long list of them in my life.

Chapter Sixteen

Rubi

I'M MAKING MY way downstairs after getting Hope his breakfast. I walk into the kitchen where the smell of coffee hits my nose, and notice Tyler is emptying out this machine with a little white cup.

"Good morning."

He smiles. "Good morning. I hope you slept well."

I chuckle. "Like the dead," I tease.

His smile falters because in truth, I cried myself to sleep in the closet. I felt alone, and if it wasn't for Hope purring and rubbing himself on my face, I don't think sleep would have ever come. My eyes must look red and puffy. I must look like shit, and Tyler notices.

"What is that?" I point to the machine he was just closing.

He raises a brow and then looks at me, realizing I have no idea what it is. I have never seen one before, and I'm curious. It must be a fancy coffeemaker of some sort since I obviously smell it.

"It's called a Keurig." He walks over and opens a lid and reaches next to the machine where there is a carousel of the same little white cups. "These are called pods, and you slip one inside like this." He slides it in and closes it. He pulls out a plastic reservoir that holds water. "This is where you pour water. You grab an empty mug, place it on the tray, and depending on how much coffee or how big the mug is, you press the respective cup size and press start."

He shows me the steps and presses start and the machine makes a whirring noise, and then the coffee pours out. Fresh and hot. It smells amazing.

He gives me a grin, like he's some sort of magician, and I suddenly feel embarrassed. He must think I'm from another planet. "I'm sorry. You must think I'm so dumb or something."

"Not at all. I didn't know how to use it when my mom bought it, to be honest." He walks over to the fridge when the machine stops and pulls out different flavors of creamer. He opens two of them and holds it close. "Which one? Caramel or coconut?"

I lean close and smell each one and decide I like the coconut one better. "Coconut."

"Good choice. I like that one too."

He pours some in and stirs it before handing it to me. I take a sip and close my eyes. The flavors of the coffee and coconut creamer explode on my tongue, warming me up instantly. "Thank you. I think I'm love with this thing."

"You can make yourself a cup anytime. I'll make sure we buy extra coconut creamer."

I don't know what changed, but Tyler has been very nice to me lately. Every day he asks if I want breakfast, and smiles when I walk down to meet him at his truck for a ride to school. He doesn't treat me bad like he did when I first arrived. I even overhead him tell one of his football friends that I was his half-sister. He wouldn't acknowledge me before, and now he is more accepting that I'm here. I wonder what changed. I wonder why Ky is saying I'm ruining his best friend's life.

After the short drive to school, Tyler parks his truck in the parking lot, and then from the corner of my eye I see Ky's car pull in the space next to us, and my stomach clenches. I open the door to the truck and see Ky in his car with Jen, and they have the top down.

"Thank you for the ride to school." She smiles and bites her lip, attempting to be sexy. "And for this morning."

My eyes scan the beautiful car with the top down. I remember when we were kids Ky and I talked about wanting a car like this when he was older. He promised I would ride in it with him like we were Batman and Robin. I was supposed to be Robin, and the only one who would ride in it with him.

"What's your favorite car?"

I grin, tilting my head and looking up to the blue sky, loving the way the clouds make funny shapes. "My favorite is a convertible."

I watch Ky's expression and he grins. "The cars that don't have a roof."

I nod yeah. "I love the fact that you can see the sky, maybe the stars at night. The wind blowing in your hair. I think it's cool that you can close it if you want to. It's like you have a choice."

"What color?" he asks.

"Um, I don't know. I haven't thought that far. I don't have a favorite. Not yet, anyway. Besides, I have to learn to drive it first."

"I would want it black. Like Batman."

"That makes sense. Since you looove Batman."

"He is the best. When I grow up, I want to have a car like Batman."

"Could I be Robin. So, I can ride in it with you?"

"I thought you like Superman."

"I do, but if I want to ride in the Batmobile with you, I will have to be Robin."

He holds his hand out and I take it. His hand is warm and clean compared to my fingernails, but he doesn't care, or he doesn't mind. "Alright, deal."

"Promise."

"I promise, Rubi. No one but you."

"Rubiana?" I hear Tyler's voice calling out my name and I shake my head, snapping out of my memory.

I look over at Tyler, and then out the passenger window where I see Jen and Ky. Jen is giggling. "Freak. I told you she has a thing for you, Ky."

Shit.

"I'm sorry. I was waiting for them to go inside the school so I can walk to my locker," I say looking at Tyler.

"Is Ky bothering you? You can tell me. I'll have another talk with him."

I open the door to climb out of his truck. "Don't worry. I can handle Ky. I'll just stay out of his way."

He nods and gets out of his truck, and I make my way inside the school. Another piece of my past. Another memory tarnished. Sometimes I think he is doing it deliberately, or maybe it's in my mind and I made up something that was really not there.

I pull out my phone and text Cesar.

Rubi: Why are guys immature assholes?

Cesar: Because we think with our dicks.

Rubi: Figured you would tell me the truth and be honest.

Cesar: Who's the asshole?

Rubi: No one important.

Not anymore.

Cesar: If he is messing with you, it's because he likes you and wants a reaction.

Rubi: Not this guy.

Cesar: Want me to fuck him up?

I snort. That would be something. As much as it sounds appealing, since Ky is an asshole to me, I would never want to see him hurt.

Rubi: No. None of that would serve any purpose except get people hurt. It wouldn't change anything.

Cesar: Always the good one. It's what I love about you, Rubi. If he keeps bothering you, will you tell me?

Rubi: No.

Cesar: Why? ;)

Rubi: Because the last guy you saw hurting me can't wipe his ass.

Cesar: That is what he gets for touching my girl.

I close my eyes, willing the memory to not pop up as I pocket my phone in my hoodie. Hoping that flashback stays in the past, buried with the rest.

"Hey, are you going to the game after school?" Abby asks, popping up out of nowhere behind my open locker door. She is always so bubbly and friendly.

I look around and notice the cheerleaders wearing their uniforms and the dancers of the band wearing theirs, walking up and down the halls. I also notice some of the football players wearing their letterman jackets. Now that I think about it, Tyler was wearing his in the kitchen when he was showing me how the coffee machine worked.

"I'm not sure. I've never been to one before. I have seen them on TV and I understand the game somewhat, but not entirely." I have also never seen Tyler practice after school, or seen him play. I guess it would be nice to see him play. I shrug my shoulders. "Yeah, why not."

"Awesome. It will be so much fun. I'll wait for you after school and we can go together."

"Okay."

***

The bell rings and I make it out of school and Abby is waiting for me in the parking lot. I sent Tyler a text telling him I was catching a ride with Abby to go to the game. He sent me a smiling face emoji with a thumbs up. I guess he liked the idea of me going to watch him play.

Her car lights flash, signaling that she unlocked her car. She drives this cute little red Mini Cooper. It kind of fits her bubbly personality. I open the door and slide in the small car.

"It's nothing fancy like what the other kids at this school drive, but I like it," she says in defense.

"I was thinking that it's cute and matches your personality. I think the other kids buy cars because they care too much about what others think."

"Except Tyler. He doesn't care what anyone thinks."

I guess she was right with the way he has been acting toward me now. He is definitely nicer to me. I turn my head and wait until she looks forward after backing out.

"You like him, don't you?"

"Who?" she asks, playing dumb. It is so obvious she has a thing for my half-brother. It is always Tyler this and Tyler that.

"Tyler."

Her cheeks flush and I knew I was right. "Don't tell him, please," she says in a pleading voice.

"Of course not. It's not my business, but I think if you don't want him to find out. Don't defend him so much unless it's absolutely necessary. Oh, and stop watching him every time he walks in a room."

"Is it that obvious?"

I nod. "Yeah, but the fact you have known him for a while doesn't make it blatantly obvious."

"Okay. I don't want him to know because I'm younger and his best friend's sister, so that makes me a no-go. It would be cliché. Younger sister has a thing for brother's best friend, right?"

I think about how that would be the same thing if Ky was different toward me, but then again, Tyler is my half-brother, and I have only known him about a month. I don't think that counts.

"I could say the same for Ky. It's the opposite."

"What?"

What is she talking about?

"The way he looks at you. I'm not the only one who has noticed. He watches you. My brother says he gets in a snippy mood when he sees you talking to Patrick at lunch. Conner teased him about it, and he got angry. He also seems to be hanging around Jen a lot. He never did that before. I was confused at first, but I think Ky secretly likes you and is using Jen as a distraction."

"Funny, he says the exact opposite. He thinks I'm dirt on his shoe and he tells me I'm nasty and I smell."

She bursts out laughing. "You don't smell, and you are not nasty. He is just being a stupid idiot. He has a bad temper since his mother left him and his dad when he was eleven, I think. I don't think he ever got over it, and I think it's why he doesn't want a girlfriend."

"That must suck. Do you think its because of what you told me about his mother?"

But I know the answer. He is afraid she will leave. *The same way you had to leave him.*

Oh my God. That is why he is angry.

"Maybe he thinks if he doesn't have one, he doesn't have to worry—"

"About another female leaving him," I finish for her.

She nods. "Yeah, I think so." She changes the subject. "Want to come over to my house and I can let you borrow something to wear. I can do your hair if you want. I bought this new blow-dryer and straightener, and I would love to try it out."

"Okay, that sounds like a lot of fun."

And oddly enough, I truly meant that.

Chapter Seventeen

Rubi

IT'S BEEN A long time since I had my hair blow-dried and straightened. I did it once when this girl named Mary swiped one from the department store when we snuck out. Just like Cesar, she turned eighteen and was sent to a job rehabilitation center, and I never heard from her again. I hope she made a life for herself somewhere.

After I started getting attention from guys in the different homes I was placed, I learned not to dress up or attract attention...so I avoided applying makeup or trying to look pretty. That sort of thing backfires when there are horny teenagers who sleep in bunkbeds above yours. One night one of them—Gus—got handsy and tried to force himself on me. He did, but Cesar was there to make the memory of that night go away. Let's just say that the same fingers that he rammed up inside me so hard were cut off a couple of days after. Surprisingly, Cesar wasn't caught, or maybe Gus was too afraid of what would happen if he opened his mouth. No one knew what he told the doctors at the hospital, and at the time I didn't care.

It wasn't the most memorable way to lose my virginity. Cesar looked at me that night and asked me if I trusted him. I was shaking so bad. I cried so much I didn't have any tears left. He held me and muffled my cries. He was my savior that night, and the following night he was also my first. The worst part was that I imagined it was Ky. Cesar was perfect. He was gentle and he told me I was beautiful. That he didn't deserve a girl like me. That I was too good for someone like him. But living the life of a drug dealer and a gang member has roughened him up. Since he has a record, he thinks it's too late for someone like him to find happiness.

He was the first guy who said that I was too good for them. But I think he was being nice because of what happened. We have been friends ever since, and he never let anyone else touch me. Of course, all good things had to come to an end after he turned eighteen. Thankfully, I have is a cellphone number and we stay in touch.

"It's packed. I have to get to the back with the band and the dance team for our half-time routine."

"I didn't know you were on the dance team."

I honestly did not know.

"Yeah, I like it, but I can't say it's easy when Jen and her friends on the cheer team interfere. They are bossy bitches, and to be honest, I don't think the routine is all that. The other schools have better routines, but every time I try to mention something, she shuts me down and says I'm too young to know any better."

"Sounds like she wants the cheer team to look better at the games. In case you haven't noticed, you are a lot prettier than any of them and you attract more attention than they do."

She swallows before looking at her reflection in the rear-view mirror. "You think so?"

I guess having an overprotective brother sucks sometimes, but she must be blind not to think guys don't sneak glances at her when she doesn't notice. My half-brother is one of them.

Abby is beautiful. She has a petite figure, and curves in all the right places. Her personality is even better. I like her, and if my half-brother wasn't so blind, he would make an effort to notice. I get that she is Chris's little sister, but honestly, they are perfect for each other.

"Yeah, I think so." I open the passenger door of her Mini Cooper. My long hair that hits right above the swell of my jean-clad butt, paired with Converse sneakers, and a long-sleeve sweater with a daring neckline showing the swell of my breast.

I drape the hoodie on my arm like a security blanket, and watch as she zips up her windbreaker jacket with the blue and red Westlake prep logo on the right front breast pocket. "I hope you have a great routine. I'll be watching from the bleachers in the right corner.

"Is Patrick going to pick you up after the game?"

I almost forgot that I agreed to go out with Patrick as friends, and I was reminded when he mentioned it at lunch earlier today. I told him it was okay to pick me up after the game. It's Friday, and there is a party after the game, win or lose, and he assured me it was cool and that we should go since I was hitching a ride with Abby.

"Yeah. He said he will be waiting for me by your car after the game."

I still don't know what car Patrick drives since I only see him at lunch and in English class. She walks backward toward the back of the bleachers where the school band is gathering to get ready to perform. "Okay, so I'll meet you at the party?"

I give her a nod as I head toward the bleachers where everyone is walking to get a seat. "Yeah. I'll see you at the party. I can't wait to see your routine."

I would love to see what moves she's got. I'm glad that Ky doesn't play on the team because that would mean I would have to watch him on the field. I'm guessing since his best friends play, he will be in the stands. He also has his harem of girls he screws on the cheer team, so I guess it's a win-win for him.

I make my way up the bleachers and find a seat on the top to the right of the stands, away from everyone trying to get better seats below.

The sun has set, and the bright lights are shining on the field. People are chatting, and the cheer squad for both teams are down on the track practicing their routines. I'm glad it's still warm despite it being the first week October. The breeze blows my hair, but it's not chilly, and the smell of popcorn carries on the wind.

I notice the guys are heading out on the field, and the refs are in the center holding the football, deep in conversation. My eyes scan the players on the field. The Westlake Prep bulldogs are playing against the Georgia High's bears. The mascots take the field and dance, making mocking gestures to each other in rivalry.

My eyes land on Tyler and I smile when he laughs at something Chris said. He scans the stands, and then surprisingly his gaze lands on me. He holds his helmet up in a mock salute, and I wave back, causing other students, some with their parents, to turn and notice me sitting alone watching the game.

Conner walks up and places a hand on Tyler's shoulder with a smile and waves at me. I duck my head, sliding my straightened hair behind my ears. He is trying to be funny, but I have noticed that since Tyler has started to be nice to me, so have the other guys on the team.

Speaking of the devil, I feel eyes boring in my skin, causing the tiny hairs to stand. My head lifts and my eyes scan the stadium seating in front of me...and five levels below I find eyes like two black orbs watching me. My gaze locks on Ky's in a challenge for a few seconds.

I avert my gaze and sweep my hair over to my left shoulder, pulling my cellphone out of my pocket, giving me something to do before the game starts. I'm not here for him. I'm here to watch Tyler dominate on the field, and watch Abby perform her routine. After five minutes, my head lifts when I hear the cheerleaders shout, and my eyes find Jen at the front. I'm assuming that means she is the captain. I could never frequent games at the other schools I attended. I was either locked up in the detention center, or I was not at a school long enough, bouncing from foster home to foster home, so I guess I can file this away as an experience.

Jen waves with her pom-poms and her fake smile as she blows a kiss to Ky seated in her line of sight. He sits still. He doesn't wave, and he doesn't blow her a kiss in return. Interesting. I guess he doesn't like showing PDA. He doesn't seem like the type anyway. He seems dark and unavailable. Everything is on his terms, and not the other way around. I guess that would make sense if you like to keep your options open and screw around with different girls.

It is the first quarter, and we have scored two touchdowns so far. I wanted to get up and cheer but feel awkward not having any friends sitting with me. I guess I will keep my excitement inside.

When Tyler would look up, I would smile letting him know I'm enjoying watching him play. I'm also getting hungry and I have twenty dollars Mr. Murray left on the table with a note telling me it was for food at school.

Standing up from my seat, I make my way the ladies' restroom before going to the concession stand by taking the side walkway. I open the door and head inside and notice that it's empty, so I choose the last stall. When I'm about to close the door, it is pushed open, and I'm slammed against the side of the stall. I'm about to scream but a hand is clamped over my mouth.

"Shh." I shake my head and try to push Ky off me, but he doesn't budge. Fuck. His fingers comb through my straight blonde hair on the side of my face. "Who are you all dolled up for? Is this for me?"

I roll my eyes and try to bite the palm of his hand, but can't get my teeth to snag on his skin. His eyes slide down to the edge of my sweater where my hoodie is wrapped around my waist, and he removes it with his free hand, sliding his knee between my thighs, holding me in place.

He has me firmly pinned so that I can't move. I can't scream or tell him to fuck off.

"Who are you all dressed up for?" he repeats. I try to speak but it comes out muffled. He smiles and he leans close to my ear. I can smell his citrus cologne, the heat if his skin and the mint from the gum in his mouth consuming me. "I'm going to remove my hand from your mouth. If you scream, I will place it back on and I will take you right here. I will slide my big fat cock inside your pussy, and you're going to like it. Nod if you understand.

I nod. He is trying to scare me. Deep down I know he wouldn't do it. I'm not scared of Ky.

His hand slides down my chin, to my neck, and stops at the swell of my breast. My eyes follow, and then they flick back up to his parted lips.

"What do you want? I have left you alone."

He watches my mouth as I speak. Slowly caressing my face with his eyes. His leg is still wedged between my thighs, his body leaning into mine. My stomach clenches and unclenches with the beat of my heart pounding inside my chest.

"I never said that I would leave you alone." His lips are close to the pulse beating frantically on the side of my neck. "I never said I wouldn't show up when I wanted, how I wanted, whenever the fuck I wanted. Because, Rubi, I'm going to show up. I'm going to do to you whatever I want."

My chest rises and falls with each breath. I look up at him and I don't know what to say. I don't know what to do. I'm at a loss for words and I can't think.

His tongue peeks out, licking his lips like I'm a meal. His lips are so close it's like we are breathing each other's air. "I want to tell you something." He brushes his lips against mine. I want to bite him. I want to fight him, but I can't. "Do you remember our first kiss?"

"You said–"

His tongue plunges inside my parted lips and I whimper as our tongue swirl and battle. We continue to kiss each other passionately as he suckles my tongue and I grab his bottom lip. I try to squeeze my thighs together because my panties are going to be ruined, I'm so wet. But I can't move because his leg is in the way.

He slides his strong hand around my neck, holding me in place as he growls in my mouth. He pulls away and his head dips as he places kisses on my breasts. My fingers slide inside the dark strands of his hair as his mouth finds the edge where my nipple begins, sliding his tongue around and flicking the engorged peak just above the cup of my bra. I'm on fire. There is no other way to explain it. When I look into his obsidian eyes, they hold a promise.

"Ky," I whisper his name, hating him, wanting him to stop, but I know deep down I don't want him to.

"Fuck," he rasps.

His hand lowers and he pulls at the band of my jeans and forcefully slides his hand inside my pants, finding my panties and pulling them hard to the side, making my body jerk.

My mouth is parted in shock, arching my neck when I feel his icy fingers against my wet heat as they glide over my clit, rubbing in circles and making me ache for him. Making me need him. Making me want him.

If he doesn't stop, I know I'll let him. Threat or no threat, I'll let him fuck me. I'll scream, but not because of him barging in the stall and trapping me. I'll scream his name when I finally come with him deep inside of me. When you fantasize about someone for so long, it's impossible to resist wanting them.

He draws his hand out, his fingers are moist and glistening from my arousal. My face flushes in embarrassment and I look away. "Look at me," he demands.

My eyes find his full of lust with the desire to fuck, he pushes his wet fingers inside of his mouth and it is so fucking hot watching him close his eyes like it's a delicacy when he sucks his fingers.

He pulls them out of his mouth, removing his leg between mine and leans close as he lowers his voice. "You have this darkness that calls to me, Rubi. A darkness I want to explore. A darkness that feeds me. I get drunk off of it like a drug. It's become my addiction because I know that it's caused by something evil that lives inside of all of us. It's an evil that is more dangerous because we all have it. It's when we act on it that it becomes something out of control. You have dealt with it for so long, but I want to know what caused it.

"Why?" I croak, closing my eyes.

He leans forward and rubs his nose up the side of my face, sniffing my skin while he grins and licks his lips. "Because when I find it," he says in a rasp. "When I see what it is, what is breaking you inside, whoever did it will understand what it means to have fucked with something that is mine." My mouth drops open as he inserts a hand between my legs and cups my pussy with his palm. "This is mine. Be ready when I come for you."

I didn't even see him shut the stall door, but after he pulls his hand away, he double-checks that my top is covering my breasts before banging shut the door on the way out, leaving me breathless.

After leaving the bathroom, I made it back to my seat to watch halftime and the band and to see Abby's routine on the dance team. It is nothing to go crazy about, but then I narrow my eyes and notice Jen, Nicole, and another girl I have seen Tyler with walking down the halls at school.

They are all laughing behind her back with their pom-poms over their faces and I bet they want Abby to look foolish when she is out there. The routine with the other girls isn't bad, but they use an old song, and the steps are out of sync with the beat. It looks like a middle school performance.

Abby looks over at me and bites her lip knowing the routine wasn't' memorable.

My eyes scan the bottom of the bleachers involuntarily, but I can't help it. What happened in the bathroom was hot. It was possessive and crazy. I should regret it, but deep down I don't. I inwardly smile because he obviously didn't find me ugly enough when he went out of his way to kiss me or taste me. I file that fact away for later. If he wants to play fuck games, I'm all for it. He wanted me to stay away from him, but the question is, can he stay away from me?

His black hair felt like fine silk between my fingers, and I could feel the definition of his chiseled back through his white shirt. His cologne lingered on my hands for a while. I really dislike my seat since I can't see Ky's reaction when Jen looks at him and smiles knowingly.

Was what happened earlier real or a lie? I shouldn't read too much into it. I got my kiss. A kiss I wondered what would feel like if I ever saw him again when I was older. But I have to admit, physically, Ky is everything.

He stands and his jeans sit low on his narrow hips, indicating a flat stomach but with strong thighs. He has a chain hooked in his jeans and tattoos placed in different areas on his skin. When he was up close, my favorite was the one that is vertically on his neck. It read: *Darkness lives in all of us*. It made sense with what he told me in the bathroom earlier.

My darkness attracts him.

But can it tame him?

Chapter Eighteen

Rubi

AFTER THE GAME, I see Abby looking defeated even though Westlake prep beat Georgia High 34-31. I catch up with her in the parking lot as I try to avoid Ky. I want to hold onto the memory of what happened earlier for a little while longer before he goes cold.

"Was it that bad?" she asks me with her bag over her shoulder with a look of defeat on her face.

I scrunch my face and tilt my head playfully. "It wasn't bad…but it wasn't memorable."

She blows a puff of air out of her mouth. "It sucked. I know it did, and I've tried to change it with the other girls, but they always need approval from the cheer captain."

I pinch my brows in confusion. "Why? It isn't her routine."

"I know and I hate the music and a lot of things about the choreography."

"Change it and don't tell them shit. Come up with a new routine and perform it at the next game. When they see the crowd likes it," I shrug a shoulder. "They can't say anything." I cup my hand over my mouth when I hear the cheer squad and the football players headed our way. "Make sure the music is bomb as fuck, and make sure you outshine them. They suck."

Abby flashes me a pearly grin as Tyler, Conner, Ky, Chris, and three other players head over with the cheerleaders not far behind, but her smile rapidly fades as they get closer and she spots Nicole. Since it is a home game, they don't have to board a bus and can leave in their respective cars.

Nicole and her grating voice filters through the conversation. "Damn, Abby. That wasn't what we practiced. You need to work on that routine."

Giving her a hard glare, I hope she trips and falls on her face. "What are you looking at, street rat?" She crosse her arms and juts her hip out. "I see you're trying to fit in."

Jen gives me a smirk, eyeing me up and down. "I think she wants to attract attention."

"Funny, what you need to worry about is your lame ass routine before you go shutting other people down. Come to think of it, didn't you come up with it?" I say, putting it out there that the whole routine was her idea, and now she is giving Abby shit about trying to embarrass her. The school for whatever reason has the cheer captain head of the dance team and cheer team.

"Come up with what?" She emphasizes the t in the end.

"That routine—and your cheer moves and the dance team's routine. Shit is lame. A third grader on TikTok comes up with a better routine than that."

"Oh, and you could do better? Don't you have to go steal something or some shit."

"Don't you have to go and get on your knees like the easy skank you are."

"Woah, ladies." Conner interrupts. "Damn."

Ky walks around Conner. "Go home, Jen."

Her eyes widen. "I thought you were taking me to the party after the game. I don't have a ride," she whines.

My eyes drift to Ky, but he doesn't meet them before responding, "Then let's leave."

It feels like I got punched in the gut. I guess the memory couldn't last another hour. I almost declined Patrick's invitation, making up an excuse, but now I'm happy I didn't. After the game ended, I was about to push send but I changed my mind.

Jen gives me a sly look before walking up to Ky and placing her hand flat on his chest. He studies her hand, but doesn't remove it. His eyes flick up, aiming directly at me for a moment, but I can't read his blank expression. As soon as his black eyes land on mine, he turns away and I try to hide my irritation. An hour ago, he was all over me. I was stupid and I caved.

"Hey, are you okay, Rubiana?" Tyler asks, getting Ky's attention, but I look away.

"I'm good."

"Do you need a ride, or are you riding with Abby?" he asks.

"I'm waiting for someone."

Tyler's eyebrows rise and he looks around, but doesn't see anyone he knows would be taking me anywhere. Chris casts a *why didn't you mention anything to me* look at Abby.

Nicole is busy shooting daggers over at Jen, and Conner slaps his teammate on his shoulder. "This is gonna be good," Conner says, looking at Ky, but my gaze remains on Tyler.

My phone vibrates in my jeans pocket, and I 'm relieved that I can distract myself by removing my phone and opening the alert to the text.

Patrick: I'm here but I don't want to get out of the car.

Rubi: Why?

Patrick: I want to keep on living, Rubi. Ky and your brother will kill me. Look to your left at the car with the parking lights on.

Shit. I forgot about that. My eyes scan the parking lot, and parked in the back with the lights on is a black Camaro.

Rubi: Black Camaro?

Patrick: Yeah.

Rubi: Give me a sec.

Pocketing my phone, I watch as Ky slides in the driver's side while Jen opens the door in a huff. Woah! What did I miss? She gets in the car, but Ky's windows are tinted, so I can't see inside.

"Is your ride here? Tyler asks.

I tear my gaze away from Ky's BMW and look up at Tyler. He has his arms crossed with the strap of his bag on his shoulder waiting for an answer. I smile inwardly because for the past couple of weeks, he has been acting like a big brother. I'm not sure if he remembers that I'm older than him.

"My ride is already here. I'll meet you at the party."

He pinches his brow when he sees me take off across the parking lot toward the Camaro.

"Do you know where it is?" he calls out.

I hold up my hand without turning around. "I'll be there. Don't worry, I won't disappear."

If he only knew how appealing that sounds, but then I have my cat Hope to think about.

I reach the Camaro and I can hear the doors unlock from the passenger side. I pull the handle to open the door and slide inside. I'm greeted with a scared shitless Patrick looking around like someone is out to get him, and a whole lot of cologne.

"Hey."

"Hey," he says, looking around to make sure Ky is backing out of the parking lot in his black BMW.

"Dude, relax. You look like a meth addict on a paranoia trip. What's with all the cologne?"

"I-I–"

"Breathe," I quip, interrupting him before he has a stuttering fit.

He inhales and lets out a breath through his mouth and starts again. "I wanted to smell good, and how do you know how a meth addict acts?"

I sigh, not wanting to tell him that part. "Where I come from, I just know. Let's go."

He places the car in gear and begins to drive down the street.

He glances at me briefly and then says, "I'm sorry about the cologne."

I'm sure it would smell good if he didn't pour the entire bottle all over himself. "It isn't bad." I glance and see his mouth breaking out into a little grin. "Keep it to a couple sprays when you're trying to impress a girl, though."

I point out the last part because I'm not dumb. It is obvious when a guy is trying to make an impression and I see the way he looks at me when he thinks I'm not looking. I thought he said we were only friends.

"Okay. Got it."

"I can't be out too late. I have to get to the party to catch a ride home with Tyler."

"Do you think you have time so I can show you something? I want to show you my drawings."

"Where is that exactly?" I notice he is driving toward my old neighborhood in West Park.

"Not far."

After a ten-minute drive and four blocks from West Lake, I can see abandoned buildings to my right with one streetlight. I recognize the buildings from when I would take the bus to meet Ky when I was younger. I notice some of the buildings now have art and graffiti on the exterior walls.

He pulls into an abandoned parking lot in front of one of the buildings. I follow him out of the car and he has a flashlight in his hands. Wait? This is his art? He is the one doing this?

He shines the flashlight on the wall, and I stand, admiring the wall painted in different colors depicting West Park and West Lake. Rich and poor.

"W-what do you think?" he asks after five minutes.

The mural is a mirror image of the way the two towns separate. Nice big estate homes on one side, and West Park with abandoned buildings, broken down cars, and small houses with overgrown grass. The kids are in the street. One street with nice cars, kids wearing nice clothes with smiles on their faces. The other kids have mismatched clothes and rusted bikes with sadness on their faces. All because one side has more money than the other. One side is looked at as better than the other.

"I think it's perfect."

He glances at me. "Really?"

"Yeah, you have talent and an eye for things."

I don't want to tell him that I know what it feels like to live on both sides. How different kids become as adults when they are raised a certain way.

"Thanks, Rubi. It means a lot coming from you."

I turn around to head back to the car and say, "Why?"

"Because I have a feeling you understand both sides.

I open the door to his car. "I guess I do. Thanks for the ride and for showing me your art." He nods before he gets in the driver's side.

I understand why he drew it on the building. It is his way to express himself and speak out the only way he knows how, and no one will judge him or know who did it. It is obvious that he feels that he doesn't belong on either side. It is not your choice where you come from. I'm not a shrink or a therapist and I am so fucked up with my own mess and I am no one to give him advice with whatever he is going through. He is obviously bullied at school. He is talented, though, but there is a part of the mural that is missing. The part that doesn't show a person's action that makes them good or bad. People from either side could be good or bad. They could make a wrong decision because they didn't know better, or judge without knowing the truth.

It is why you shouldn't judge people. We all have our demons and skeletons in our closet.

Chapter Nineteen

Rubi

I'M WALKING UP the perfect lighted path toward the white house with the muffled sounds of music playing inside. As I step closer, I can hear laughter and people trying to talk over the music. I spot Ky's BMW and Tyler's truck in the driveway between the rows of cars parked at the curb.

Patrick offered to get some food before dropping me off, but I declined. I can't go missing for too much time. If Tyler tells Stephen that he doesn't know where I am, I'm in deep shit.

I walk inside the medium-sized mansion, and the crowd of drunk kids are sprawled all over the nice house. The music is blaring through the built-in speakers mounted on the ceilings. Beats the shit out of an old boom box the older kids stole from a pawn shop back from where I came from.

"You came!" I turn and see Abby practically running up to me.

"Hey, where is Tyler?"

The light in her eyes dim and she points behind her. "He is upstairs in one of the rooms. The guys went up there."

I realize this scene isn't for me and I want to get out of here. This isn't my type of crowd.

I walk up the staircase and I open the door to the left, and when I open the door, I freeze. Nicole and Jen are naked and facing each other. Ky is sitting on the floor at the foot of the bed, but his back is to me.

What the fuck is this? They are both naked from the waist up, but Ky is just ...watching them.

"What the fuck are you doing!" Jen screeches, failing with the attempt to cover herself.

I don't answer her because I'm stunned. Ky whips his body around, and the wicked gleam in his eyes flashes in challenge. He smiles but I glare at him. This isn't funny.

"Come in and close the door," he demands, standing up.

Not wanting to be part of his little orgy fest, I turn around, but he is right behind me, placing a hand on the door and putting pressure against it.

"You're staying."

"I don't want to be part of whatever you have going on in here."

I'm disappointed. I'm furious. I'm jealous. I'm jealous because of what happened earlier tonight, and now he is in here with both of them.

"Who said I wanted you to be part of anything that has to do with them. Don't be a coward, Rubi. Stay."

He backs up a step, and I feel his hand grip my wrist over the sleeve of my sweater, tugging on my arm to follow him. I should turn around and open the door to get out of the room, but I'm curious. He doesn't want me to participate. Can I stomach if he participates? If he decides to fuck them in front of me?

"It's okay, Rubi," he says, softly nudging his head in the direction of the couch situated with a direct view of the bed. My eyes land on the profile of his face with the two stuck-up snobs behind him on the bed. They are like a silhouette of two women about to make out. "I don't bite." He continues as he leans close to my ear and whispers, "Yet."

Goosebumps snake over the skin of my neck in a direct line to the heat between my thighs. If I turn around, he will think I'm a coward. It will also cause the bitches behind him to continue to talk shit behind my back. There is only so much I can take before I punch both of them in their faces. And that is something I can't afford to do. Too risky.

So I let him tug me toward the dark blue couch, and he sits down with his legs spread wide, tapping repeatedly to the space he has made between his legs that's just big enough for me to sit in.

"Are you serious, Ky?" Jen says in a sarcastic voice. "What do you want us to do with the street rat here."

He leans back and spreads his arms wide on the couch like it's his room. Like he owns the place. He gives her an evil smirk. His black eyes are hard when he looks at Jen and then at Nicole.

"Then Nicole will stay. She does whatever I want. No one is forcing anyone here to do anything they don't want. You are free to leave."

Jen snaps her head toward Nicole as realization dawns across her features. Ding-Ding-Ding. She just realized her little friend has been going behind her back and is really a backstabbing bitch just like her. They're perfect for each other.

"Fine," Jen says through clenched teeth, giving Nicole a vicious glare.

He waves his finger and says, "Continue."

Both of them begin kissing and touching each other. This is obviously for Ky's benefit. This is some sick macho bullshit.

"Sit," he quips.

I really want to smack him right now, but like I said, it will make me look like a coward. So I do as he asks, and sit in the space in front of him. He pushes himself back and his crotch his snug to my backside. I'm glad I'm wearing jeans. Nicole has her tongue down Jen's throat, but her eyes flick to where Ky and I are sitting like we are a couple. He pulls me back against him so that my back is to his chest, and slides my hair to the side, pulling the hood of my sweater down. I can feel the warmth of his breath as he exhales through his nose. My skin pricks in awareness like the heat being turned on when you're cold. His warmth is all I feel all over my body. I'm aware of him and only him because everything in my heart has only been about him for so long.

It is hard to just let go and forget him. When we were kids there was always this spark. An electric energy that tethered us together. But now it's almost severed, held together by the thinnest thread.

Maybe it's his hate for me, or me hating him for what he has become, or what he has done to me. Because my love for him is what kept me alive. It's the type of love that gave me hope. He was the only love I ever knew was true, and it's the only love I ever wished for.

It is the only thing that I can think of for why I am sitting here. Maybe it is because I don't want him in the room alone with them. In my mind, Ky is mine even if he doesn't want to be. Even if he pushes me way, hurts me with his words, and ruins all our memories. Because before them, it was us. Before them, he was mine.

I try to keep my eyes trained somewhere on the walls of the bedroom and not hearing the kissing noises or the moans from Nicole and Jen. I don't feel Ky getting hard behind me. I can tell his crotch is still pressed up behind me, but I can feel every breath he takes even if I can't see his eyes.

"Are you watching, Rubi?" I swallow, not wanting to look, not wanting to answer because I don't care about them. Deep down, I only care about him.

I remain still, not trying to move, but his breath near the lobe of my ear has me hyperaware that I'm this close to him. It reminds me of when we were kids, and he was showing me how to plant a flower. I loved the little white petals of the daisies so much that I wanted to always have them, but didn't know how to plant the seeds, much less afford to buy the seeds to grow them myself.

It is why I had them tattooed on my arm with his name in bold black letters that I hide underneath my long sleeves and with a Band-Aid the first day of school. Two letters to remind me of the boy who held a sadness in his heart just like my own. His memories were the only good ones I had. The first day of school I placed a Band-Aid over those letters to hide them from prying eyes, even wearing my hoodie I didn't want other students to ask about what it meant. Then after the milk incident I was really glad I had the Band-Aid on since I lost my shield when the hoodie got wet.

"Are you watching?" he asks again, and I nod, hoping he doesn't notice that I'm not. That I am staring at a dark speck on the wall by a chest of drawers. But he calls me out on the lie. "Liar," he whispers.

I stiffen when I feel his warm fingers in the band of my jeans under the hoodie. His fingers expertly undo the top button, and I hold my breath when the zipper gives way. I can't hear it, but I feel it against the skin of my lower belly. I should pull away, but I know I can't.

I won't.

He slides his hand inside my jeans, and my head tilts back when I feel his finger touch the nub of my clit over my panties and whispers, "Do you know why they do what I say, Rubi? It is because humans are possessive and territorial creatures by nature. In their case, they are trying to claim a territory they think they are entitled to because someone told them that they were pretty."

I'm panting, trying to listen to his words while the tension is building between my legs, increasing by the second. I feel out of breath and swallow the saliva that has pooled in my throat, trying to hold back a moan from escaping my lips. "It feels good, doesn't it, Rubi? To feel how I'm breaking you. Admit it. Admit that you want me inside you. Admit that you want what they want."

I won't admit it. I would, but he's playing with me. Tears pool in the corner of my eyes because I do want to feel him inside me, but I know it won't mean anything except him making his point. He craves control and feeds off it.

I begin to grind myself shamelessly on his fingers and he chuckles in my hear. "Hmm… you like it, don't you, Rubi, the feel of me fucking you with my fingers like the puppet master pulling your strings?"

I'm wet, hot, and ashamed of the way I'm letting him play me. This is a game to him. A way to break me because I left him. He wants to hurt me, but he doesn't understand why I left, that I had no choice.

No one understands why I held on for so long. Why I endured the pain. Why I stayed silent and took it. It was all for him. My mother was a piece of shit who gave up on me since the day I was born. She made sure she told me every chance she could what a mistake I was. She also treated me and let everyone else around treat me like the mistake she claimed I was.

My stepfather hated that I would sneak out while he was at work, while my mother was getting her next fix with her drug of choice, meth. Meth was her favorite and she would do anything to get it. I just didn't want to stick around to be part of it. I didn't want to watch her kill herself or look at me with soulless eyes as she checked out.

It was always the last time, I would tell myself, but I couldn't let Ky go. One day led to the next and the next. I was an addict and Ky was my addiction. He was my drug, and I would do anything for the next hit, just like my mother. Hers was the euphoria, and mine was a day spent with a boy who stole my heart at eleven years old and never gave it back.

I can feel his erection behind me hardening by the second when he slides his fingers inside my wet slit. I bite my lip, drawing blood to hold back the moan and feeling like my vocal cords are going to snap like a guitar string. Nicole and Jen are forgotten like background noise.

"You're so wet for me, Rubi. You don't want to talk, so I'm going to make you feel," he says, punishing me by sliding his fingers deep inside to my G-spot. I arch my back, about to come. "I'm going to love when you scream."

Nicole and Jen are moaning while Nicole sucks on Jen's pussy, but Ky doesn't seem interest like a teenaged guy would be. His face is on the side of my neck with his lips rasping against my skin when he speaks. His hard cock is growing into a steel blade against my ass. I push back against it so he knows I can feel him.

"Come for me, Rubi. Show me how much you want me. How much you need me," he says as he relentlessly fucks me with his fingers. I can't take it anymore and I come. I come hard, clenching his fingers and wishing it was the cock that is currently pressed up on my ass behind me. Stars explode in the backs of my eyes like a white light from the flash of a camera.

I can hear moaning, but I'm relieved when my head clears from the intense orgasm he gave me. It's then that I realize the sound is coming from Jen and she is currently watching Ky as she comes, confused that he isn't even looking at her.

He pulls his fingers out of me and slides his hand out of my jeans, holding it up to my line of vision. "Here, Rubi. Taste your shame."

He bites the skin of my neck and I recoil like I've been slapped, and scramble off the couch, glaring at him. His eyes black like a possessed demon reminding me of a black heaven, his stare cold and dangerous. Unrecognizable.

He smiles. "You are no different." He motions to Nicole, licking her lips after sucking Jen off. "Except they're better. At least they fight and beg for what they want."

"You think it makes you any better to watch them beg and fight, huh? Makes it right for them to do whatever it is you ask," I say through clenched teeth.

He is right. He knew I would be ashamed of how I let him use me. I'm mad that he compared me to less than them. He is no better than they are…or maybe he is worse.

"At least I enjoy it."

Not wanting to look at his face and hear him spit anymore of his shit. I storm out of the bedroom in a fit of rage down the stairs. I find Tyler talking to a brunette with his arm resting above her head, lost in conversation. His eyes lift when he spots me.

"Hey, I was looking for you. Abby said she saw you when you arrived."

The brunette gives me an eye roll, probably hearing more rumors about me that I'm a poor orphan trying to destroy Tyler's perfect life, and that I'm a thief trying to get a free ride.

I ignore her and grab Tyler by the arm. "Hey, chill out, we were talking."

I angle my head and curl my lip in a snarl. "Sorry, bitch. I have to get home, and he is my ride. You know…I have this thing called probation and I have to be home." She glances at Tyler to see what he will say, or if he will tell me to get lost, but his mouth turns into a grimace and he shoots me a guilty expression because he was the one who started the rumors about me when I first arrived at Westlake Prep. I should have let Patrick take me home since he backed out of going in when he saw how many people were here. I think he was afraid of what people would do or say if we showed up together, but I told Abby I would show up.

"Let's go," he says quietly, and we walk out while the brunette gives me a glare.

I don't even care what they say about me anymore or what they think. It doesn't define me. I still have two hours before my curfew to be home, but I need to get out of here before Ky comes out with the two skanks he was with upstairs. He is probably going at it with them after I left. I've had enough of his humiliation for one night. I need to be alone. In my closet so I can cry and wallow in self-pity over a guy who doesn't care about me.

Just like my mother did.

Chapter Twenty

Rubi

I WALK INSIDE the house trying to tip-toe around my mother. She is sprawled on the couch lying on her side. Her eyes are like saucers. They remind me of a cat's eyes when their pupils dilate. I remember watching the stray cat Moe's pupil dilate when my stepfather would come out. They received money in the mail, and they said it was because my mother applied for help from the state, and she had a kid, so she was supposed to get free money. My mom said I was good for something because my real father didn't want me. She said I should be grateful that she kept me and didn't abort me. She would tell me that all the time. When I tried to leave and thought I could do it on my own one night after they smoked that stuff and passed out. I left the whole day and came back that same night when I was hungry and couldn't get food. Especially, when I would get funny looks from people, and I was scared of homeless people who would talk to themselves causing me to run the whole way home.

    I saw my stepfather's truck in the driveway, and I'm hoping he is in the room passed out from whatever he took or smoked. The water was cut off today. I had to get my water bottle and fill it so I can brush my teeth and wash the best I could. It happens every two months when they forget to pay the bill and it gets shut off. So I'm used to this routine.

I'm tip-toeing to my room, and when I push the door open, my hope that he didn't notice me gone is short lived. He is sitting with his stained tank top from working at Lou's mechanic shop. He smells like death, beer and that stuff he smokes. It makes him angry and mean.

My hands begin to tremble because I know what is to come. The last time was three days ago, and the fresh wounds on my back were finally not stinging as much.

"Where were you, brat?"

I swallow and he can see it in my eyes. He knows I went to visit Ky. He can probably tell from the fresh dirt stains on my jeans from kneeling on the grass. Ky was showing me how he learned to plant flowers today. I stay silent hoping his mind will move on to something else like he does sometimes. Just... sometimes. Today, I'm not so lucky. I can see it. I can smell it. He wants to hurt me for whatever reason. He says it's because I go visit Ky. I made the mistake and blurted it out. It is my biggest regret. A regret I must pay for every time. But I keep going to see him.

"You went to see that boy again, didn'tcha? You sneakin' behind me and your mother's back, you little tramp," he snarls, saliva sputtering out of his mouth.

His eyes, red rimmed, look like an owl. He is on the bad stuff. The stuff that smells like death when he exhales it into the air. I cover my nose and run to hide in the closet so he can't find me when he turns around after his eyes roll back inside his skull. Or so they can't find me.

The others who come here to do the same.

He has a brown leather whip in his hand. The same kind I remember seeing in my history book at school. The teacher said it was called a bullwhip. I recognized the color and the shape, except the one he used was smaller, and he started using it after I threw away all the belts in the house. My stepfather blames his other friends for stealing them. I won't tell him any different.

"You know the drill. You go see that boy and you pay the price. Being a little whore will cost ya, brat."

I kneel on the stained carpet with burn holes that hurt my feet if I'm barefoot.

"Take off your shirt, Rubi. Turn around and kneel."

I do as he asks because it will only be two hits instead of five if I do as he says. He only uses the whip when I go see Ky. The other times he uses his hand or just pulls my hair.

I kneel after I take off my shirt and cross my arms over my chest and close my eyes shut. Wack! The sting burns and then gets really hot like a fire is spreading in its wake across my skin.

Wack! My tears leak and I take it. I take it because he will think I learned my lesson and leave me alone. The throbbing pain causes a sob to escape my throat and my bottom lip to tremble. My hands start to shake from the pain. It hurts so bad. The tears keep falling down my cheeks. I feel something like a rain drop slide down my back. The second hit always draws blood. My mother and stepfather do not allow me to have friends. I don't why. When I ask, they scream at me and tell me it's because they said so, and then they shove me inside my room and close the door.

But the marks that are left are marks I will bear for him. A mark I will take because it allows me another day to see my best friend. The only one who talks to me and makes me feel wanted. He is the brightest part of my day, and the only one who can make me smile. I'll keep taking the punishment because Ky is worth it. He is my everything.

I jolt and my eyes pop open when I feel a warm ball of fur near my cheek purring. I snuggle my head against Hope, but then I look down at my long t-shirt and notice I'm on the bed again. Hope stretches his paws, and then I hear something jingle when he moves. I pet his head and pinch my eyebrows when I feel a collar with a bell around his neck.

"How did you get this, huh? Who did you let place a collar around your neck?"

I wonder how he got it? Hope is not friendly with everyone, and he doesn't' like anything on him. He's always in my room waiting for me until I get home. I talk to him when I'm feeling sad, and before I go to sleep. Sometimes I wish he talked back, but sometimes you just want to be heard. Not to be judged or told you don't belong, or that no one wants you. Just someone... to listen.

I don't know why I keep waking up in the bed when I fall asleep in the closet. It has happened two or three times a week for a while now. That's a worry for another day, I guess. So I get up from the bed and freshen up in the bathroom to head downstairs for breakfast. It's Saturday, and usually Stephen and Caroline go out shopping.

"Hey, I put fresh water in the Keurig," Tyler says with what appears to be a cup with a shaker in his hand.

"Thanks."

He starts to shake the cup and what looks like some powder with water. While I get a cup of coffee, I see from the corner of my eye him leaning on the counter.

"When you got to the party last night, how come you were upstairs?"

My heart begins to pace. Did Ky tell him?

I clear my throat as the humming of the Keurig begins to do its thing, "I was looking for you. They said you were upstairs. Don't you remember when I came down and asked where you were so you could take me home?"

I try to play off what happened last night as best I could. I don't want him to find out about me and Ky. It would raise a lot of questions. The types of questions I don't want to answer.

"I wasn't upstairs. All the people upstairs are screwing in the rooms."

My lips form a thin line and I look away toward the coffeemaker so he doesn't see that I knew what was going up upstairs, and that I was in the room with Ky watching and participating.

"Got it."

"Hey, do you want to come with me?"

I pause.

Is he serious? Where?

"Where?" I ask, taking a sip of the warm coffee after I pour, stir the creamer, and replace the coconut yumminess back in the fridge.

"Boxing gym."

I turn around and lean on the counter with my coffee in hand and raise my brows. "You box?"

"Yeah. It's kickboxing, technically. When I can, if I don't have football, and always on the weekends. You want to come instead of being stuck alone all day in the house. We will see what we can get into afterward?"

"Alright."

How bad can it be? At least I won't be stuck here with nothing to do.

"Awesome."

"Hey, Tyler?"

"Yeah?"

"Do you know who put the collar with the little bell on Hope?"

He shakes his head. "No. Dad has been working on a project for a client, and Mom has been going to work selling houses again, and she always gets home after we are already here. She would have told me. She gets excited when she does stuff like that. Why?"

I lick my lips and place the cup in the sink, pumping the dish soap holder and turning the faucet on to wash the cup and place it on the dry rack.

"I was trying to figure out how he got it, is all."

And now I'm even more intrigued about where that collar came from.

Chapter Twenty-One

Rubi

WE MAKE IT to the boxing gym, and when I jump out of Tyler's truck my stomach drops. A black BMW looking very much like Ky's is parked two spots over.

"Rubi..." Tyler calls out to me, nudging his head toward the entrance. "Come on. It's this way."

I follow him inside, and the smell of rubber, sweat, and cool air from the air conditioning greets me. I can hear smacks, hard breathing, and male conversation going on behind the black and red wall with the counter in front. The black and gray speckled floor feels like rubber under my Converse sneakers.

Tyler has his gym bag strung over his shoulder. I follow him behind the wall, and there are three boxing rings in the middle of the massive place. There is also a MMA ring to the right. Boxing equipment is set along both sides of the walls that run parallel. Mats, weights, red punching bags, everything you would need to kickbox.

There is a man instructing a class of younger kids to the left. I notice small bleachers where people can sit if they are here just to watch. I can see some guys working out with the punching bags to the left, and some at various other areas doing their workouts with weights. I can't believe Tyler also does kickboxing besides football.

"I'm going to change. You have a seat over there. If you're thirsty, get something from the front and give them my name and they will charge it to my account."

How nice. It beats the shit out of finding an empty water bottle and getting water for free from the water fountain.

"Okay," I say instead.

I walk up to the bleachers and spot Abby.

"Oh my God, Rubi. You're here. This is awesome."

I nod. "Yeah, Tyler asked me if I would come."

Her mouth breaks into a smile. "Chris likes when I come. We get to hang out and eat after."

I sit next to her, adjusting my hoodie and sliding my two long braids out and over the front of my chest. "You come and watch all the time?"

Her eyes light up when Tyler walks out of the locker room with shorts minus the shirt. I bet she does with the way her eyes are following Tyler to the punching bags.

I follow her line of sight and my chest tightens. Crap. He is here.

I didn't know he trained with Tyler. He doesn't have a shirt on, and I have better view of all the random tattoos placed all over his body. A tattoo that looks like a big Band-Aid over his heart catches my attention, and then I stare at his ab muscles as they flex with each punch and kick he lands on the bag. His body is perfect. Ky can also fight. I have seen plenty of kids get into fights, and I have never seen them close their fist and land a punch that perfect.

It makes sense why the students at Westlake Prep respect him. None of the bigger guys mess with Ky.

My eyes continue to scroll down his perfect body. His arms are bulging with a sheen of sweat, and his dark hair looks like a raven's wings. His hair is so black, it is almost blue, and is now shiny and wet. I remember feeling his solid body behind me on the couch. Now I know why people fear him when he gets in their face. Ky can kick someone's ass.

"Yeah. I think it makes me feel safe that my brother can protect me."

I know how you feel, Abby. I wish I had one of those when I was younger. The closest I had was Cesar.

I secretly wanted it to be with the boy who has turned into a man. The same one I'm looking at hit the bag like it is the enemy.

Ky stops hitting the bag and is breathing hard, his body is dripping in sweat, making him look like a girl's wet dream. His black eyes look around the gym, and then they land on me like he could feel me watching him. His eyes don't widen like he is surprised. He doesn't smile. He just watches me.

My eyes lock on his like we are waiting to see who blinks first. Who pulls away from the challenge? But the spell is broken when Abby shouts.

"Hey, Ky. Look who's here."

His mouth breaks in a small grin when his eyes flick to Abby. A grin I'm jealous of because it is not meant for me. I get a stare, but she gets a grin, and for a spit second, I hate Abby.

She has been really nice to me since I met her, so I'll do her a solid.

"Abby."

"Yeah?"

I look around to make sure no one is directly around us so they won't hear what I'm about to tell her. She eyes me curiously as she waits for me to speak.

"Spill. I know you like him."

She looks down at her hands. "Of course, I have known him since I was in sixth grade. He is my brother's best friend."

Nice try, Abbi. She keeps fidgeting like a shoplifter when they get caught. "Relax, Abby. I'm not gonna stand up and shout it to everyone. Especially in front of Tyler and your brother."

Her shoulders sag in relief and her eyes lift up and land on mine. "I have had a crush on him since eighth grade, but he doesn't know, obviously. He doesn't look at me like that."

I glance over to where the guys are talking, but we are too far away to hear what they are saying. Ky is facing away from me, and Tyler isn't looking this way and is blocking Chris so he can't see us.

"Ignore him."

"What?"

I have caught Tyler checking her out before. He likes her physically and is always polite to her, but he doesn't see her that way. He won't make a move because she is always bubbly and all smiles in front of everyone. He sees her as cute Abby. He knows she is off-limits, and if anyone saw him checking her out and thinking about her in a sexual way, they will point it out and tell her brother.

Observing Tyler with girls at school and at the party, I notice that if a girl is all over him, he loses interest. Tyler likes a challenge. Something he can't have. In this case, Abby is the perfect challenge.

"Ignore him. Don't smile when he looks over. Don't go up to him at school and make it a point to say hi. If he looks at you, look away. Stop giving him all of your attention. Don't make it easy on the person you really like to get your attention."

"Oh." She scoots next to me on the bench and my head lowers as she says above a whisper, "Is that how you got Ky to like you?"

My head lifts and I turn to look at her. "He doesn't like me. He hates me. There is nothing about me that he likes except to see me suffer."

"Then why does he stare at you all the time? The expression in his eyes looks different when you are around. I don't think he even realizes that he does it. When you two were in a stare off a minute ago, it was like he was communicating with you in a language only the two of you know. It is like you two share a big secret."

"He doesn't seem thrilled," I deadpan.

She snorts. "He doesn't stare at the girls he sleeps with. He is cold. Distant." She gives me a side glance. "Except with you. To be honest, it is hot and sexy the way he looks at you."

"What do you think people are saying when he looks at me?"

I know it isn't true, but I want to know what she thinks because if she thinks this way, maybe it is what other people assume. People like Jen and Nicole.

My eyes find Ky and he is staring at me again. Tyler and Chris are on the other side of the gym. Ky is waiting behind the instructor giving the younger kids their lesson. It is like he is trying to see if we are talking about him, but I know we are too far away, and it's impossible from where we are sitting with all the noise from the gym.

"It's like you already belonged to him before you came here, and if someone touches you, he will beat them like he did to that punching bag."

Giving her a wry smile, I know what she just said is impossible, "Crazy because we both know he doesn't. He only thinks I'm a threat to Tyler."

She waves her hand in a way that tells me she thinks that is bullshit. "I don't think you are a threat to Tyler. I think the opposite. I think you are just what Tyler needs in his life. A sister."

I wish that were true, Abby. A girl like me doesn't have it easy.

The instructor comes up to Ky and says something to him that has him stepping forward. He instructs the kids in position, and I can't help but notice the way his back muscles ripple with each movement he makes. When one of the boys is off balance, he walks over and instructs him on how to position his body. Some of the other kids start laughing. Surprisingly, Ky tells them to stop and to kneel. He tells them that making fun of someone else will not be tolerated.

So he's okay with not bullying in certain circumstances then…interesting. This is the side of Ky I remember seeing when we were kids. The side that would never allow another kid to make fun of someone else. The side that is gentle when he explains something to make sure you get it right. He tells the ones kneeling to apologize. The boys stand and walk over to the kid they were making fun of.

He must apologize because they shake hands, and all is back to normal. Ky stands in front of the group of kids in the same pose and begins to shadow punch with each count. Every kid follows in sync with each punch, showing them how to defend themselves. He isn't showing them how to hurt someone. I pick up a few of the words as he explains the movements, and he always uses the word defend. He is showing them that defending yourself with your fist is the last resort, and that you shouldn't make fun of others who are learning something important.

When Ky is finished with the group of students, he turns to face Chris and Tyler as they walk over.

"Come on," Chris says, motioning to Abby.

She gets up and smiles, and then Tyler does the same, motioning me with his finger. "You, too"

I pinch my brows, confused as to why he wants me to walk over to them on the mat. When Abby and I both face them, Ky walks up.

"Come here," Ky says, nudging his head over to the punching bags hanging to the side.

I hesitate and look at Abby, but I already see her walking away, trailing Tyler and Chris to the other side by the mirrors and leaving me alone with Ky. Shit.

When I turn around, Ky is waiting for me by the black punching bag. "I'm not going to hurt you, so you can stop being afraid," he says. I walk over to stand in front of the bag facing him, and he moves behind me and whispers, "Yet. But this lesson isn't about me and you. This lesson is about someone else hurting you, cornering you against the wall or in a bathroom."

My heart begins to hammer in my chest. He listened. He remembers what I said in the bathroom at the party. I turn my head and my nostrils flare from the scent of his sweat mixed with his cologne. He doesn't smell bad but good. I can feel the heat of his skin and imagine how it would feel against mine with nothing between us.

He tugs on the back of my hoodie and says, "Before we start, I think it would be better if you take the hoodie off."

I freeze for a split second and I shake my head. I can't take my hoodie off, not because I don't have a T-shirt that covers what I don't want others to see, but it would expose the two letters I don't want him to know are imprinted on my skin between the daisy tattoos. I don't have a Band-Aid to cover it up today. Tyler never mentioned I would participate in gym.

"It is okay, I'm good."

He leans close, his breath ghosting my ear. "What's wrong, Rubi? Are you afraid to show me what I want to see." I stay motionless. Frozen in place because his words are hitting close to the truth.

He laughs through his nose. "I'm messing with you. Come on." He stands behind me and my body relaxes. I look down and see his hands pop up around me with his palms facing up. "Don't freak out. I'm going to place my hands on your hips and guide you into the correct fighting position to land a proper punch, alright?" I nod and he lowers his voice and says, "The next time a man corners you and you feel threatened, Rubi. You don't slap him in the face. You need to know how to land a proper punch without hurting yourself, because an attacker can be stronger than you, but knowing the proper way to defend yourself can save your life."

"Okay," I respond.

I pinch my brows when he places his hands on my waist, and I'm aware of his fingers over the fabric of my sweater that are firm, causing tingles to snake over my skin.

"Make sure you maintain your balance," he says softly, moving me in the proper fighting stance.

For the next hour Ky shows me how to throw a perfect punch on the punching bag. When I get the hang of it, he praises me. He gives me a slight grin when I hit the bag over and over, letting out all the frustration and anger I have inside. It feels satisfying imagining that I'm defending myself against my stepfather, and the night that asshole tried to rape me. I hit the bag over and over, zeroing in on the place wear my fist connects with the bag. I blank out, and I can't hear when I get tunnel vision and my name is being called out.

"Rubiana!" I hear Ky raise his voice, my name echoing around me.

I close my eyes and blink, dropping my arms that I have now realized are burning from the effort. My chest is rising and falling with each breath I take trying to fill my lungs with air. I look up when I feel strong arms wrapping around me, and turn my head to see who is holding me. Ky.

"It's okay," he says softly. "It's okay," he repeats, and I notice the intimate way his mouth is near where my neck meets my shoulder.

Tyler and Chris are walking over. Tyler's eyes flick between me and Ky almost as if he is trying to figure out if there is more going on between us than we let on.

I'm relieved when Chris breaks the tension when he raises his eyebrows and says, "Damn, Rubiana. I would hate to be on your bad side. You wouldn't stop hitting the bag."

"If Ky is showing her how to land a punch, I wouldn't get in her way. That was insane. You wouldn't stop," Abby chimes in with a grin.

"I'm sorry," I say out of breath. "I got carried away and it felt good."

Ky chuckles near my ear and I feel it vibrate over my skin with his chin still resting on my shoulder. "You did great, and you are a fast learner. I will show you some more next time," he says, pulling away, but not without his nose rubbing on the fabric of my hoodie like he was inhaling my scent.

I'm hot, and the skin underneath my hoodie and shirt has a sheen of sweat, but I shiver from feeling him so close, and from the fact that he said he would show me more in the future. And I liked it.

After Tyler, Chris, and Ky are ready to leave from the locker room, I'm back in Tyler's truck.

"I still can't believe you three are into kickboxing."

"Yeah. Ky got us into it. He is really good. He could actually go pro if he wanted."

I believe him because I saw him firsthand. I really loved the way he taught those kids. He is a great teacher. Caring. Patient.

"So how come he treats people at school differently?"

Tyler sighs. "He learned kickboxing when he went to Thailand with his father on business when he was like twelve. He learned and loved it so much, his dad convinced his instructor to come to the states and open the gym with him. Basically, the gym belongs to Ky now that he is eighteen. He will also own part of the company when his father steps down from the architecture firm. Dad, Ky's dad, and Chris's dad own the architecture firm together. Ky will learn the business side of things hands on. I'm not sure if he is deciding to go to college. He doesn't talk about it. Ky is...complicated but Chris and I will go to college to study architecture."

"Is that what you want?"

I ask because I'm not sure if he likes drawing buildings, but then again, I don't know Tyler that well.

"Yeah, I want to work alongside my best friends. I trust them and they trust me. Ky has had it rough out of the three of us." He clears his throat. "I'm not saying you haven't. I'm not comparing––" he trails off.

I slide my hands inside the pocket of my hoodie and look out the window to watch the shadows cast by the sun. The leaves are beginning to fall off the trees as they prepare for fall since it is already October.

"It's cool, Tyler. It's not your fault I was dealt a shitty hand at life. I'm used to it."

He glances at me briefly as he stops at a red light. "Used to what?"

I look out the tinted glass of the passenger-side window of his nice truck. "I'm used to not having anything. If I do have something, it is always taken away somehow. After a while, you figure out that maybe it was never meant to be, and you just have to accept it."

"Accept what? I don't think I understand."

I dig my nails inside the palm of my hand in the pocket of my faded black hoodie and tell him the truth of what I know. What I am to everyone. What I mean to everyone.

"That you mean nothing."

The sound of his phone ringing interrupts the silence, and he answers as the light turns green.

"Yeah. When? Right now?" He glances at me when he makes a right turn down a side street that I notice is Ky's street, where his house is.

"I'm down the street. I'll drop Rubi off and then head over. Are you sure? I'll be right there, "he says and then hangs up. "That was Ky. He is having a little get together at his house."

"Wouldn't you want to drop me off first?"

The last time I came to visit him at the back of his house didn't end so well. I don't think he would appreciate me showing up again. I don't think I have the energy to deal with him if he reverts to being an ass again.

"It's cool. He said he didn't mind on the phone just now."

My spider senses are on high alert. That doesn't sound like Ky.

Chapter Twenty-Two

Rubi

I FOLLOW TYLER nervously through the front door. My eyes take in the wood color floors, cream walls, and dark and white-colored accents. The house is a work of art. Simplistic, cold, and reminds me of something sterile. Lifeless. It is modern luxury, and the house looks like the ones I have seen on TV. The type of homes that realtors put on the market that is ready to move in, but lacks any warmth. I wonder what his mother and father are like.

Are they caring? Do they love him? I'm sure they do if they give him a life where everything is at his disposal. He has traveled extensively and drives the car that looks like the one he always wanted.

First thing I notice is that there are no pictures of anyone. The staircase handrails are metal and glass and looks like a house you would see in a movie. I thought I would feel warm when I finally got to see the way he lived growing up, but all I feel is cold. All I see is emptiness.

I guess we both share something similar, emptiness. We know how it feels because this place screams it. Depressing and alone.

"You made it," I hear Ky's voice coming through the open patio.

"Yeah, what's up. What are going to get into?" Tyler asks.

Ky's gaze lands on mine. "We need to make a run later."

A run. A run for what? To me, a run means picking up drugs. It is what my stepfather used to say when he was running low on meth or heroin.

A cold, sinking feeling has me looking at Ky and trying to see if he is on anything, but I don't see it. I would be able to tell.

"Rubiana."

A hand passes an inch in front of my face trying to get my attention. I blink and look up.

"We were calling you and you were spacing out again," Tyler says, and his hand falls to his side.

Ky places his hands together and points in my direction with his index fingers. "I'm letting you stay and hang out with us because of Tyler. This is your only warning. Don't steal my shit or anything in this house, or you will be arrested. Got it?"

"What the fuck, Ky!"

Ky ignores Tyler's outburst. His eyes never leaving mine. He wants to make his point. My eyes sting, and the pressure begins to build in the top of my nose, but I won't break. I'm nothing I remind myself. I'm nothing but a potential problem.

"Don't worry, there is nothing here to steal. It is too cold and empty in here for my taste," I say sarcastically and walk outside to the patio.

I don't want to be in this house. Funny how I longed to be allowed inside of this house for so long. I imagined it would look like a palace. A place where it was clean, smelled good, and his mom would bake cookies.

Parents who would eat dinner at the dining table and talk about their day, or discuss where we would like to go on vacation like Tyler, Caroline, and Stephen do almost every night. I imagined when a guest is in their home like Tyler's friends, they would make them feel welcome. In the beginning I didn't feel warmth when I sat at their table because I have to look at a man and remind myself that he never wanted me. I always thought Ky had it better.

I'm sitting in a chair away from the group of people he calls friends. Tyler is sitting next to a group of girls from the cheerleading team. The only ones missing are Jen and Nicole. Abby is watching Tyler and her brother with the girls, and is trying not to glance at Tyler.

Ky is sitting sandwiched by two brunettes who are eyeing him like a prime steak, smiling at something condescending he must be saying because Ky doesn't smile when he talks to them. He looks disinterested in anything they have to say, but he keeps his arms around them. He keeps them close and probably decides which one he will fuck—if not both of them—before the night is over.

He doesn't stare at me like he did at the gym. It is like I'm not even here, but that is okay. My body is here sitting in a chair at his house, but my mind is counting the days until graduation. The days until I can leave everything and everyone behind. All the memories will look like the pile in Ky's backyard. Burned to ashes, forgotten like a pile of dirt. It is funny how he is worried about me stealing from him. Maybe that is why he never invited me inside all those years ago. I looked like a homeless kid from the street.

"Oh my God, Abby I would love to say you nailed that routine at the game, but I don't know...there was something off." One of the girls says to Abby, giving her a smile that screams fake bitch.

They are putting her shit out there so they can get Tyler's attention to point out that Abby sucks because she is prettier and has a way better personality than these skanks.

"What do you think, Tyler? "the blonde one next to her asks.

He grimaces, and Abby's face falls with a frown. My eyes land on the blonde talking shit.

Chris gets up and turns on the music, probably trying to help his sister out with the topic of conversation. I really hate those girls. Chris glances over at me, and something passes over his face. I think he feels bad that I'm sitting outside.

It's okay, Chris. I am the outsider.

He holds out his phone in my direction. "You want to pick something to dance to, Rubiana?"

"I don't think she can dance or knows how, Chris," one of the brunettes sitting next to Ky adds.

I roll my eyes and take his phone. I open to see a music app that basically has everything if you just enter the name of the song or artist. My eyes lift to Chris because I wish I had this.

"Play anything you want. Let's see what you got," he says playfully.

"You think you can keep up?" I ask in challenge.

He shrugs his shoulders. "I'm no expert, but I can definitely keep up."

"I doubt if she knows how, Chris. You can sit down, Rubiana. Don't embarrass yourself," Ky says sarcastically from his seat.

He is challenging me, and at the same time giving me the coward's way out and sitting back down.

"Let's see what you got, Chris. I'll go easy on you."

He chuckles, but he blushes. He is nervous.

"Do you know how to dance reggaeton?"

"No, but I can keep up," he assures me.

Abby smiles when I give her brother a grin and hand him his phone back. All eyes are on us in the center of the patio with the fan's cooling the area from the afternoon heat. It isn't stifling, but dancing while wearing a hoodie is not the best idea, but I can't take it off. It is my security blanket, and I have the tattoo situation I'm trying to hide.

The song I chose, "Tití Me Preguntó" by Bad Bunny, begins to play, and I start to move side to side and grind my body against Chris and have him follow my steps. His mouth drops open like a fish. His eyes go wide when I place his hands on my hips as I begin to move to the fast beat closer to him. I turn and grind my hips and bend my knees so my butt brushes up against him, and when his hands slide lower, I see him fall to the side like a domino.

My mind is trying to catch up with what just happened. Chris is on the floor trying to get up, and is getting in Ky's face.

"Oh, shit!" Abby says with a shriek.

Tyler shoves himself between them. "What's up, brother? What the fuck is wrong with you, Ky?"

I step back as Chris gets up, adjusting his clothes. "What the fuck is wrong with you, Ky? Have you lost your fucking mind?"

My eyes flick to Ky, and his expression is angry, like he wants to commit murder. He is trying to push Tyler out of the way, but Tyler is all up in his face. Ky's nose flares. His hands are in tight fists. "What the fuck are you doing, Chris? Is that how you want your boys to treat Abby? What are you teaching your sister, huh? Rubiana may be the type, but she isn't."

"I think your outta line, Ky? Watch how you talk about, Rubiana," Tyler growls.

I'm grateful Tyler is sticking up for me. He doesn't have to defend my honor. Of course, that is the reason he pushed Chris to the floor. I'm trash in Ky's eyes.

The other girls are silent. My eyes find Abby and she gives me an apologetic expression.

"Fuck you, Ky." His head whips in my direction and the smile that breaks across his lips is wicked and full of anger.

"You're a hypocrite. Sitting their treating every chick like a piece of meat. What are you trying to show, Abby? That it's perfectly okay to be talked to like that?"

One of the brunette's who was sitting next to Ky snorts "You're just jealous. He wants us, not a dirty, homeless piece of shit like you. It's no wonder you know how to dance like that. It's how whores dance."

I snort. "Why, because I can move better than that lame ass routine you all pull. Two-stepping with no rhythm. A five-year-old can come up with a better routine than that shit you call dancing, or whatever you all do. Your whole cheer squad is wack as fuck. You all should be banned. I had to practically bleach my eyes. Abby did the best she could with that shit you sprung on her. The routine came from the source. A bunch of plastic, overprivileged loser skanks with no rhythm."

The brunette's face turns into a frown and I snicker.

"They only say it's good and go along with it because you're all a bunch of thirsty bitches who would do anything for attention."

"Get out!" Ky roars.

I shake my head. "Gladly."

I turn to leave, and Tyler stops me. "I'll take you, Rubiana."

"I'll walk back. Stay with your friends."

"Tyler, we need to head out. The run," Chris says, checking his phone and looking between Tyler and Ky.

"Fuck, I almost forgot." Tyler runs his hand through his hair. "Alright, let's go." Tyler's eyes find mine. "Get in my truck, Rubiana. I can't let you walk. I'll take you afterwards."

Chapter Twenty-Three

Rubi

THE CHEERLEADING BITCHES head home, and we are heading to West Park. Ky is in the passenger side, and Abby, Chris, and I are in the back. I'm sitting right behind Ky and notice that the houses begin to look like abandon shacks the farther we go. We are heading to the warehouse district. It is where drug deals go down, but I'm confused. Why would Tyler, Chris, and Ky be involved in anything like this. Then it hits me.

This is how they keep the gangs and drugs out of Westlake prep. They are controlling it, but then that means they know Cesar, if not someone under him. They don't know how dangerous Cesar is. He doesn't fuck around and has nothing to lose. Fuck. I lean forward and glance at Abby and she looks nervous.

I lean forward. "Hey, I thought you were dropping us off?"

"Tyler said afterwards," Ky quips.

Shit. The guys seem calm like they do this all the time. I bet that they do, and I now know why they are so respected in school. They are the bad boys of West Lake who control the gangs from coming into Westlake prep.

Tyler stops in the middle of the road. There are abandoned warehouses to the left and right. It is dark already, and the light from the truck shines bright into the three black cars blocking the street. Tyler gets out first, and I'm about to tell him to stop, but he is out before my voice escapes my lips.

I stare at the exchange, and I notice Tyler gesture with his hands after he hands him money from his pocket and I recognize the person he hands it to, Cesar, but he walks back to his car and Tyler tells him something. I'm about to text Cesar, but then the driver's side door opens, and Tyler is furious.

"What happened? Where is it?"

Tyler shakes his head. "It's not Henry this time. It's the other asshole, and he says he is taking our money and not giving us shit."

"What the fuck! Has he lost his fucking mind. Does he know who he is messing with?" Ky says through clenched teeth.

"Who the fuck is this asshole?" Chris chimes in, leaning forward in the middle seat.

"We can take them. Fuck these assholes. We had an agreement after we fucked their little crew up last time when they wanted to come to our school and funnel their shit through there. They don't run West Park. Yo–" he trails off when Ky gives him a glare.

"Fuck, dude, that means no weed," Chris says with disappointment. "I need that shit to calm the fuck down."

Not wanting to hear anymore, I open the door to the truck and jump down.

"Rubiana!" Tyler shouts at me, but I slam the door shut.

"Rubi, get in the fucking truck!" Ky shouts behind me. "It's dangerous."

I turn around and I place my hands up so they can all see that it's okay. "I got it," I shout back.

I walk up to the guys who are making no attempt to hide the fact that they are strapped with handguns.

"Hey, little princess. I think you should listen to your boyfriend," the one with the blue shirt and the cross tattoo under his eye says.

"She fine, though," the other to his right says and wipes his mouth as he leans back on the car.

"Si, esta bonita," the one standing in front of Cesar's car.

"I'm not here to talk to any of you. I came to talk to him." I point as Cesar spots me through the windshield of the Challenger he is sitting in.

His face breaks into a friendly smile as he gets out of the driver's side.

"*Mi nena preciosa*," Cesar says, greeting me.

My eyes look at his handsome face with his faded haircut and tattoos all over his arms and neck.

"Hey, handsome."

"I see you can't let the hoodies go. Remember what I said, you're beautiful inside and out. That your half-brother who just came to see me?"

"How did you know that?" I ask.

I'm not surprised. Cesar knows everything, but he doesn't answer me. So I ask another question. "What is it that they are trying to buy? Why did you take their money?"

He smiles and comes up to me, pushing my hoodie off my head in front of the lights of his car. I can see his face clearly, and he can see mine now as his eyes look over the features of my face.

"I don't want that stuff around you. It's weed, Molly's, and Addy's. It is the crap your half-brother's friends pay premium for, apparently. They all do it. Except your half-brother and the guy sitting next to him in his truck. That *cabrón* has a little temper, but he isn't a drug user. Dabbles in a little weed and drinks, but that's about it."

"He can fight, though," the guy to his right says.

"Yeah, that fool is no joke. He can fuck a guy up. He's a little crazy upstairs in the head, if you know what I mean. I saw it with my own eyes," the one with the blue shirt adds.

Cesar smiles and places a kiss on my forehead. "I miss you, princess. Are you staying out of trouble?"

I nod. "I'm trying. People don't like me there. I'm scum from the foster system trying to rain on their parade."

He smiles and sucks his teeth. "They are just jealous you don't need fancy clothes and a fancy upbringing to be beautiful."

I smile shyly. "You were always a smooth talker, Cesar."

"What can I say, it's what you love about me the most."

I look down at my sneakers. "Will you at least give them their money back?" I look up at his handsome face as he caresses my cheek. "I don't take drugs. You know why, but it looks like they have some sort of agreement."

The light in his eyes leaves and he pinches in eyebrows in confusion. "They told you that."

"Not exactly."

He looks up at Tyler's truck for a second like he is thinking. Deciding. His gaze lands on mine and he grins. "The one sitting in the passenger seat is looking at me like he wants to kill me. The fighter. Is he your boyfriend?"

I giggle. "I don't have a boyfriend. No one would want to sleep next to a monster."

His jaw clenches and he glares at Tyler's truck. "He said something to you, princess?"

I shake my head telling him no. I would never tell him what they do to me at school. The way they make fun of me or call me names. The stupid pranks they pull because if he knew and got involved, they would take him to jail after he was done with them.

"No, you know I wouldn't put myself out there like that. I would never let them see. I'm not wanted, remember?"

He rubs his lips together and caresses my cheek with the backs of his fingers and grins. "I love that you protect me, *nena*." He gives me a tight hug and I place my forehead against his chest, breathing in his cologne. "You're gorgeous. Everything about you is phenomenal, and I would kill anyone who hurts you, my angel. If I were a different man, I would never let you go. I want a better life for you, and you need to be where you are right now. It's safer than out here and I can't offer you what you deserve, Rubi. I wish I could."

"But you make me feel safe," I say on a sob.

He pulls away and lifts my chin with his finger so I can meet his eyes. "I wouldn't be able to keep you safe and give you all the beautiful things you deserve. You should never settle for less, Rubi. If someone doesn't show you that you are worth everything and can give you everything that you want, then they aren't good enough for you. I can't give up what I do for you, Rubi. I can't."

He reaches behind me, and it's a bag with I'm guessing are the drugs they came to get. He holds it in front of me so I can take it. "Tell them no meth, cocaine, or heroin. I won't put that shit around you out of respect."

I nod. "Okay."

He places a soft kiss near my mouth. "I think you should go back before he jumps out of the fancy truck like Jet Li and wants to kick my ass." He says the last part on a chuckle.

"I'll call you."

"I'll always answer you, *nena*. Vaya con Dios."

He always tells me to go with God. I miss him.

When I reach the truck, Chris opens the back passenger door and I step up and lift myself to get inside. Once I'm seated and the door is closed, all their eyes are on me. I toss the package on the center console. "He says no meth, cocaine, or heroin."

"How do you know him? He is the leader of the most dangerous gang in West Park. He's a drug dealer, Rubiana," Tyler says sternly.

"Is he your boyfriend?" Ky asks.

"I know him from the foster system."

"I bet you know him a little more than that," Ky snaps.

I shake my head. "No. He just looked out for me. Not all the kids in the foster system are nice."

"I wonder what you did to get the most dangerous one to look out for you," Ky mocks.

What is his problem? I got him the shit they wanted. He wasn't going to give it to them if it weren't for me.

"We got the shit and I have to thank you, Rubi. I need the weed. It is how I cope with school, football, and the pressure of graduating," Chris says.

Gee, you have it so bad. I want to tell Chris that he doesn't know what it is to live with pressure, but I don't. It's not worth it.

"Poor guy, it must be awful being you," I say sarcastically.

Chapter Twenty-Four

Rubi

I CLOSE MY locker with a slam. Whore written across it vertically, and I want to punch whoever did it in their face. Really? I'm a whore now.

I have been hearing whispers about me being at the party, and that I was seen entering one of the bedrooms. I can't lie and say I didn't go in because I did. What gets me on edge is that no one is talking about Jen and Nicole or even Ky. I guess anything that I can be linked to would be taken out of proportion and would make me out to be this nasty person with all the labels. Street rat, scum, trash, dirty, I stink, freak, and now whore. They are all toddlers, I swear.

I'm walking toward the cafeteria when I'm pushed into a dark alcove, and then I'm shoved inside a room and the door slams shut. I open my mouth to scream when a hand clamps over my mouth and pushed up against a wall. My eyes are trying to adjust in the dark, and when I can refocus, my eyes land on hard black eyes.

"Did you fuck him?"

What? Who is he talking about? Then it dawns on me. Cesar. He is asking if I fucked Cesar. Should I lie or should I tell him the truth?

I manage to push my face away from his hand and take a deep breath. "What the fuck is wrong with you, Ky, huh? Why do you care?"

"Did you?" he asks through clenched teeth. "Did you fuck him?" he asks again.

I push against his hard chest, but it feels like I'm pushing against a concrete wall. He won't move. He won't budge.

"I'll tell you if you tell me who wrote whore on my locker and is spreading rumors about me at the party." Nothing. I'm met with silence.

His arms are caging me in the small room that looks like a storage closet. It is too dark, so I can't see anything besides the tiny stream of light coming from under the door highlighting his face. When someone goes silent it's because they know, or they had something to do with what I'm asking.

His fingers tip my chin up so I can focus on him. "I told them to do it. It was me."

"Why?"

"You asked who was behind it and I told you, so now it is my turn."

I want to kick and punch him. I want to hurt him for hurting me. For treating me like I'm nothing. I'll tell him and I know why he is mad. He thinks I chose Cesar after I left and never came back to him but he doesn't understand.

"Yes," I whisper. I watch as his fists curl against the wall by my head and I close my eyes.

"Why? Why him?" He chokes on the last part like he is in agony.

My eyes begin to well with tears. "Because he was there for me when they tried to rape me." I close my eyes and tears run hot down my cheeks. His breathing begins to pick up like he is struggling for air, but he doesn't speak. "I was sixteen, and that is the age of consent in the state of Georgia. One of the teenagers kept coming on to me trying to convince me to have sex. I was staying with a couple who liked to take in kids so they could collect a check. There were six of us and I was the only female at the time. Cesar had just gotten back from a stint in juvie, and he was supposed to come back that night. No one messed with him because of who he was. I was coming out of the bathroom and he was waiting for me like a predator. He pinned me hard against the wall and said he was going to take it because no one cared enough about me anyway. He shoved his fingers so hard into me that I felt the trickle of blood. I tried to scream and scratch him, but he was bigger and stronger than me. He was about to shove his dick inside me when Cesar saw him and dragged him outside through the door. I was on the floor in pain. Cesar came back and cleaned me up. He waited and he talked to me about what happened, and then one night, he took me to another room and he made me forget. He took it away because I wouldn't eat and I would stay up at night afraid."

"What did he take away, Rubi? He fucked you. You gave him what wasn't his in the first place."

I sobbed and lowered my head. "He made me forget. He made me feel beautiful and he never stopped telling me that I was anything less than beautiful. No one had ever whispered to me and told me that I was pretty, or that I meant something to someone." I grip him by the shirt with my hands, not caring that I had tears coming out of my eyes as I pulled him close so he could hear me. "He also never told anyone to call me a whore." I push him back and run out of the closet.

Chapter Twenty-Five

Rubi

AFTER THE WEEK of hell and avoiding Ky at all costs, ashamed that I revealed something so personal, I never told anyone that story...and now I told Ky. I was angry, hurt, and I'm just tired of him.

Plus, I keep waking up in the bed. Bags of cat food and kitty litter also keep popping up in my room. One day I noticed a new litter box. It is a self-cleaning one. I refuse to ask Caroline because I don't want to see the look of pity she gives me all the time. I can only take so much. It is bad enough I get it from Stephen.

But today is Saturday and it's finally my birthday. Tyler says they are doing something for me at Ky's house because he has a heated pool, and his father is away somewhere, but I notice they said father and not parents. Weird.

I brush my teeth and make my way to Tyler's room and knock. When he opens the door, he is in his boxers, and I think he has someone in there. But he is blocking the door and it really isn't my business.

"Rubiana," he says, pulling the door closed behind him. Whoever it is, he doesn't want me to know. I get it...privacy.

"I'm sorry to interrupt, but I wanted to ask if you think having a party is really a good idea. Especially at Ky's house. You know he isn't too fond of me. He practically kicked me out of his house last weekend. And I don't want any more drama."

His expression turns serious, and he crosses his arms over his chest. "Did Ky say or do anything to you. He is supposed to back off and stop bothering you."

"No. Nothing like that. I'm just not used to a party, or think it is necessary," I lie about the first part.

What I want to say is: *He cornered me in the bathroom during your game, had people call me names and graffiti my locker. Spread rumors that I'm a whore and finger fucked me on a couch in front of two cheerleaders eating each other out. He has been a total gentleman, and the little fact that he hates me all because I left him a goodbye letter and didn't contact him because I had been stuck in foster care since I was eleven years old was just the icing on the proverbial birthday cake.*

He looks relieved and gives me a grin. "We want to throw you a birthday party. Mom had a cake made to cut at the house after. We will have a little party with Abby, Chris, Ky, and some kids from school. It will be cool, I promise. We can leave early if you want."

I don't want to seem ungrateful, so I cave. "Alright, I will give it a try. I don't want to disappoint Caroline. She has been really nice to me, and I haven't thanked her for getting Hope food and kitty litter," I say as I walk backward toward my room to get ready and he looks confused, but I don't want to keep him from whoever he has in his room. I run my mouth off topic not really knowing what to say. "The new litter box is super cool, and it cleans itself."

I don't want Tyler to think I'm ungrateful even though it bothers me that Caroline tries to be nice out of pity.

He smiles and shakes his head, turning the handle and letting himself in his room. "I'll see you in an hour downstairs."

I close the door and open my closet to grab a pair of old ripped jean shorts and a hoodie to get ready. I don't have that many options, but it is not like I'm getting in the pool, so I figure I'll just wear a bra under the sweater, so I don't melt from the heat. Caroline tried to convince me to get a swimsuit, but I declined and told her the truth. I don't know how to swim. I never got the chance to learn. They don't take foster kids swimming, and none of the houses I was sent to had a swimming pool, or access to one.

I get to Ky's house and follow Tyler through the front door and out to the back patio. There is grunge rock playing, and I can hear people laughing and jumping in the pool.

I follow Tyler as he walks out and spots Ky and says, "Hey, Ky, what's up?"

I look around and see people sitting around the patio, and when I think everything is going to be cool, Jen and Nicole are here with the same brunettes who were chatting up Ky last weekend.

Ky walks up to Tyler and gives him a bro hug, or whatever guys do to greet each other. I can hear Tyler mutter something to Ky, but he just shrugs his shoulders.

"I told Amber from the cheer team she could come when she called me earlier and asked what I was up to. Jen and Nicole obviously invited themselves."

"Come on, Ky," Tyler says giving him a look like he disagrees with whoever Amber is on the cheer team.

I don't know what Tyler said to Ky, but I'm guessing Tyler isn't happy about Jen and Nicole showing up, which I can appreciate. My thoughts go to the conversation Tyler and I had in front of his room. I don't have to stay long, and we could just leave.

"Happy birthday, Rubi!" Abby comes running up to me, giving me a hug, and I give her an awkward smile. I don't know how to act at a birthday party for myself. This is all new to me.

"It's official. You're legal," Ky says with a smirk. "Happy birthday, Rubi. It's not much, and I hope you don't mind, but some people invited themselves. I don't know what you usually do on your birthday, or what you like to do, so whatever you want to eat or do, we can figure it out."

I don't know if he is being genuine, or he has something up his sleeve. He hasn't bothered me since the day I told him about Cesar in the closet at school. I don't know what to do or say, but all I can do is tell him thank you, I guess.

"Thank you," I say, looking around at people drinking and laughing. My gaze lands on his and I wave my hand toward the patio. "I'm okay. You didn't have to do all this, but thank you."

"Hey, Rubi. Want to go for a swim? Do you have your swimsuit on under your clothes?" Abby asks me as she walks in my direction.

I bite my lip and give her a weak smile. "I'm good, Abby. I'm not really much of a swimmer."

"Okay, but if you change your mind, I'll join you, alright."

I want to share with her that I can't swim. I'll probably drown in front of all these people, and they will be celebrating my demise instead of my birth. I know she is trying to help by including me, but I can't tell her that.

"Oh, I bought you something." She walks quickly to a table and holds out a gift bag hanging from her fingers. I take it and peer inside. "It's black. I hope you like it. Maybe you'll wear it out sometime, or something like that."

I dig inside the tissue and pull out a beautiful black mini dress. I'm in love with it, but I hold back the frown that wants to break my smile. It exposes a lot of skin on the back part.

"Do you like it? If you don't, it is okay. We can go together and pick another one out."

I swallow the lump that threatens to choke me and say, "It's really nice, Abby. Thank you. You didn't have to do that."

It's not because I can't wear it, or maybe it is, but it's because no one has ever gifted me anything for my birthday.

"I think it would look great on you."

I give her a smile, holding in that lump from creeping out. I bet it would if I never stepped out of my room with it on, or if I could wear my hoodie over it. Maybe I'll wear it when I graduate and move out on my own and meet someone who would take me out on a date.

My eyes flick to Ky, and he is just watching me hold the dress, and I look away, folding and placing it back in the bag. I hope he can't read my thoughts about how I feel about the dress.

"Thanks, Abby. That was really nice of you," Tyler says.

"I wanted Rubi to have something nice," she says, averting her gaze. "Anyway, Noah is here, and I want to say hi. Rubi, you can come along if you want. We can go hang out by the pool."

"Noah?"

"Yeah, Noah. He is on the football team. Second string, but that is because he is a junior like me."

"Actually, it's because he sucks," Tyler points out.

"Doesn't mean he isn't cute."

Tyler's head snaps in her direction and he snorts "Noah, cute. Pssh...he is average, at best."

"He isn't a bad guy, Tyler," Ky says. "We can still kick his ass if you want so he doesn't get any ideas with Abby, but that would make you look like--"

Tyler interrupts Ky and says, "Like a guy looking out for his boy's sister."

"Yeah, whatever," Ky snaps and walks away.

"Don't pay attention to Ky. He gets in these moods and gets angry and has to let it out at the boxing gym."

"Why?"

Abbi looks worriedly at Tyler and then at me. Something is missing. What am I missing?

"Go ahead Abby, tell her."

"One day after Ky's mom left, Ky snapped. He became mentally unstable. Withdrawn. Angry."

I look over at him and he looks annoyed.

Abby clears her throat and continues and tells me more of the story about Ky and his mom. "When he was fourteen, she contacted him so she could meet up with him. He was nervous that he was finally going to see his mom again. He hadn't seen her in three years. No visits. No phone calls. Nothing. It was always Ky and his father. His father is cold and distant. He has had multiple women come and go. The most they do is stay the night. Nothing serious. Anyway, all we know is that the day he was supposed to meet her at a café in town, she didn't make it. She was killed in a car accident, and the worst part of it was that she was pregnant by a man she had married. Ky was always cold and distant when we met him, but when his mother died, he didn't cry or show any emotion. I think he stopped caring. He doesn't have girlfriends or girls stay over at his house. He was just ...angry all the time. His father took him to a psychiatrist, and all we know is that Ky has...issues."

"That sucks. I know how it feels to have a mother who doesn't care."

Tyler stares at his shoes, and Abbi's expression softens as they hear me talk about the woman who had me and wasn't supposed to. The one who hated my existence.

"Where is she now, if you don't mind me asking?" Abby asks and Tyler clears his throat.

"She's dead. She died of a meth overdose around the same time my stepfather landed in jail for child abuse."

"I'm so sorry, Rubi. It was messed up to ask. I'm really sorry."

"It's cool, Abby. She wasn't a good person. Let's go say hi to Noah," I say, changing the subject because I didn't want this conversation to be this heavy on my birthday.

Tyler lifts his head as Abby walks away. "If you like her do something about it or someone else will...someone like Noah," I tell him.

I'm walking out on the patio toward the pool when I see Ky standing to the side with Jen and Nicole, and they are playing around with the hose. Amber gives them a once over and waves at me sarcastically. Ky looks up and says something to her that I can't hear.

"Hey, birthday girl, how about a swim?" someone shouts from behind me, and a gush of water in a powerful stream hits my back, and they keep walking forward, not allowing me to get out of the way. I can't see, and I'm sputtering water from my mouth, trying to breathe, but I stumble backward and fall in the pool. Water surrounds me and I'm panicking. I thrash my arms until they burn and know that I have to remove my hoodie or I'll drown. I manage to get the hoodie off, somehow, but I'm sinking.

Strong arms grab me and pull me out of the water until I'm lying in the fetal position on the edge of the pool. I'm coughing and gasping for air, and then I hear it. The gasps and voices of these strangers.

My braids are plastered to my cheeks.

"Holy shit!"

"Oh my God!"

"Are those scars all over her back?"

"Dude, it looks like she was tortured. Look at all the scars on her back."

"Damn, that's horrible. Who would do that to someone?"

Tears begin to pool in my eyes as I try to cover myself, thankful that I'm wearing a bra that covers my nipples, but my back is exposed, and everyone can see what I've tried to hide this whole time.

I can hear Tyler shouting. He is livid, and all I want to do is go home and cry in my closet because I know that the rest of the year at Westlake is going to be even worse than it already has been. I just want to go home. I want to go to sleep and forget about this day, about my birthday, because now I'm the freak they say I am.

Chapter Twenty-Six

Ky

I TAKE MY shirt off and hand it to Chris so he can cover Rubi. My eyes are trying to focus from the blind rage I feel from what just happened. I couldn't jump in before Tyler because I snatched the hose away from Jen and Nicole, and was busy kicking them out of the house and telling them to never come back.

I hate her for leaving me, but I would never do something like that on her birthday, or any day for that matter. I promised Tyler I would be nice. I want to go to her, but I can't. Tyler is in her face, and I can't tear my eyes away from counting the marks on her back. There are so many. Raised scars in red and white colors that mar her beautiful skin.

It's obvious why she wears the hoodies and never takes them off. It is why she looked at the dress Abby gave her with a sad expression because she knew she wouldn't be able to wear it.

"What the fuck, Ky! Why? Why did you invite them? What have you done? I want to kill you! She could have drowned. She obviously doesn't know how to swim, you asshole. I hope this wasn't one of your pranks. I told you to leave her alone," he says through clenched teeth.

Pain radiates on the side of my jaw, and I think Tyler just punched me, but I'm numb.

Chris appears out of nowhere, and I look at where Rubi is, and Abbi is making sure she is covered. Each of them are watching out for her.

"Tyler, chill. He's bleeding. You split his lip wide open," Chris says.

"Good, I hope the bitch tries to hit me back so I can drop his ass." My eyes dart to Rubi again, but tears are falling down her cheeks and it breaks me. It breaks me because he is right. If it weren't for me, they wouldn't be here. Those bitches would have tried to hurt her, and even though Tyler got to her in time, they managed to hurt her in an even worse way.

"Don't you dare look at her, you piece of shit," Tyler spits in my face. "You ruined her day, and since you're so curious about it, I'll tell you. Maybe you will understand what torture and abuse is. When someone doesn't love you and treats you like you are less than a dog. You want to know, huh. Do you? Answer me!" Tyler pushes me and I stumble back. I can't fight back. Not for this. Not when she is crying and broken. I promised to break her, but not like this, not after witnessing her pain.

"I read her file. I wasn't supposed to, but I did, and you know how she got those scars? She used to sneak off and see this little boy she thought was everything to her. She wouldn't say his name or where she would go. Her piece of shit mother was so high, her stepfather would beat her every time he found out, but she kept taking it and taking it. All for a piece of shit boy who probably wasn't worth the scars she has to wear on her skin forever. The therapist thought the little boy was made up."

I think I'm about to throw up. I touch my face and my cheeks are wet. Tyler grips my hair and slaps my shirt on my chest. "It was a mistake to bring her here, so you stay away from her permanently because the last thing she needs is anything from you. Crying isn't going to change anything. I have to hear her sobs at night, and I'm almost positive tonight will be no different. Now, thanks to you, I will have to hear my sister cry herself to sleep because I was too stupid to trust you on her birthday. She has never had a birthday, and after today, I don't think she will ever want one, you selfish asshole."

The things he is telling me pull out a memory from my mind I had thought were long buried. Something I missed but couldn't figure out. There were signs, but I was just kid. We were both just kids.

"Hey, why are you making that face? Does something hurt?"

"No, I think I hurt myself when I was climbing the fence, it will go away in a few days. I think it's because I don't exercise that much."

"Are you sure, Rubi? I could get you a Band-Aid if you scraped your knee."

She scrunches her nose in that cute little way that I like. "It's okay. I'll be fine."

"I'll try to add wood so I can make it easier for you to climb over." She smiles.

Her smile is beautiful. It reminds me of the sun and the moon because they both give light, and the world needs it just like I need her. I need her light. She is the most beautiful light I have ever seen.

After everyone leaves my house, I sit down on my bed and pull out the book where I kept her last letter and the dried-up daisy, and I open it and read it again and again. I sit on my bed, and I cry. I finally cry for her like I didn't for my mother. I could never cry for my mother, but I cried for Rubi. I cried because I lost her smile. I lost my light. A light I didn't deserve. I was the cause of her pain. She left because she couldn't take it anymore, and I was too stupid to notice. I knew she lived on the poor side of town. I saw her dirty clothes, and she managed to always smell good for some reason. Like she sprayed perfume on herself before coming over. I didn't care if she sprayed it or not. I wanted her anyway I could have her, and little did I know that having her in my life meant that she paid for it.

"I'm sorry," I sob to anyone who can hear me. "I'm so sorry, Rubi."

Chapter Twenty-Seven

Ky

I KNOCK ON the front door because I want to see Rubi. I knock and ring the doorbell a few times. Finally, I hear the lock turn, and when the door opens, Mr. Murray is standing on the threshold.

"What can I do you for you, Ky?"

I know I look like shit, but I need to see her. I need to tell her I'm sorry. I need to hold her. I need to make it right.

"I want to apologize to Rubi for what happened today. I didn't know they would do that. They invited themselves, and I'm sorry."

My apology doesn't mean shit, but I need to see her.

"Ky, I don't know how clear I'm going to make this. I never thought I would be saying this, but I need for you to understand something." He crosses his arms over his chest and straightens to his full height. "You are the last person I want around Rubi. I don't want you near her. To you, Rubi doesn't exist. Tyler told me what happened, and I'm ashamed he trusted you to throw her a little party. Tyler holds himself accountable for not wanting Rubi here in the beginning, but now he understands her. Rubi has been through a lot, and it is my fault, but I will not allow a psychotic punk kid with abandonment issues to fuck up my daughter. Stay the hell away from her." And with that, he turns and slams the door in my face.

It could have been worse. A lot worse. So I guess I will have to go with plan B.

I climb the same way up that I do most of the nights. I grimace when my shoulder brushes against my lip. It is already swelling. I make it over the rain gutter and climb to the window and slide it up a bit. I train my ear to see if she is in her closet, but can't hear anything. Hope jumps up on the windowsill and begins to purr. I can hear the little bell I bought so I know where he is at all times. I don't want him to escape because then Rubi would be devastated.

I slide the bag with the little box I brought with me and place it on the bench in front of the window. Hope jumps down and it allows me to slide inside the room, making minimal noise. The cat tries to sniff the box and I pull it away.

"Not for you, buddy, I bought you the good stuff over there," I whisper.

I got him the canned cat food that has chicken in it because they gave Rubi the food that smells like rotten fish, and the litter box is horrible. Cat shit stinks like ass. I bought her one of those fancy self-cleaning litter boxes. It was a bitch getting that through the window when no one was home and she was sound asleep, though.

Rubi is really a deep sleeper. She doesn't flinch when I carry her to the bed after she stops crying in her sleep. The bastard in me wanted her to pay for leaving me, but now I know why. I know why she didn't come back when I was the cause of all of her pain for the entire year.

I take each step slowly, so I don't make noise, and I pull the closet door open and find her like I always do when I come in to see her. Curled up in a little ball with sobs escaping her body from crying. She is wearing an oversized man's with long sleeves. Imagining another man's t-shirt on her body has me gritting my teeth. Jealousy eats me from the inside when I see that fabric. I want to rip it off her body.

I'm careful picking her up and lying her on the bed. I need to really talk to her about that. Maybe I'll stay the night. When she wakes up, I'll be the first thing she sees, and she will remember when I tell her how sorry I am. I won't stop until she accepts every apology I have to offer. I won't stop until I get her back. I don't think I could ever let Rubi go. Not when I just found her again, and not when she is within my grasp.

I tuck her in and slide in beside her, holding her close to my chest. I take in her scent mixed with pool water and I just breathe her in. I take in the fullness of her lips I like to kiss so much. If she only knew how much I like her taste. She's addicting and she is mine. Rubi will always be mine because she is my flower and I'm her earth. I take out a piece of paper from her desk and write her a note and leave it near her phone so she can wake up and read it just in case I don't get to tell her what I want to say. Sometimes writing how you feel makes what you mean more genuine. I lie back on the bed letting sleep claim me as my eyes close and I fall asleep.

Chapter Twenty-Eight

Rubi

I'M WARM AND I feel safe. Safer than I have ever felt before, and then I remember the pool. Did I die? Am I dreaming? My body feels like it is on a cloud, and when my eyes open, I see the face that has haunted my dreams. The face that I want to see up close in slumber, but somehow is so far out my reach when I'm awake. I look at the window and see the sun is already up. It is still early because I don't hear voices or footsteps coming from the hallway.

I must be dreaming. I take a deep breath, close my eyes, and open them again. His face is still there, and then I look down to where my body is snuggled up against his, and then I realize that this isn't a dream. It's real, and I'm in bed with Ky. I turn and look at my door I know I locked because I checked it three times after I ran into my room.

I didn't even stop to see the cake Caroline got for me because I was so upset. After I removed the wet clothes that were plastered on my skin, I grabbed an old t-shirt and pulled it over my head and then I ran inside the closet with Hope and cried myself to sleep, wishing I could forget that any of it had ever happened. My eyes find my phone on the nightstand with a piece of paper next to it.

I look over at Ky and he is still sound asleep. I reach for the paper to see what it says.

> I'm sorry about yesterday. I didn't know they would do that or that you couldn't swim. I would never hurt you like that, Rubi. I will hold you if you allow it, I will dry your tears and replace all the years of your pain. I will make up for everything I did or said that caused you to cry. I'm sorry, Rubi. Please, let me be with you.
>
> Ps: That dickface Cesar was right. You are beautiful, but what he doesn't know is that you are my flower, Rubi, and I am your earth. We have always belonged together.
>
> Ky

I read the letter over and over. I read it at least six times. I don't know what to do or say. Ky is...Ky. He is moody, and I should be kicking him out and screaming at him, but I can't. I turn around and give him my back, trying to make sense of his written apology. He has done so much to hurt me. But I don't think many people get to hear words of apology from him, especially written on paper.

I can hear his steady breathing behind me, and I stare at the wall feeling numb. I don't want to see anyone at school. I don't want to hear the whispers or the names they will call me. I shouldn't care about any of them, but it reminds me of him. I don't care what they think of me. It is the reminder that it happened. When the memories play in my head like a loop, all I can hear is his voice. I smell the scent of death in the air, and I can feel the dirty matted carpet under my knees.

I tense when I feel warm fingers on my lower back. I can feel Tyler's shirt pull up and over my raised skin. I overheard Tyler screaming at him. He was shouting at Ky, and I think he was just staring at him with silent tears running down his cheeks, listening. He was listening to what I feared. Now it made sense why Tyler was being so nice to me, because he knew almost all my secrets.

When my shirt is past the middle of my back, I can feel his fingers unsnap my bra. It gives way, and I remain still. He wants to see. He wants to see the scars of my pain. The ones that I wear permanently as a reminder of my time with him. The many scars I will wear on my skin for the rest of my life, for him. Everyone thought I made up the story about the boy I would go and visit. The one who meant everything to me.

But I kept the biggest secret of all from him, that I was beaten almost every time I went to spend time with him. To see his smile and for him to look at me with those dark eyes silently telling me that I was his heaven.

Being with him felt right.

It felt like I belonged with him.

It was perfect.

We were perfect, because nothing mattered, and it was just us under the sun sharing things we wanted to know about each other. Not the ugly things, but the things we liked. The things that mattered to us the most. Each other.

It was magic.

We were magic.

When I would fall asleep, I wished to the stars that I could do it all over again. I wished to the moon to give me one more day. Every night I wished for one more day with him.

His fingers slide over the raised skin. He traces each scar with the pads of his fingers and then I hear it. The sound of him crying. I never thought I would ever hear him cry. I didn't think guys cried.

But Ky does.

He cries, and I'm not sure he has ever cried, but right now he is sobbing.

For me.

It doesn't mean I will just forgive him, but I'll let him see it just this once. I'll let him see the scars of my pain. The reminder of my scars that are seared onto my skin and tethered to my inner soul. The proof that I have cried tears of pain that burned down my cheeks all for him.

He wraps his arm around my waist and pulls me to him in a spoon position. He is soft and gentle and places kisses all over my back while he traces his finger over the tattoos of the daisies on my arm. I don't hide it from him. I don't have a Band-Aid to place over it or a marker to cover the two letters written in bold letters over my forearm.

If the scars of my past aren't enough to prove to him how important he was to me, the tattoo that's a permanent part of my skin will.

Two letters that mean more than anything to me, and now he has seen proof of my secret. He has seen each and every one of them.

KY

After a while, I can hear footsteps in the hallway, probably Tyler getting up. It means his time is almost up before someone knocks on my door to see how I'm doing. I turn around on the bed to tell him he needs to leave, but when my eyes find his, they caress my face like a total embrace. Two black diamonds, glassy from sleep, watching me like they're full of moments from a story book read to me at night

"You have to leave," I whisper.

"I'll go for now, but I'll never leave you and I'll never let you leave me."

"It's over, Ky. It's too late." I reach over and take the note he wrote me and hand it to him. He looks down at it with a pained expression with his lip that is still swollen. "You got what you wanted. You broke me. Now all I want is for you to leave me alone." I pause, my eyes welling up with tears as I look him deep in his eyes, because letting him go is the hardest thing I have ever done, but telling him to forget me is even worse. "You need to forget about me. You told me to never see you the other day. Now I ask you to do the same. Don't come back, Ky."

His looks down at the note like it is a fire that he cannot touch, or he will get burned. His eyes travel back up to my face, his expression unreadable. He pushes to get up, and in one motion his hand grips the back of my neck, dragging my face to his. Before I can protest, he presses his lips against mine in a single kiss. His firm lips against mine just like we did when we were eleven. My heart flutters in my chest, and before I close my eyes he pulls back and rasps, "Never." He gets up and I watch as he expertly exits the bedroom window.

Hope jumps on the bed and begins to purr in the same spot Ky was just lying on and rubs his head against my hand so I can pet him. When I get to the collar where his bell jingles, I see it. A little charm with his name engraved, but when I flip it over, it has a letter K and R engraved on the other side. It was Ky. It was him coming in my room this whole time. My head turns to the nightstand, and I see a small box. I sit up and reach for so I can open it. It is a mini gourmet chocolate cake with *Happy Birthday, Rubi* written across it. I smile to myself because this is the first cake I have ever eaten for my birthday and I know why he picked this particular one. I told him I liked chocolate when we were kids. He remembers everything we said to each other...just like I do.

Chapter Twenty-Nine

Ky

I LEFT HER the box of cake with *Happy Birthday, Rubi* written across it on her nightstand. It was a mini cake I found in a gourmet bakery. It was chocolate. She told me one day all those years ago that her favorite flavor was chocolate.

We asked each other what our favorite candy was, and she said anything chocolate. There is nothing I don't remember about her. I remember every curve of her face, and the two little freckles that are on her small nose. I remember her long straight hair when she would let it down and it would blow in the wind. But what I loved the most about her was her smile. Her smile hit me like a punch in the gut when it would break from her lips.

I open my locker and tape the worn letter with the flower on the inside of the door. I wanted to remind myself why I kept it. Because I could never let her go and I never will. I just hope she can forgive me.

"Ky, I need to talk to you."

I turn around and Jen is standing behind me holding her book against her chest. I know she isn't sorry about what she did because she was jealous of Rubi since the night at the party when I told her to make out with Nicole out of spite. I have known Jen and Nicole since middle school. They didn't think I was good looking back then. They thought they were the popular girls and could have any guy. These were the types of girls who would bully other girls who weren't pretty or didn't have a nice body. The type who thought Patrick was cute when he didn't stutter. Patrick used to bully me. He used to push me and trip me when I was in fifth and sixth grade. These were the types of kids Rubi and I hated. The type I use and treat like shit now because tit for tat. I'm the type who doesn't feel sorry for hurting a girl I care about. The one girl I have eyes for. The one who was asleep in my arms the day before yesterday and will make sure to never let her get away again.

"There is nothing I have to say to you. I told you to leave me alone."

"I'm sorry, Ky. Please. I know it was wrong, but you wanted us to mess with her."

"And I told you to stop. A long time ago. What part of that didn't you understand?"

Students in the halls are giving us curious stares. I'm sure they are trying to overhear our conversation. So I'll give them something that will spread like wildfire.

"Get off my dick, Jen! I told you I don't want you anymore. What you did to her at her birthday, you can bet your ass I'm going to make you pay for it. Now I suggest you leave me alone."

Her eyes widen in horror.

I just embarrassed her, and everyone heard it. By this afternoon, everyone will know that I canceled her ass. And this is just the beginning.

I turn around, leaving her slack-jawed in the hallway, and I see a familiar figure in a black hoodie behind a locker. I walk up to Rubi, but she doesn't notice me, or she does and doesn't want to acknowledge me, and that is fine. I'll give her time.

There are a lot of things we need to discuss. Details about her past because I need names and locations. I hope she doesn't think I'm going to let what happened to her go, because that is just not going to happen. Tyler's dad called me psychotic, and maybe I am. Maybe I'm fucked up.

Rubi is broken, and I know I didn't help her cause since she arrived at Westlake, but I plan to change all that. Piece by piece I will put all the broken parts back the way I want them. And she will like it because I did it. I'm the only one who cared and the only one who understands her.

She closes the door of her locker, and our eyes are fixated on each other. I love to stare at her even when I hated her for leaving me. Even when she was not looking, I would stare. I tried not to, but I can't help it. I want to make sure I memorize everything about her and don't want to miss something. And the weird part about it is, I always find something new. Something I missed the last time I saw her. She was my favorite person since I first met her, and she always will be.

The dreams I have had about her throughout the years she was gone make sense. Maybe it was her soul crying out for me to save her. Maybe it was the connection we have that was telling us there was something wrong. Whatever it was, I could see her, but I couldn't see her face in those dreams, and now I can, and I can't help but stare.

"Are you okay?" I ask.

Her eyes glance downward, and her lips are pulled inward, forming a thin line. I know I royally fucked up with her. Her brother and father don't want me around her, but I was never one to listen, and always did whatever the fuck I wanted. Like right now.

"Do you want to get out of here?"

That causes her to lift her head quickly, her eyes are angry, and I think I know why. It doesn't take a genius to figure it out, but the anger I see reflected in her eyes is different.

"I don't want to talk to you. I don't want you around me. I already told you to leave me alone." She leans close and I smile because that is not going happen. "I hate you. And stop coming into my room."

I like how she doesn't back down. I like how she isn't going to make this easy, but I have the rest of the year to convince her. To keep her. Because she isn't going anywhere.

I walk toward her until her back hits the locker, and my nose is rubbing against her cheek, and my lips are close to her ear. I lick her earlobe and I whisper, "Make me."

She pushes against me, and I chuckle. This is going to be fun. She doesn't know how crazy I can get. They fear me in Westlake for a reason. There is a reason Cesar didn't call us out when we did the run. I'm sure he kept that bit to himself. She doesn't know that I'm always two steps ahead. I'm always in control. She holds secrets about her past. She has every right to hate me but she will understand why everyone here fears me.

"Leave me alone, Ky."

"Never, princess. *Nunca. Yo no soy quien tu piensas. Pero ahora los vas a entender, preciosa.*" Her eyes widen.

I will never leave you alone. I'm not who you think I am, but you will understand, beautiful.

My mouth breaks into a smile. We all have secrets, Rubi. We all have our pain. We try to hide it, but sooner or later, it claims us.

She doesn't know that I know Spanish. Just one of the many things she doesn't know about me. I have been patient. I've been waiting.

I hear her intake of breath when she spies someone behind me. I turn and I chuckle.

"Patrick..." she calls out as he is passing by. "What happened?"

He spots me and his eyes go wide. "Hey, Patty. Nice make-up. Next time, find another girl to show your drawings to," I mock, giving him a wink.

Rubi shoves me from behind, but it's like being pushed by a five-year-old. "Did you do that? Did you hit him?"

I turn around and fiddle with the hem of her hoodie, and she tries to step back, but the lockers behind her prevents her escape as I cage her in. My eyes make a slow ascent up her body, and I meet her eyes. "Did you think I would let that slide? You in a car alone with a guy who wants to fuck you. Did you think it was a coincidence when you were dropped off at the party, you ended up in that room with me?" Her lips part and her breathing picks up. She's piecing together my intentions.

I lean in and I rasp against her cheek, "I didn't fuck them after you ran out. I was too busy sucking your cum off my fingers. In case you were wondering, you taste sweet." Her eyes go wide. Her tongue keeps peeking out as she moistens her lips. Lips I want wrapped around my cock. "No te pongas nerviosa, princessa. I wouldn't hurt you, but I will make you scream."

I can hear Tyler shout down the hallway. "Get away from her, Ky."

"Gotta go, princess. I need your little brother to feel like he can protect you. I think he knows he doesn't stand a chance, but I'll see you tonight." I walk away, giving her a knowing smile. "Same time. Same place. Oh, and I left you something in your closet, and don't worry, I fed Hope for you."

Chapter Thirty

Rubi

WHAT THE FUCK was that? Tyler reaches me just as Ky walks away. It was him. The whole time I thought I was crazy. I thought I needed mental help because I was sleepwalking. I know he has been coming into my room but who knows for how long. I'm trying to rack my brain to see when I first noticed things appearing. He must have heard me crying in the closet. He was the one carrying me and placing me in the bed. I want to say it's romantic, but it's more disturbing, actually.

"What did he say to you, Rubi. Did he hurt you?"

I shake my head. "He was apologizing." Not the whole truth, but he did say he was sorry. I don't think he was behind the prank at the party, but he feels responsible because he could have prevented it. "Why would you think he would hurt me?"

Tyler runs his hands over his face and his expression looks torn. "Ky is unstable sometimes. He does things."

"What kind of things?"

I can see Tyler visibly swallow. There is something missing. Something he doesn't want to say.

"I can't tell you that. All I can say is that you need to stay away from him, Rubi. Ky can be dangerous. I regret the day I vented to him about you showing up. I don't know what the fuck is wrong with him, but he has taken it to a whole other level. He has always been cool, but since you...it's like something woke up the psycho."

It doesn't make sense. The letter he left on my nightstand. It doesn't add up completely, but then he was talking to me in Spanish. There is something I'm missing. There is more to Ky than he is letting on. Tyler is making it seem like Ky is fucked up. That he is dangerous to be around. I have seen fucked up, but there are countless levels of crazy when people you love are involved.

I spot Patrick coming out of the bathroom and his eyes widen when he sees me. I grimace at the shiner that is on his left eye. Jesus, Ky.

"I-I need to stay away from you, Rubi. He will kill me if I t-touch you."

"He is not going to kill you. I'm sorry, but I need to ask you how did he know that we went somewhere? How did he find out, Patrick?"

"He knows a lot of things. He isn't who you think he is, Rubi. Stay away from him. He is obsessed with you. He made that perfectly clear when he gave me this," he says pointing at the shiner on his eyes and continues, " he says that you are his and that no one is to touch you."

"What do you mean, Patrick? He hates me."

Patrick shakes his head, and his good eye is trained on my face. "Obsession can be confused with hate. He doesn't hate you. It's more powerful than that. He controls things, and Ky always gets what he wants."

"What do you think he wants, Patrick?"

"He wants...you, Rubi. He wants you and he is never going to stop."

Patrick is talking crazy. He must be scared because Ky is stronger and bigger than he is.

"Patrick, I'm sorry."

"I gotta get to class, Rubi." He walks back in the opposite direction. "Remember what I said, stay away from him."

Easier said than done, in algebra class he sits right behind me, and I can feel him watching me. I can hear him breathing. I couldn't even concentrate on the day's lesson because I'm aware of him.

I open the page of my book and scrunch my nose because of the lingering smell of cheese. I try to get to the right page she instructed, but it's stuck together. I take a frustrating deep breath and sigh.

I jolt when I hear the sound of a book slam close and look up. When I turn my head, Ky is standing right next to me grabbing my textbook and replacing it with his.

Everyone watches as he walks up to the front of the class, and the teacher raises her eyebrows when she sees him come forward with my textbook in his hand.

"Is there a problem Ky?" she asks.

He looks straight ahead and turns toward the trash. He drops the book with a thud into the garbage can. "I'm just taking out the trash."

She lowers her eyes she can see above her reading glasses and notices it was my textbook. "Is that Rubiana's textbook you threw out, Mr. Reeves?" She questions him in a stern voice.

He waves his fingers toward the smart board. "It's not your concern. Do continue. As you can see, I have replaced it for her."

The teacher opens and closes her mouth, but nothing comes out. She turns around and resumes writing on the board.

What has gotten into him? It's not that I don't appreciate him giving me his textbook that doesn't smell like rotting cheese, but why the drastic change? Tyler glances at me from the corner of my eye, and the others in the class are just staring at him behind me, probably just as confused, but no one says anything. No one questions Ky.

It is lunch time and I sit at my normal seat waiting for Patrick. He is the only one I talk to during lunch but when I place my tray on the table and sit down but when I look over the next table and see Patrick is sitting at the table purposely away from me.

"Patrick," I whisper-yell, trying not to attract attention.

He turns around and I gesture with my hands like what the hell is he doing over there. He shakes his head and I sag in my seat feeling defeated. Great. The only person I could talk to at lunch just got beat up by the school bully because of me. I can't blame him, to be honest.

More people begin to come in the cafeteria as they begin to sit down, and they whisper and laugh as they pass by me sitting alone like an outcast, but I don't care. Let them laugh. Let them talk about me. I still wear my hoodies like I'm used to because why stop now. It has become part of me and who I am. I don't need to change because they saw the scars on my back, and the last thing they need to see is the two letters tattooed on my arm like a stupid school girl infatuated with a boy who torments me. I was relieved that no one pointed it out at the pool party. They were so focused on the visible scars on my back.

The table moves when someone sits next to me like they are sitting on a seesaw. I turn my head and I see that it's Conner.

"What the hell do you want, Conner?" I ask, opening the chocolate milk carton.

He gives me a predatory smile that has my hairs on my back rising. "I don't care about the scars, you know. What everyone is trying to find out is how you got them, but to me it doesn't make a difference." He leans closer and lowers his voice. "I do care about what you have in between your legs."

"Fuck off," I snarl. "Get away from me."

"Or what? No one cares about you here. Not even your half-brother. He is just playing nice for his daddy. But I don't care about all that. I know a nice piece of ass when I see one."

I stiffen and my heart breaks. Is that true? Tyler still doesn't want me here? Is it all an act and he's playing me until I leave?

A shadow appears over the table behind me, and I can feel the tension. The presence of his energy without looking back and seeing that it is Ky.

"What the fuck are you doing here, Conner?"

He looks up and smirks. "Having a little chat with the freak."

"Call her that one more time and we will see you looking like one."

Conner's smirks droops into a frown and he pinches his brows in confusion. He is probably just as confused as the rest of us by Ky's sudden demeanor. Ky sits opposite Conner on the other side of me like I'm the center of a sandwich as they face each other.

Ky brushes the tiny hair behind my ear that escapes my braid. "She is pretty, isn't she, Conner?" My insides begin to turn to mush, but there is a hard edge to his voice. I can sense the danger that is emanating from him.

"I-I thought you said she smelled and was ugly," Conner stammers.

Ky laughs through his nose and leans close, his lips inches from my cheek, but he is looking at Conner when he says, "I lied." He angles his head and I feel his eyes trailing down my face. My hands are frozen in place not wanting to move.

"Dude, what the fuck is wrong with you? One minute you–"

"How much do you like football, Conner? Ky interrupts him.

"It's my life, but you already know that."

"Hmm." He sucks his teeth and leans close to whisper in my ear. "Drink your chocolate milk before it gets hot, baby. Eat." He then leans back slightly and his eyes flick to Conner, all calm and collected. "You didn't answer my question, Conner?"

"Yes, she is pretty." Conner replies in a hard tone.

"Since football is your life and it is all you care about. I suggest you get the fuck up and leave Rubiana alone. This is your second warning...there won't be a third," Ky tells him. "You wouldn't want to be forced to find something else to do with your life once you graduate or... you might not get to graduate."

Conner suddenly gets up and he shakes his head. "You have fucking lost your mind, Ky. You need help."

Ky laughs manically. "Yeah, well, at least I don't force myself on girls."

I look up and Conner's eyes narrow, and I think Ky struck a nerve. A nerve that hits close to home. I believe Ky for some reason, but I also know that Ky is acting strange.

"Says the one who fucks the entire cheerleading and dance team. I don't force myself on girls."

"Yeah, keep telling yourself that," Ky deadpans.

"What are you doing, Ky?" Tyler asks as he walks up behind me.

Ky moves to get up from the table, but before he stands, he whispers, "My time is up, preciosa. I'll catch you later." He stands and taps Tyler's shoulder. "I'm just making sure Conner was behaving...we wouldn't want Noah to take his QB spot, now, would we?"

"I told you to leave her alone, Ky," Tyler warns, but Ky walks out of the cafeteria without a backward glance.

He didn't even eat. He didn't sit at the table with the cheerleaders and jocks, and now I'm confused.

"Stay away from him, Rubi."

I look up at Tyler, not trusting his motives now. I'm not sure if his kindness is all an act. "Why? Why are you so worried about Ky?"

"I can't talk to you about it here. Maybe some other time, but trust me. Stay away from him. He likes to play games. The kind where you always lose."

Chapter Thirty-One

Ky

I WALK INSIDE my house after school, hating the fact that Tyler is busting my balls about Rubiana. After the incident at the pool party, he is on a mission to keep me from talking to her. I couldn't stand that Rubiana was forced to smell rotten eggs because of me when she took out her textbook. I was behind most of the pranks and offensive name calling, but that was before. Before I knew the real reason she left me.

Tyler has no idea I was the boy she talked about. The one she would sneak off to see and pay for in abuse when she would get home. I was so blind and stupid. She must think I'm the biggest piece of shit, but I have to change that. Her thinking like that about me just won't do.

My father is sitting alone in the living room nursing a glass of whisky in his hand. When he sees me approach, he places the tumbler on the glass table in the center. "Good, you're home. I have something to discuss with you."

My father waiting for me to get home can only mean one thing, someone has called him to complain about his only son's anger issues. My instability.

"Yes, sir," I answer politely, taking a seat.

I respect my father...he has always been there for me. But I know that the only time he wants to have a talk is when he is covering up for me, or wants me to follow the rules or to cover up for me and tells me how he is going to do it. I can thank my father for the few things he made sure to give me besides money and the ability to fuck girls whenever I want. He made sure when kids in seventh grade began bullying me and I came home with a black eye and a note from the principal about how sorry she was for me getting hurt, he said I needed to stop being a pussy and defend myself.

"Stephen Murray called me about your behavior. He says he wants you to stay away from his daughter. She's troubled."

Annoyance flickers through me, but I shrug my shoulders and lean back in my seat. "And?"

My father smiles and with eyes just like mine that gleam with awareness he is telling me that he knows. He made the connection. He knew I was playing with a little girl in the yard behind the house, but he didn't think she was a threat since I never brought her inside the house. I knew not to because I didn't want my father to stop her from visiting me. My father is not only a businessman with part ownership of an architecture firm. He wants me to take over his architect firm after I graduate and work there for a couple of years. A firm that Tyler and Christian's father all work for. The three of them are partners, and it's also how I met the guys. Eventually the three of us will take over. It was all planned since middle school, all of us following in our fathers' footsteps. My father also has other businesses, mainly drugs he funnels to Georgia from Florida.

It was then that I kind of understood why my mother left him, but there were other reasons. Apparently, I have other issues that were diagnosed when I was kid, and it got worse after Rubi left.

My father leans forward, removing his suit jacket, and when he is done, he says, "There are two types of men in this world, and it depends on what lessons they have learned that defines them. You have learned different types of lessons that makes you who you are. I have allowed you to do as you wish in return for you following my rules. What is it with this girl that you can't seem to leave alone? It has been a long time, and you have plenty of fish to keep yourself busy. Stephen does what he is told, and I don't want him giving me a headache. I know who she is, Ky. I'm not stupid, but your infatuation with this girl cannot interfere with business."

"Who said it was infatuation? What does she have to do with our business?"

I'm confused about what Rubi has to do with what my father wants me involved in that affects him. I run the crew that pushes the drugs through West Park. Cesar is a two-bit drug dealer who does a good job keeping quiet and doing what he is told. They all answer to me, but when Cesar touched Rubi, something in me snapped. I was holding back sitting in the truck. Watching. I was putting the pieces together as to how they knew each other.

There is no way my father knows about Cesar and Rubi. Richard Reeves gives two fucks about the kids who have a fucked-up life and are sent into the foster system. To him, they are potential employees. The problem I have with Cesar is that he touched what wasn't his to touch. The only thing that holds me back from slitting his throat is the fact that Rubi said he saved her from being raped.

"Rubiana Murray is the oldest child of Stephen Murray, and she is heir to his estate and since Caroline is unstable and had a little mishap taking more pills than she should have. She needs to sign a release that relinquishes her rights to his estate if he dies. He left a will that indicates he would leave everything to his oldest child. In this case, she is the oldest. She needs to sign it so she can leave it to her half-brother since that was his intention, but things are complicated now. How would it look if he asked that of her and she refuses. Do you understand?"

So, the plot thickens. "Is that the reason he showed up and took her in? So that she would find out later and didn't sign she would magically disappear? She said she is leaving after graduation?"

I'm not letting her leave to go anywhere, but he doesn't need to know that.

"And?" He volleys back with a grin. "What makes you think she will sign her stake of a billion-dollar empire once she finds out it exists and that she has a right to it. The court found out where Stephen was and would have told her who he was. If she found out, she could go after it. He never spent a dime on her. She is entitled to his financial support."

"But I'm the bad guy. And Tyler?"

"Does what his father tells him like you and Chris do. Well, Chris and Tyler. You're still a wild card, I'm afraid." He picks up his drink and downs the rest, placing the cup down on the table with a clink. "Do we need to call the psychiatrist and have this mishap cleared up?"

I was diagnosed with borderline personality disorder after my mom and Rubi left. They think it was because of my mother that I became angry, but the truth was, it was Rubi. She meant more to me than my mother because we had more of a connection. I had more of a connection. An obsession they called it, but she was gone.

I ignore the psychiatry question and focus on more important matters. The subject of me leaving Rubi alone. That is not going to happen.

"So that is why Stephen took her in?"

My father raises a brow and responds, "Maybe. But I would have done the same, so it doesn't matter. It's done, and after the stunt at the pool, he thinks you were behind it all and he wants you to leave her alone for obvious reasons. He needs to convince her to sign the papers and not make it obvious his true intentions. There are stipulations in the company's agreement Stephen signed when he thought it was just Caroline and Tyler. Rubi's existence is a problem. A loose thread."

I lean back on the loveseat and arch my neck and look up at the ceiling. "He wants her to sign over her stake before he agrees to let her go on her merry way, but he doesn't know one little detail. Something no one knows. Something he never counted on."

"What is that?"

I rest my head on the back cushion and flick my eyes to look at my father, giving him an impenetrable stare. "She's mine."

Chapter Thirty-Two

Rubi

IT HAS BEEN three days since I Ky has been in my room. I try to stay awake at night waiting for him, but I can't stay up that long. I have even left a crack in the closet to see if he comes through the window.

I haven't seen him in school either. It is like he vanished. But every night, instead of waking up in the closet, I wake up in the bed, so he is around. When I turn to reach for my phone to shut off my alarm, there is a daisy on my nightstand, but no note or message. It's just sitting there next to my phone on the charger like a gift. A reminder. The second day I found another one, I even checked my cellphone like a desperate idiot to see if he put his number in, but nothing. The same thing happened this morning with the daisy.

I've looked for him in the halls at school and during math class. During lunch, I ignore the whispers and stares of everyone. I'm past caring what they think of me or what some of them saw at the party. I still find notes in my locker calling me freak, whore, and countless other names. I ignore all of it because what is the point. I can't fight everyone. My focus is on Ky and where he is.

I wonder if something happened to him, and I don't want to ask Tyler because all it will do is raise questions when he has repeatedly told me to stay away from him.

I haven't told anyone that he sneaks in my room, and I don't plan to because I don't want to cause more problems. He annoys me. He excites me. He terrifies me. But most of all, no one knows we have a history, or that we have met before. And I want to keep it that way.

If I tell anyone that he comes through my window, they might think I'm stupid and crazy because there is no proof he has been in my room. If they confront them, he will probably deny it and make it worse for me at the house and at school. I'm still pissed off at him for the rumors and pranks. I'm not going to deny that I'm not, but I also cannot deny that I want to see him.

I am even tempted to jump the fence in Ky's backyard to see if he is home, but then I remember that day I ran into him in his backyard and how well that went. There is no telling what mood Ky is in, or what he is really capable of.

I close my locker when the bell rings and I see Abby walk up to me with a smile. "Hey," she says, walking up to me.

"Hey, what's up?"

She looks at me with excitement in her eyes. "Are you going to the state fair tonight?"

I pinch my brows because I forgot all about it. I never really cared about the fair because I have never been to one.

"No. Why?"

"Oh, I thought Tyler would have invited you to go since he is taking someone."

Her eyes go flat for a second, and she looks down at her shoes. I feel bad for her, but I have to tell her the truth.

"Nope. He never mentioned it. He probably didn't want me to be the third wheel. Why, are you going?"

I hate pointing that out to her, but it is most likely the reason he never mentioned anything, and besides, I don't have money. My thoughts go to Ky, wondering if he is going and if he is, then with who. But I push those thoughts down because he hasn't made an appearance. Abby is clearly disappointed that Tyler is taking someone else and not her, that much is obvious. I get it.

She looks up and she smiles, brushing it off. "Anyway, Chris always takes me, but this year Noah asked me to go with him. Chris has to go along or I can't go, though. I didn't want Chris to tag along. So I wanted to ask if you wanted to come with us. It would be so much fun, and don't worry, it will be our treat."

Good for her. She is taking my advice in not being hung up on Tyler and ignoring him by going with Noah. If I agree to go, it means I'll be accompanying her brother Chris, but I wonder what Tyler and Ky would think about me going along with Chris. I have my suspicion that Chris sent Abby to ask me to go on a double date.

Despite being an adult, I'm still on probation until I finish school, so I have to be back before curfew. However, I can't help but think about Ky's previous reaction when Chris danced with me at his house. Although, he criticized my dancing and said it was a bad influence on Abby, Ky doesn't have any real interest in me, so it shouldn't matter to him. He has sex with other girls and has no reason to get upset. It's not like I belong to him.

I return her smile and accept. "Okay. I'll come along."

She beams. "Yes," she says, emphasizing the S. "I promise. It will be so much fun. We will be around to pick you up at six."

• • •

I check my reflection in the mirror and make sure I look okay. I don't know why, but I apply some lip gloss I had stashed away in my things. I'm not going to lie and say I'm not excited to go, because I am. It is something else I can file away that I have done.

I'm wearing the same jeans Abby gifted me. She told me she didn't need them when she lent them to me the day I went to the football game, and the bonus was that they were brand new. I turn to the side to make sure the red long-sleeve shirt doesn't ride up my back, exposing my scars. It is a bit too small, but was one of the nicest things that were in one the boxes of donated clothes they give to foster kids, but I didn't want to wear a hoodie. Not tonight.

I jolt, placing my hand over my chest when Hope jumps up on the dresser, purring while he gets in a sitting position. He cocks his head to the side wanting a rub and likes to be petted on his neck. I saw Ky doing it the day he snuck in my room. I reach out with my hand and pet him the same way I saw Ky do it before he climbed out my window that Sunday morning.

"I know, buddy. I miss him, too," I say softly.

There is no logical reason for me to want Ky to continue to be in my life after the way he has treated me. I guess the few moments when I looked into his eyes, black as midnight, and he kissed me, it was like we were transported back in time when we were kids. And now that we are older, we are just picking up where we left off. But then his caustic words would douse the fire he created, leaving me cold and confused. Making me want more.

Knock. Knock.

I sigh and turn toward the door when I hear Caroline's voice. "Rubiana, Abby and Chris are here."

Tyler left an hour ago. I didn't tell him that Abby invited me to go with Chris and Noah. He acted like nothing was amiss, and it was just another day going to the school. I walk over and open the door to see Caroline standing in the hallway.

She smiles, her expression going soft when she looks me up and down. "You look very pretty, Rubiana."

I lower my eyes to the floor, not used to someone paying me a compliment. I look up to acknowledge her kind words.

"Thank you," I reply with a small smile.

"I know we said your curfew was eleven, but since you're out with Abby and Chris, we can push it to midnight. It is Friday and all."

I'm annoyed that she is pointing it out right now in front of everyone.

"Okay," I say quietly.

What can I say, even if I'm an adult, they have control as part of my sentence. Pointing it out that I'm an adult will not help my cause to not feel embarrassed. I still don't have a plan after graduation. To be honest, I'm scared. Maybe I can get a job after school, but now is not the time to think about that.

She steps to the side, and I shut the door behind me. When I make it downstairs, I find Abby, Noah, and Chris waiting for me by the foyer.

"Hi." They all greet me at the same time.

I give them a small wave. "Hey. Thanks again for inviting me."

Chris steps forward, his soft brown eyes landing on my face. His dark blonde hair is styled to the side. It looks like he made an effort tonight more than he usually does, and I still get the suspicion that he asked Abby for me to come along.

It is not that I don't find Chris attractive, because he is. He is wearing a gray Henley that he fills out nicely, and dark blue jeans that sit low on his narrow waist. He has a straight nose, and is the exact opposite of Ky. And herein lies the problem, he isn't Ky.

He doesn't make my stomach clench or my heart race when he is near. He doesn't have obsidian eyes that can look deep in mine like he knows what I'm thinking or the secrets I keep in my soul. He doesn't stare at me and doesn't care who is watching. Chris also doesn't have dark straight hair that I want to sink my fingers into, or firm lips that I want pressed everywhere against my skin.

Chris's mouth breaks into a smile and nudges his head toward the front door. "Come on, let's go."

Stephen comes out of the kitchen with a small smile. "Have fun, you guys. And Chris?"

"Yes, sir?"

"Please, have Rubiana back home by midnight."

Chris glances at me and grins. I inwardly cringe, but look away, embarrassed.

"Of course. Yes, sir."

Chapter Thirty-Three

Ky

I WATCH AS Chris, Noah, and Abby walk out of Tyler's house with Rubi. I didn't think Chris had a set of balls on him to actually show up and take Rubi along with him. I was overseeing a shipment from Florida to Georgia for my father and making sure it was distributed properly on the other side of town. My father uses me from time to time so that he doesn't show the world his evil that he covers up with the architecture firm.

I also visited my psychiatrist and have an appointment with my fucking therapist tomorrow. I think my dad telling me to get myself checked out is my father's way of telling me to get a grip on Rubi coming back into my life.

I didn't want to leave, but I still manage to leave a daisy for Rubi so she doesn't think I was lying to her when I promised that I would never leave her. I hate that she sleeps in the closet, but with all the abuse she has gone through, I don't blame her for being afraid. But that is what gets to me, her being afraid. She should never be afraid. Especially when she has me.

I might ask the therapist what he thinks of people who sleep in closets. Maybe I can get a better idea in understanding Rubi without asking her so many questions about her past.

he loves me ~~*NOT*~~

I watch as Chris holds the door for Rubi to get in the front passenger of his Maserati. I watch from a safe distance, allowing me to have a perfect view of watching her pathetic attempt at a smile when he stands there like a moron waiting for her to get in. My cock strains in my pants at the sight of the way the jeans she is wearing hugs her ass. The way the red shirt is molded to her breasts, causing my cock to ache wanting to sink deep inside her while I listen to the way she says my name from her pouty lips.

Before she finally gets in, I see her give a slight nod at something Abby says to her, probably encouraging her to sit in the front with her brother while she slides in the backseat with Noah.

The poor guy does not stand a chance with Abby. I see the way Noah looks at her like he is eating her alive, while her brother isn't around or is too blind to notice. He is my friend, but a fucking idiot at times. He is clueless and doesn't notice that his little sister has a thing for Tyler. And Tyler is too busy battling his guilt because he wants to sink his dick in his best friend's little sister. It is funny they think that I don't k know their secret, but I do. Last year was the one night Tyler slipped and went too far with Abby.

They didn't see me that night they were in the pool at my house, and they thought Chris and I were asleep. It was late and we were hanging out at my house on the patio. It got really late and we decided to crash at my place.

Chris and I had dozed off on the couch, but my eyes snapped open from hearing a splash in the pool. I padded my way to the corner of the patio door and my eyes skirted the pool to where the splashing came from. I spotted them both in the corner of the deep end where a little bench was built.

I saw him push her off him after his tongue was down her throat and her legs were wrapped around his waist, grinding on his cock. I never said anything to anyone or confronted him about it because it wasn't my problem. To be honest, I didn't care, but now that Tyler doesn't want me around Rubi, I think I'll use it to my advantage.

I'll make it my mission for Noah to move in on Abby. The way I see it, Tyler doesn't deserve a girl like Abby. She is too pure-hearted and kind. Innocent. And Tyler... isn't. Tyler and Chris are almost just as bad as I am. Almost. They go on runs with me to West Park to pick up and drop off drugs. They know about my father's dealings, and are part of what we do to some extent. I'm capable of things they aren't. Like eliminating the threat to the problem. They assist me and go along with it. They also like to go to the parties on the other side of town, slumming it with the public-school girls from West Park.

But now I have a bigger problem. Chris is taking my girl to the fair, acting like she really wants to go him. I follow Chris as he pulls out, making his way to the fair. I hope they didn't think because I had to go on a run, I wouldn't show up. I also have to teach Rubi a lesson about going out with another guy who isn't me.

Chapter Thirty-Four

Rubi

AFTER CHRIS AND Noah buy us tickets, we stand in line for the first ride and I look up to find that I'm nervous and feel awkward. My first thought when I saw the bright lights and the smell of popcorn and cotton candy was that I wanted to experience this with Ky.

I shake my head to push the thought of him away, and try to have a good time.

"Have you been on this one before?" he asks.

I look up and see the giant looping rollercoaster called the Ring of Fire that goes about sixty feet high. I don't want to tell him that I have never been on anything because I'm tired of being pitied and looked upon as the poor girl who grew up in the foster system. So, I decide to not tell the truth or lie.

I simply shrug my shoulders and respond. "I don't know. I can't remember."

I look forward and notice Noah talking animatedly to Abby, but she is distracted with looking over at the next ride. My eyes follow and my stomach drops when I see Tyler with Amber, waiting to get on the next ride that looks like a pirate ship swinging from one end to the other. My stomach is in knots from both Tyler seeing me here with Chris and Abby and for getting on the ride in front of me.

Will I throw up and get sick?

"I admit, I have been on it a couple of times. It isn't so bad. Don't worry, I'll hold you if you get scared," Chris says.

I bet you would. If that comment right there is any indication, I think Chris likes me. I have no idea why if I'm the pariah at school, and my back looks like an endangered manatee and boats have ridden all over my back. There isn't much going for me, I'm also poor and have a juvenile record and I won't be his family's favorite, except for Abby. She likes everyone who isn't a bitch to her.

The sound of the rollercoaster going in circles on the track, and the people screaming like their life depends on it has my stomach clenching and unclenching in fearful anticipation of not knowing how it is going to feel being upside down that high in the air.

When it is our turn to get on, my hands are clammy. After I pull the harness over my shoulders, the operator checks it, and I clip it between my thighs with a click.

"Relax, I'm right here," Chris says.

I close my eyes trying to calm myself down. Chris grips my hand as the ride begins to slide forward on the track, and my stomach somersaults when it goes higher. Holy shit.

A scream escapes my throat, and I remove my hand from Chris's grip and it feels like I'm flying in the air reminding of wishing I could fly like Superman if I was a kid. My mind flashes to a memory of me and Ky.

"Why do you like Superman?" Ky asks.

"I don't know," I answer.

"What do you mean, you don't know. I told you why I like Batman. It is because no one knows he is Batman, he kills the bad guy, has pretty girlfriends, and has a cool car.

I lower my head and try to think of the best way to really answer him without giving too much of the real reason away. "I guess because he can fly away whenever he needs to, and he has special powers to save people. He can also walk around as Clark Kent without anyone knowing who he is. I also like that he has one true love, Louis Lane. He even gives up his powers to be with her."

Ky scrunches his nose like he smelled something foul, and I hope it isn't me. I made sure I made a stop at the drug store to spray some of the body spray on my clothes. I sigh in relief when he says, "But that makes him weak if he gave up his powers. He wouldn't be able to save her. That is why Batman is better. He doesn't have to give up anything for a girl."

I roll my eyes. "That means he doesn't love anyone, and he is lonely."

He lays on the blanket and smiles, looking at the clouds in the sky as they slides in front of the sun, a daisy in his hand that he is twirling the stem between his fingers. His black eyes dart to my mine, and he holds out the single daisy. I extend my hand and take the stem in my fingers, feeling the thin, soft stem on the pads of my fingers.

"That is why you can't be Robin."

I draw my eyebrows together in confusion, at the same time feeling deflated. Robin is Batman's sidekick. His friend. Does it mean he doesn't see me as his friend?

Ky raises himself on his elbow, touching the tips of my hair, and he smiles. "You're Catwoman." I smile, and suddenly he leans close and presses his lips on mine. Fireworks explode when I close my eyes, and butterflies swarm in my stomach.

The ride stops and it feels like I was transported in time.

"Did you like it?" Chris asks.

I wasn't paying attention. I was daydreaming of the guy I can't get out of my mind.

"It was okay," I lie.

We meet up with Abby and Noah. I can't help but notice Abby looking over to see Tyler with Amber. I raise my brow to let her know that she is being obvious, and she tears her eyes away and looks up at me with a fake smile.

We pass by fun houses and the house of mirrors and that one intrigues me and I want to go in. Noah pulls Abby to another ride, and Chris looks at me, and then in the direction of the restroom.

"Uh, I'm going to go to the restroom for a second. Are you okay waiting here?"

Wanting to go to the house of mirrors, I simply smile. "Sure, go ahead. I'll be checking the house of mirrors out."

He looks relieved and walks backward toward the men's restroom. "Okay. I'll be right out."

Take your time. I turn to the entrance to the ride. Well, it isn't exactly a ride because you walk through a maze of mirrors until you get to the other side and exit, hopefully without bumping your face. I show the ride attendant my unlimited band that gives access to all the rides, and enter the maze of mirrors, looking at my reflection and feeling my way through the tight spaces.

Every turn I make, I come to a frustrating dead end and turn in the opposite direction until I reach the back. I see a shadow to my right, and feel the hairs on the back of my neck rise, but when I look, I sigh in relief. It is just my reflection. I keep moving, holding my hands out like I'm a blind person and making sure I don't bump my head because my eyes are playing tricks on me.

When I turn, it is dark, and I can't see the entrance or exit anymore, A hand covers my mouth and I pull back, muffling a scream until I'm pushed up against the interior metal siding of the trailer.

My eyes widen, and I'm about to panic when I hear, "Shh." My chest is rising and falling with each breath. I close my eyes, making sure I can breathe through my nose, but a hand is still plastered over my mouth. "You have been a bad girl, *preciosa*." I give a weighted sigh in relief. Ky. "I think I need to teach you a lesson about going out with someone who isn't me. I'm going to remove my hand, and if you scream, I'll make sure you regret it. Nod if you understand."

Anger and excitement trickles through my veins. My stomach flipping like the ride I was just on makes me want to clench my thighs, feeling his breath ghosting my neck as he speaks. I nod because it is the only choice I have in order to talk. I want to ask where the hell he has been.

When he releases his hand over my mouth, his eyes bore into mine. "Where have you been?" I query.

He tilts his head to the side. "Aww. Miss me?"

I'm instantly annoyed with his sarcasm and his little games. "Obviously not."

He gives me a devilish grin. "You want to be a smartass?" He lifts his lips with a maniacal smile that has goosebumps raising on my skin. He pushed me in between three of the mirrors with only one way out, and he is blocking me by standing behind me. He forcibly turns my head, and there is a clear view to the entrance from his angle. I can see Chris with his arms folded across his chest waiting for me.

"You see that? He is pathetic, isn't he? Waiting for you like a pussy. Thinking he can convince you to like him. Too bad I'm always a step ahead."

"What are you talking about?"

Ky slides his nose on the skin by my neck, making my legs buckle as his teeth follow, lightly scraping my skin. He holds me against him. "Hmm. I can tell you missed me. Nothing that concerns you for now. All in due time."

I wonder what he means. Ky is talking crazy. He thinks he can just show up and I'll fold and fall at his feet without answers. Fuck him.

"Let me go," I say through clenched teeth, trying to wiggle away from his grasp, but he is holding me tight against his chest. The ridge of his cock pocking me in my back. "See what you do to me." I arch because my nipples are hard, and I want him. I want to feel him, and he senses it. "Did you think I was going to let you go. Did you think I was playing around when I said I'll never leave you." He slides his other hand inside my shirt and finds my erect nipple. "Is this for me, Rubi? Are your tits for me?" He pinches my nipple and I'm about to cry out, but his other hand covers my mouth. "Now. Now. If you scream, then someone will come, and what Is the fun in that, huh? You like mirrors?"

My eyes widen when I see my reflection and his eyes staring right back at me. "I was trying to be nice and remove my hand, but you are being a bad girl. So I'll just let you watch. Understood?"

I nod my head because his cock is hard like a steel rod behind me, and he bends his knees and grinds his hips so I can feel him. He wants me to feel how hard I make him, and my panties are wet. I won't be surprised if the crotch area of my jeans doesn't have a wet spot seeping through.

"I have missed you, Rubi," he whispers. "I hope you liked the little flowers I left you. A token of my friendship. Now I need to show you a token of my possession."

I whimper, because at the same time he is rubbing himself on my backside, his other hand is rubbing the crotch of my jeans where my clit is rubbing against the rough fabric. The friction he is causing is driving me wild, but I know it is wrong. There is nothing right about what he does to me, and it's messing with my head. It is dirty, and my mind is screaming at how shameful it is while at the same time I'm watching Chris wait for me. I know there is not much time before Chris starts to get worried and asks the operator to come and look for me, but I have a feeling Ky is aware of that. That doesn't stop him from cornering me and doing what he wants.

This is the part of Ky that scares me but thrills me at the same time. I know that sounds crazy and his actions are borderline psychotic, but I have dealt with crazy and the depraved. Maybe I'm used to it. Maybe in some twisted way I'm so fucked up that I like that he does it. In the back of my mind, it is probably why I don't tell Stephen or Caroline that he sneaks in my room, because the little eleven-year-old girl inside of me is hoping she gets her best friend back. But that is crazy because eleven-year-old Ky is gone. He grew up, and now all he wants to do is make me pay for leaving him.

"I'm not going to stop coming for you, Rubi. This is your last warning. You saw what happened to Patty for taking you on a joy ride to show you his hideous art. It's a shame all that hard work went to waste on those buildings. I think he understands now to stay away from you." He kisses the skin below my ear and rasps. "Now you defy me and go to the fair with one of my friends." Tsk. "I hate to make him my enemy, but for you, I just might. It won't stop me from ruining his chance at playing football ever again for touching you. Make sure he keeps his hands to himself."

I'm panting, and my nose flares like a bull waiting to fight. What the fuck is wrong with him? He has lost his mind.

"What are you going to do? Hurt every guy who comes near me or touches me?"

"Ding. Ding Ding. I knew you were a fast learner." He licks my ear lobe, causing electric currents to snake down my spine. I close my eyes, battling the want and anger coursing through me, but he continues, "The fate of everyone around you depends on what you allow and what they do to you...and I'm the judge."

"You're fucking crazy?"

I said it. I hope it sinks in what I think of him because the things he is saying are psychotic, and he is obviously stalking me. Since I showed up, he has been watching me, waiting, sneaking into my room and placing me in my bed, even watching me sleep.

"Some have called me worse, but in your case, I'd rather go with obsessed. We don't have much time, *preciosa*. I want to give Chris the benefit of the doubt before I have to teach him not to fuck with what is mine."

"I'm not yours," I snap.

I'm irritated with him. He thinks he can do whatever he wants by pulling the strings. He thinks he has control. I'm about to scream, but he clamps his hand over my mouth, muffling the sound from escaping my lips. Then he bites my neck hard enough to leave a mark, sucking on my tender skin as he tears his mouth away.

He pushes me away from him on a laugh. "I'll see you later tonight, Rubi. I can finish what I started because I love to see the look on your face when you come."

Tears have collected in the corner of my eyes because I'm angry and pissed off at him. But most of all, I'm angry at myself for letting him do this to me.

Chapter Thirty-Five

Rubi

I EXIT THE ride and see Chris waiting for me. His eyes widen when he finally spots me. I tried to see the damage Ky inflicted on my neck by looking in the last mirror but it was warped. It was so red and I had no choice but to undo my braids to cover it.

"Did you get lost in there?"

No, your best friend is a freak and stalked me until he cornered me to whisper crazy shit in my ear and bite me, warning me not to let you touch me. But I don't say that.

Instead, I point at my wild hair. "I was busy taking out my braids. They were giving me a headache. The mirrors were better in there than the bathroom," I lie.

He rubs his chin, probably skeptical about my reason for taking so long, but the conscious part of my brain is telling me how stupid I must sound because we both know I didn't go to the bathroom.

He reaches out and touches the tip of my hair, and my brain is screaming for him to stop. I'm not sure if Ky is still watching me, but of course he is. He said he was. Chris's fate rests in my hands because I have a feeling Ky doesn't care that they are friends. He will hurt Chris for touching me. I think what he did to Patrick is just skimming the surface of what Ky is capable of.

So I do the smart thing—the sensible thing—and step back so he can't touch my hair. "Your hair down looks good on you. I like it."

No. No. Please don't like me or find me attractive. I rub my lips together and look around. Anywhere but at him or his eyes, afraid of what I might find if I take a look. Want. Desire. Everything but friendship. I would even prefer pity at this point. I couldn't stomach being the cause of someone getting hurt because Ky has suddenly decided that no one can touch me, or was I too blind to notice and that was always his intention.

My stomach uncoils when I spot Abby and Noah, and then my heart races when I also see Tyler and Amber following close behind. Abby has a grim look on her face that she is trying to hide by walking faster than Noah. I'm sure seeing Tyler with Amber is causing her pain.

At least he isn't a psycho, Abby. Trying to do something that makes sense that would help someone out, I look past Abby once she reaches me. "Hey, Tyler. I didn't know you and Amber were a thing?"

Yeah, asshole. You didn't tell me to come along because you are trying to hide something.

Tyler stops and glances nervously at Abby, and then back at Amber like he was walking on a ledge and now realizes he could fall over. "A-Amber invited me and I said yes," he stammers nervously.

"Oh, I had no idea."

"What is it to you, freak?" Amber says in a snarky tone, sliding her hand through Tyler's arm and giving Abby a knowing smile. Bitch. I wonder why she is interested in Tyler all of a sudden? I didn't think Tyler was into Amber. I have never seen him stare at her or check her out. The only person I have ever seen him look at is Abby when he thinks no one is watching.

Tyler looks between Chris and me. "I didn't know you were coming to the fair, either, Rubiana. You should have said something, and I would have taken you," he replies, but is looking directly at Chris.

Interesting. I'm not the only one with secrets. But what gets to me is that he isn't defending me from Amber calling me a freak. I'm not sure if I should be pissed off more that he didn't tell me he was going to the fair with her, or that he isn't defending me like I have gotten used to. I shouldn't expect much from him but secretly I did.

"I guess it doesn't matter now. We are all here together." I emphasize the last part even though I had no intention of it being a date between Chris and me or anything like that. I just wanted to go along for the experience, but I'm also glad that I came for Abby's piece of mind, and now for moral support.

I also don't miss the way Tyler is scowling at Noah. So he does care that Abby is here with someone else. When I think the night couldn't get any worse, the hairs on the back of my neck rise, causing the spot on my neck to throb where Ky sank his teeth, bruising the skin.

"What's up, guys? I thought you all might have gone this way," Ky says with a smile, walking up to us. He gives me a wicked smirk. "Nice hair, Rubiana. I hope you have a tie so when you go on the rides it doesn't get too tangled." *Asshole.*

"How was therapy?" Tyler asks, raising a brow.

Ky laughs through his nose, raising his perfect eyebrows up and down. "It was good. It was...crazy." His obsidian eyes land on mine, but I don't miss the way his eyes roam down body, not caring who is watching. "We all go a little mad from time to time."

Ky was at therapy? Is he really crazy? But if he was, they wouldn't allow him in school. Would they? Maybe I am dealing with a psycho. Is that why Tyler is always warning me to stay away from Ky? Now he is making it a point in making it known that was where Ky was when he was absent from school.

I watch as everyone looks away, not wanting to poke the bear any further, but that doesn't stop Ky. I don't think anything can stop Ky from saying or doing what he wants. Ky suddenly turns to Amber, giving her a wicked smile. I swear, watching him is like Dr. Jekyll and Mr. Hyde making an appearance, but you don't know in which order or which side of Ky you are getting.

Amber looks nervous when she glances at Ky, and for some reason, in spite of everything, I get jealous when he looks at her and she looks back. "I told you he would say yes?"

Her eyes widen, probably embarrassed that he is outing her. Amber asked Tyler to the fair and he said yes? It wasn't his idea, but I wonder why he agreed to go with her when I have seen her around Ky. Why would she need to ask Ky about it? Then, I remember that he invited her at the poor attempt of a birthday party they threw for me.

She is probably the one behind having the word freak painted on my locker at school. My stomach coils in rage, and I ignore all the warning bells going off in my head telling me to let it go and not cause more trouble for myself or anyone else.

Amber's lips lift in a grin. "Yes, he did."

Ky winks at Tyler. "So, how was it, Tyler?"

"How was what, Ky?" he drawls, but I can tell in his eyes that he's worried.

Ky knows something, and I can't figure out what. This all so fucked up. I can feel it. The ball is about to drop.

"Oh, come on, you didn't think anyone could see you two up in the Ferris wheel. She does give a good blowjob, doesn't she?"

My eyes go wide, and I look at Abby, watching the sadness cross her features. The hurt reflected in her eyes when she lifts her gaze at Tyler mixing with the hurt of my own feelings. The fucked-up way that I care that he is praising her. I clench my teeth so hard I feel like they are going to snap off. I want to hurt Ky the same way he is hurting me and Abby. Fuck him.

Chris is standing next to me with a surprised expression aimed at Tyler, probably not believing that he allowed Amber to suck him off on the ride. Poor Noah doesn't know if he should let the ground swallow him up. The air around us is stifling and full of awkward tension masking the true anger that is bubbling underneath, waiting to come out.

He could go fuck himself and get another blowjob from Amber since he liked it so much. My fingers touch Chris's hand, and he looks down, watching me entwine my fingers with his. I look over at the row of games with hanging stuffed animals and spot the one you have to throw a ball and hit the empty glass beer bottles.

"Hey, do you want to go play that game over there with the beer bottles? "I ask softly, leaning into him.

His eyes light up like he just won the game without even playing, and nods. "Yeah, sounds like a great idea. Hey, Noah?" Noah lifts his head. "Why don't we win us a couple of bears."

"Yeah, I think that is a good idea. Abby liked the yellow one when we passed by." That has Abby's attention, and before she turns to leave with Noah in the direction of the game, I can't help the way she glares at Tyler and Ky, leaving them alone with Amber.

I can't help myself when I pass by them. "Hey, Amber?" She glances at me with condescension. "I think the Ferris wheel has room for three...

My eyes flick to Ky.

Checkmate.

Chapter Thirty-Six

Ky

I WATCH RUBI defy my warning and walk off with Chris. I can't help the way my hands twitch when I see her hand in his, or the way she leaned into him. Rubi wants to test me. She wants to push to see if I'm bluffing or capable of fulfilling my promises. I guess what I did to Patrick wasn't enough.

Tyler steps closer to me. "What the fuck, Ky?" He growls.

My mouth got the best of me when I let the cat out of the bag about his little fun on the Ferris wheel. I saw them when I made my way to the back of the house of mirrors to play with my girl.

I saw the way Rubi was upset that her half-bother hurt poor little Abby's feelings. I guess Abby and Rubi have gotten closer than I thought. It wasn't my intention to hurt Rubi for insinuating that Amber had sucked me off before. It was long before Rubi showed up.

"What's wrong, Tyler? I was just telling the truth." I smile when I glance at Amber. "Right, Amber?"

She places the palm of her hand on Tyler's chest, but he looks at it like a fly just landed on his shirt and he wants to swat it away. Good girl. Amber has wanted to fuck Tyler since sophomore year when he made the varsity football team, but he was too busy eye fucking Abby to notice. You would be surprised what you can get other girls to spill when they want you to sleep with them. In my case, Jen.

I wonder how Tyler must be feeling that he saw Abby come to the fair with Noah. Instead of him tagging along with her and Chris so he can keep a close eye on Abby, now he must feel like complete shit that she knows he was getting his rocks off on a ride with none other than Amber. Her nemesis on the cheer team, and the one who loves to point out that Abby's dance routine sucks. *How does it feel, asshole?*

Tyler's eyes narrow on me, but my eyes dart over to where the beer bottle game is to more important matters. Rubi

"I guess. It isn't a lie. It was what we were doing, and I am good at it," Amber purrs.

Liar.

"You're playing a dangerous game, Ky," Tyler warns, pushing Amber's hand off his chest.

I pull out my vape and take a hit of the marijuana oil I picked up from the shipment from Florida. It calms me down and I need to calm down like right now. I want to walk over there and throw baseballs at Chris like a person you stone to death, but I did warn her. I'll let him off this time and I won't fuck with him too bad. I'll get him where it hurts, though. But I have to teach Rubi not to defy me again.

My hard stare lands on Tyler like a snake ready to strike. Amber must see the look in my eyes that I'm not fucking around, because she drops her gaze and looks away.

My mind is thinking of all the fucked-up ways I can make him hurt and take away what he loves the most. I don't do well with threats. Especially ones that are made so I stay away from Rubi. He thinks I don't know his daddy's little plan, and that he wants Rubi to give up what is rightfully hers. I don't give a fuck if he thinks he deserves it more than she does. She deserves everything, and I'm not going to let anyone take anything more from her. They will have to get through me first.

"Who said this was a game, Tyler? You better watch what you say and how you say it, or it will get worse. A lot worse."

"Fuck you, and stay away from Rubi," he snarls.

I angle my head and I lean close to his ear and whisper, "Good luck." I lean back and my mouth breaks into a maniacal grin. "There's always a choice, Tyler. Remember that." My eyes flick to Amber and then back to him. "You could've said no."

...

I'm waiting outside by the side of the house deep in the shadows where no one can see me watching Rubi struggle as she takes the huge red bear out of Chris's arms. I had to watch him win the bear that I was supposed win for her that put a smile on her face. I never wanted to hit someone so hard before to wipe off that smug grin and replace it with pain while he watched my girl's eyes light up.

It doesn't take a genius to figure out that this was her first time at a fair, or the fact that Chris was nervous after I showed up. They left right after he won her the bear, using the excuse that they couldn't go on any more rides because they had to carry the fucker around the rest of the time. I check the time, and it is only 7:30. She only went on one ride and the house of mirrors, but that doesn't' count because she didn't enjoy it like I wanted her too.

I wait until she is inside the house so I can make my way into her room and wait for her. I replaced the mechanism on her window after the first day of school so she couldn't lock it. Even if they did put a lock, nothing would stop me from changing it or gaining access to her room.

I hear footsteps from the hallway, and I sit and wait with Hope in my lap. Petting him while he purrs the way he likes it by his neck. I like Hope because she picked him, and he is the only animal that gets to sleep with her besides me.

I hear her open and shut her bedroom door, flicking the lock and then checking to make sure the door is indeed locked so no one can get in.

Smart girl.

She does it out of habit. Sometimes I love that she does it, but other times it makes me angry that she has to because it means she lives in fear every night. In and out of the closet. It is also why she spends most of her time in her room. I sit outside her window at times to watch her. She doesn't know I watch her, but I do. I know her habits, like the one where she doesn't come out of the bathroom unless she has clothes on so I don't get to see her dress.

I am not sure if she knows that it is pointless to lock her door when the real monster gets in her room no matter what. I will be anyone's fucking nightmare if they touch her. It's a shame she doesn't know it yet, but she will.

I hear her drop the fucking bear in the corner of her room that I want to douse in gasoline and light on fire. I'll deal with that later. I'm patiently waiting in the corner of the dark closet while she freshens up in the bathroom, which serves my purpose for this visit nicely. I love it when she takes a shower, and I can smell her clean scent when I carry her to the bed from the closet.

When she walks out of the bathroom, I hear her bare feet on the wood padding her way to the bed, the rustling of the comforter when she pulls it off and drags it toward the closet. I sit and wait in the corner holding my breath. One. Two. Three.

Who's afraid of the big bad wolf?

Chapter Thirty-Seven

Rubi

MY THOUGHTS WERE on Ky the whole time, while from a distance, his eyes were burning holes in my back. He watched Chris play the game and try to hit the beer bottles, and all I could hear was the sound of the glass breaking. Every throw he landed caused a feeling to stir in the pit of my stomach, like my insides were cracking and splintering inside because the wrong guy was playing the game beside me. The wrong person was attempting to win the bear I wanted.

I know it was messed up to think that way, but I did, I wanted Chris to lose. It was my idea to get away from the hurt Ky inflicted, but I didn't want him to win and I know that must make me a bad person. A fucked-up person, because in that moment, I was no better than Ky. I could tell Chris was nervous. Ky made his appearance, and he didn't shy away from the fact that he was watching us. He was talking to Amber and Tyler, and in that moment, I wish I was a bug so I could fly over and hear what was being said. It was hard planting the fake smile on my face when he finally broke the last bottle, loudly declaring that he won.

I was also glad he decided to take me home first, and that he didn't attempt to kiss me because now that Ky was not there, I would have stopped him if he tried. I pull the knob to slide the closet open, and when I bend down to make my bed on the closet floor, I jump back when Hope rushes out. The scream is lodged in my throat because a large hand clamps over my mouth for the second time tonight. My eyes go wide and my nostrils flare to fill my lungs with oxygen. My heart rams in my throat when a hard body is on top of mine, taking me to the wood floor. A large hand is placed on the back of my head to make sure it doesn't hit the floor. When my eyes focus, I know who it is before my mind can make a connection. I can smell his clean scent and the heat of his body over mine.

"Shh. It's me, but I think you already knew that," he whispers near my ear. His nose rakes along my skin toward my neck. His mouth kisses the spot where he bit me, traitorous tingles erupt along my neck, straight to the nipples under my thin white t-shirt poking through. His gaze travels down to where they are betraying me, telling him that they want him. That what he does affects me, and I like it.

I should thrash and scream, but there is no use. He is strong, and I don't know if he will hurt me by the time someone comes through the door, but then I remember that he could have hurt me a long time ago. He just likes to mess with me, and I as stupid as it may sound, I miss him in my room. For some strange reason, I feel safe when he is in here with me.

"Let go of me," I mutter under his hand.

I try to lift my hips to get him off of me, but I realize that was a mistake because Ky is between my legs, and his cock is hard through his jeans that are rubbing over my boy shorts right at the apex of my thighs.

"I suggest you stop lifting those pretty hips, or tonight will end a lot differently than I had planned. I'm going to remove my hand."

I nod. My body relaxes and I feel the pressure over my mouth dissipate. He removes his hand, but his other hand is on the back of my neck. "Get off me," I whisper.

His left arm frames my face, but he keeps his other hand behind my neck, making my neck arch so I can meet his eyes. His expression is soft, and his thumb caresses the area where my pulse is throbbing with every beat of my heart. Frantic.

"You looked beautiful tonight, Rubi. You always did."

My chest is rising and falling with each breath I take. His gaze is doing it again, sucking me into a different world. A different dimension where it is just us and nothing else matters. Our own little bubble.

"Why are you here? What do you want?"

"To make you pay for defying me, Rubi."

My breath hitches in my throat. Fear and anticipation mixing together inside my veins. He wants to make me pay, but then he is calling me beautiful. I must have a confused look over my face because he pushes himself up.

"Come on," he says, helping me up by taking my hand so I can stand. "I'm taking you out."

I can't go out anywhere, I'm on probation, remember? Curfew?"

"It's not curfew yet, and they don't check on you after you get home."

How does he know that? And I can't believe I'm debating this with him. My answer should be no because Ky is obviously trouble.

"How do you know that?"

He walks over to the window and pulls it up, throwing me the pair of jeans I was wearing earlier, and my bra. I catch it and glare at him when he doesn't turn around. He leans on the window, waiting.

I'm not going to lie and say I'm not excited, because I am. He wants to take me somewhere, even if it's to a cemetery where he can bury me and no one be any the wiser. I'm intrigued because I have not been out alone with Ky since we were kids. The first day of school doesn't count because I jumped out of his car after ten minutes of bickering. This time, I'll make sure he brings me back. Hopefully.

After a few minutes of contemplation in my head. He is still leaning on the windowsill, challenging me with his stare. My eyes narrow because he knows how I feel about my scars on my back. I know he doesn't care that they are on my skin. The fact that I'm attracted to him doesn't help if I turn around, he will see my ugly scars versus my perky breasts already hard and waiting to be free from the confines of my t-shirt.

I hesitate when my fingers find the hem of my shirt. Our eyes are locked. He slowly blinks, and his bottom lips snags between his teeth, making him look sexy. I blink back, and his next words are like reassuring caresses over my skin.

"It doesn't matter if I see the front or your back, Rubi. You're beautiful. It doesn't matter which side I see first."

Tears well up in my eyes that I refuse to let fall. Maybe this is his way to mess with me, because nothing about the scars on my back are beautiful.

I turn around and lift my shirt so I can put on my bra. I hear the intake of his breath, and a single tear slides down my cheek. If he wanted me to pay for defying him, he just did. He can tell me I look beautiful all he wants, but that is a lie. There is nothing beautiful about something so broken and ugly.

I might as well get used to that reaction.

I lower my head, letting my damp hair fall forward once I put my bra on. Another tear falls, and I let out a slow breath to keep from sniffling as the hot tears fall to the wood floor like fat rain drops. My pride is hanging by a thread. The only thing I can think of is to be alone so I can wallow in self-pity.

"I think it's best if you go now," I manage to say on a shaky breath. My voice so low it is almost a whisper.

I know I did this to myself, but it's better this way. To remind him that I'm not worth the trouble, and I'm not much to look at.

"I'm not here to pity you, Rubi. Put your shirt and jeans on. Let's go."

I turn around and he can see that I've been crying. A normal guy would come and hold me. A normal guy would do anything to comfort me, or even tell me that it is okay. But Ky is not a normal guy. He is cold, distant, and crazy. In a way, I prefer him to act this way than lie. What is better than a lie but the truth? They say the truth will set you free. I have learned to accept my truths.

No one loves me.

I'm damaged.

I'm broken.

I'm ugly.

Even to Ky.

Chapter Thirty-Eight

Rubi

I'M IN THE car with Ky, and he hasn't said a word since we left the house. He made sure the window was left in a way that was easy to get back inside. I guess that is how he has been able to get in and out of my room. The cabin of the car is quiet, and it feels like the silence is going to strangle me, but when I look at the screen of the dash, there are so many buttons, I'm not sure what to press to play some music.

I pull out my phone so it can give me something to do while he drives to who knows where. I'm about to scroll through my social media when he presses the screen and "Angels Fall" by Breaking Benjamin begins to play. He reaches behind to the back seat without swerving and hands me a bag.

"I got this for you." I open the bag and I notice there is a jean skater skirt. I glance at him, and he says, "Put it on."

"Why?"

"Because we're going to play a game."

"What if I don't want to play? What does playing a game have anything to do with wearing a skirt?"

I look up and notice we are back at the fair. The lights shining bright from the rides moving, swinging people around. The parking lot is still full of cars. You can hear the screams of people from a distance. There are lines of people in the front buying tickets.

He turns his head with a hard glint in his eyes. "A game I want to play with you, Rubi. It is part of the game. Like a uniform. Since you have such a hard time listening to what I tell you to do. This is the way I will make you understand. I brought you back here because we are going to play a game called twenty-two rides."

Twenty-two rides? I have never heard of it, but there are many things I haven't heard of and I'm curious. What does that game have to do with the fair and wearing a jean skirt?

"I have never heard of that game?"

He leans close and looks down at my thighs, slowly trailing up until he reaches my mouth. "Put the skirt on, Rubi."

I sigh and look around but remember that his windows are tinted pitch black. I unbutton my jeans and lift my ass to slide them off. He doesn't move, watching me fumble with the bag and the skirt. I slide the skirt over my thighs, and notice it is a tad short, but I think that was his intention.

"You have pretty thighs, Rubi. I'm going to love dirtying them."

I suck in a breath when his lips are an inch from mine. His hand slides up my thighs until they are in the center of my panties under the skirt. The tip of his finger ghosting the fabric where my clit is throbbing to be touched.

"Ky," I whisper, the movement causing my lip to brush delicately against his.

"Open your legs, *preciosa*. I want to see how wet you are for me." I open my legs because I am wet for him, and I want him to touch me. I want to play his game because he makes me feel alive. His mouth crashes against mine, and a whimper escapes my lips. His other hand is in my hair, and the tip of his finger pinches my clit over my panties as I gasp in his mouth.

"Hmm," he hums. His tongue swirling with mine.

I arch my back and he releases my clit from pinching it.

I'm on fire.

I grind my hips, seeking more. I want him to fuck me with his fingers. My hands slide in the soft strands of his black hair, getting lost in his kiss. Getting lost in him.

I moan when his slides my panties to the side and glides his finger over my slit. He doesn't stop kissing me. He slides in the first finger, and I open my legs shamelessly so he can sink in deeper.

"Yes," I moan.

"I'm going to make you come so many times, Rubi."

"Please," I plead.

I'm past feeling ashamed. I want to feel. I want to come so bad my body is betraying my mind that is telling me to stop. Ky has a twisted mind, but my body likes what he does to me physically.

He chuckles. "There she is. Don't worry, baby. I'm going to break you some more and you're going to like it. Beg for it."

I hope this isn't a cruel joke and that he doesn't hurt me. He slides in a second finger, stretching me. "Fuck, you're so tight."

My pussy clenches his fingers as my orgasm builds. His lips slide down my jaw to my neck, and he sucks and nibbles on the skin, probably leaving more marks I will have to explain how I got them. He bites and I gasp. "Let go, baby. I'll catch you."

I come hard, but he quickly slides his fingers out and I instantly feel the loss. He picks something up. It is small and shaped like a bullet, and before I can protest, he slides it into my pussy.

I gasp. "What are you doing?"

He smiles, making sure it's seated inside me. When he is done, he lifts his hand to his mouth and licks his fingers. It is sexy watching his tongue savoring me. "What do you think I'm doing? We are playing my game now."

My gut flips, making my nerves and thighs tremor. My heart pounds inside my chest, unease sliding into me when I glance around. He pulls my chin to face him, and I can smell my arousal on his fingers. My emotions are flipping upside down like a coin swirling around to see which side it is going to land.

He then picks up a remote and it has buttons on it. He presses it. A vibration begins inside my pussy causing electric currents to shoot up my clit. My breaths are coming out fast and it feels good. My cheeks grow hot when he presses the button again, increasing the vibration that also causes the pressure to build. It is almost painful, but delicious at the same time.

"Please," I beg.

He shuts it off and hands me a hoodie. "Put this on...it might get cold out," he says quietly.

He opens the driver's side door to get out, pressing the button to shut the car off. "You're taking me back to the fair?"

He leans down, giving me a devilish smile. "How did you think I was going to make you scream, Rubi?" He bites his bottom lip. "This is going to be fun. Oh, and don't run, because I'll find you. Starting tonight, you will understand that there is nothing you can do to get rid of me."

"You're crazy. You don't own me, Ky. If I want to leave, I'll leave."

He shakes his head slowly. "But that's just it, Rubi. I have always been crazy. You think you have to keep the monsters out by locking your door and hiding in the closet. What if I told you the only monster you have under your bed is me."

I lean back in the seat of the car. "You're talking psycho again."

But, I let him kiss me, bite me, and fuck me with his fingers, even allow him to slide a bullet-sized vibrator in my pussy knowing that he has a remote. He shuts the door and walks around the car and opens mine, grabbing me by the arm so I have no choice to get out. He slams the door shut with a thud and pushes me up against the car.

His forehead presses against mine, our noses almost touching. Panic begins to squeeze my stomach. "Let me see if I can make myself clear for you so that you understand. Your soul is not safe. Your mind is not safe. *You* are not safe."

What is he talking about? What does he mean, I am not safe. Am I safe at the house? With him?

He brushes his lips near my ear. Awareness creeping down my throat. If I run, I know he will catch me. And then what? He will just show up. One thing I have noticed, Tyler says to stay away from him, but he doesn't do anything about it. No one does. Ky wants to fuck with me because he knows he can. He wants to play. So, let's play. But his next words has fear gripping me in its embrace. Like shadows dancing, warning me it's too late to back out. Telling me it's too late to run away.

I feel his breath ghosting my skin near my ear. We must look like lovers in a passionate embrace right before we head into the fair. I close my eyes, and his words travel inside me, wreaking havoc within. "I have watched you at night, Rubi. When you think no one is watching. When you think no one is there. You like to sleep in the closet, leaving a crack in the door so you can see what is there in the dark, but if you keep watching long enough, you will eventually see what you should be afraid of. Me."

"What are you talking about?"

Fear is clawing within me. He watches me. It isn't that he just shows up and puts me to sleep.

"I have been watching you the whole time." He rolls his forehead over mine. "Since the first day you arrived, and there is nothing you can do to stop me. So, be a good girl, and let's see how loud you scream." He kisses me, and the darkness in his eyes I remember seeing when we were kids is present. "It is not how you create fear, Rubi. It how you release it to save the ones you love."

Thank you for reading and if possible, leaving a review. If you what to continue and read He Loves Me, book 2. Scan the Qr code for release dates or to pre-order. You can also preorder and find the link to retailers by visiting carmennrosales.com.

About The Author

CARMEN ROSALES is an emerging author of Steamy, and Dark Romance. She also writes horror under a pseudonym Delilah Croww because why not? Join her VIP list and Newsletter- www.carmenrosales.com

She loves spending time with her family. When she is not writing, she is reading. She is an Army veteran and is currently completing her Doctorate Degree in Business and has the love and support of her husband and five children. She loves to see a review and interact with her readers.

Scan the Qr link. Follow her on social media and stay up to date with her new releases. Visit her shop where can also purchase signed copies. Book boxes coming soon!

Acknowledgements

I would like to thank all my readers and new readers for purchasing my book and giving me chance. I hope you liked He Loves Me Not and hope you decide to read He Loves Me.

From the bottom of my heart, thank you.

I would like to thank my editor, Elaine York—thank you for being honest and teaching how to be a better writer. I could not have done this without your time and effort.

To all my, bloggers, ARC readers, readers, book cover designer and CandiKanePr.

Thank you for everything.

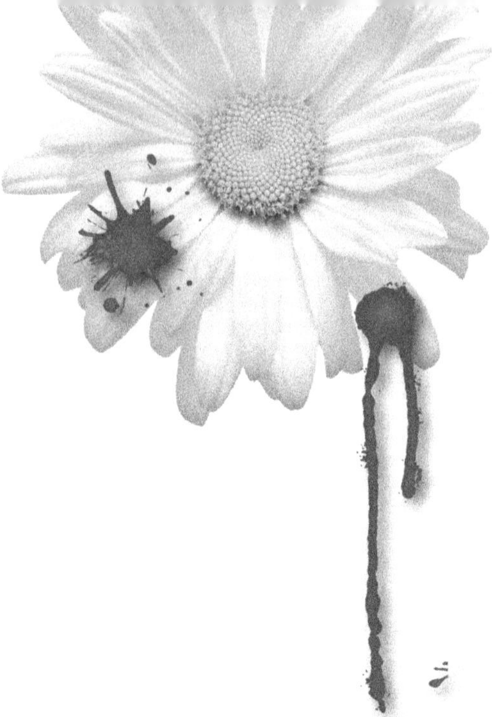

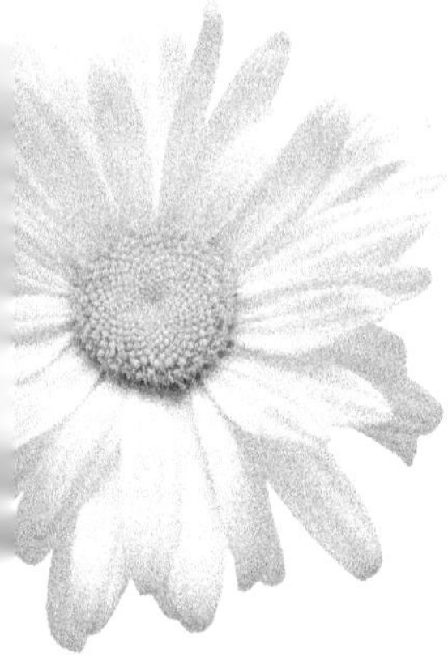